'Cold Coffee in Asmara is a compelling narrative; a gripping, well-researched account of an oppressive regime, reflecting the angst of the people and weariness of spirit in search of a better life. An informative novel reflecting the author's lived experience and visual style of storytelling.'

Nageen Hyat, Rights and social activist,
film-maker and founder director of the Nomad Gallery,
Islamabad, Pakistan

'A beautifully written novel with a flow of words and themes to fill the mind. It's a story of love and redemption in a hostile environment. It is one which reading groups will enjoy and those of an enquiring mind will find much satisfaction in its chapters. It leaves me feeling educated and privileged to have been with such stoic and resourceful people on their journey.'

Miller Caldwell,
Novelist and humanitarian, Dumfries, Scotland

'A highly visual writer, who paints his scenes beautifully in words – and takes the reader into the lives of communities around the world whose voices are seldom heard. A moving and rewarding read, touching on important global issues we should not ignore.'

Anton Levy Amoo, Artist, Leicester, UK

COLD
COFFEE *in*
ASMARA

<small>ANDREW GOSS</small>

The Book Guild Ltd

First published in Great Britain in 2024 by
The Book Guild Ltd
Unit E2 Airfield Business Park,
Harrison Road, Market Harborough,
Leicestershire. LE16 7UL
Tel: 0116 2792299
www.bookguild.co.uk
Email: info@bookguild.co.uk
Twitter: @bookguild

Typeset in 12pt Adobe Jenson Pro

Printed and bound in the UK by TJ Books LTD, Padstow, Cornwall

ISBN 978 1916668 300

British Library Cataloguing in Publication Data.
A catalogue record for this book is available from the British Library.

For **Claire,** for her untiring love and support.

For **Lula** and countless children like her.

And for those 'mercenaries, missionaries and misfits' who strive to improve the lives of others overseas.

With grateful thanks to my mother, **Nora Anni Bellamy**.

"In the midst of suffering there is a sweetness in life."
Lorenzo Mancini

PROLOGUE

WHEN TRAUMATISED AID worker John Cousins arrives in north-east Africa, he hopes to find a sense of peace among a gentle people rebuilding their lives following a bitter and prolonged war. In Eritrea he begins to forget his own emotional pain and lay to rest the ghosts of his previous mission in Pakistan. Will the work with fellow aid worker and nurse Hannah Johnson help heal the scars of his personal grief? And what is the secret of her own past?

Across the desert plains bordering the Sudan to the stifling humidity of the Red Sea coastline, the rocky highland uplands of the mountains to the minefields of the Ethiopian border regions, both aid workers begin a remarkable journey of self-discovery among a people struggling to survive against the weight of poverty and disease. It is here that they begin to discover a new meaning in life.

Cold Coffee in Asmara is an uplifting story of loss and redemption in a remote part of the world where European, Arab and African influences collide. Though it spotlights challenging humanitarian issues, it is essentially a story of hope.

The novel is the second in the author's trilogy focusing on the trials and triumphs of those less fortunate in under-reported corners of the globe, who live their lives in the face of overwhelming odds, and where the lines between life and death are often finely drawn.

It follows on from *The Humanitarian*, highlighting stories of courage, compassion and resilience of those living still in the shadow of the world's richest nations.

> *"I sat with my anger long enough until she told
> me her real name was grief."*
>
> **CS Lewis**

CHAPTER ONE

T HE WOMEN WHO gathered that morning at the solitary thatched hut in the desert were painted in silhouette against the low sun which still glowed orange over the arid terrain. Most carried small children concealed under loose white shawls, to protect them against the heat and the dust that would rise in intensity with each advancing hour. Many had trekked several hours in darkness from their scattered settlements across the silent, barren landscape in the simple hope of ensuring their children might receive basic medical care. And there they waited, their brown faces and hands brought into sharp contrast by the brightness of their white cotton garments upon which the first breaking light began to reflect its brilliance. They were the nomadic people of the plains which swept down from the highlands towards the Sudanese border.

Inside the hut there was a flurry of activity as nurses prepared their limited equipment for the task before them. Supplies were still being hurriedly unloaded from the two

1

Land Cruisers which were parked adjacent and passed into the structure. This was the only basic health unit within a day's walk for hundreds of families, and it arrived on a weekly basis. Here, the medical field team would weigh and monitor a stream of malnourished infants, watched in silence by mothers whose eyes betrayed the harshness of their lives. Some would receive injections from the African nurses, perhaps some tablets too. The women would then be handed packets of fortified food to provide additional nutrition for their children before returning to the desert.

Eritrea was suffering acute food insecurity following a protracted and costly thirty-year war with Ethiopia, its neighbour in the south. A steady stream of refugees was still pouring back across the border from the Sudan where they had fled from conflict, now to reclaim their abandoned settlements, despite the hardships they would inevitably face. Conditions could surely be no more difficult than those that continued to exist in the UN camps. At least that was the belief; that the return promised a better life than had existed before the long years of war. This was their country, the land of their ancestors.

Finally, the nurses were ready and, one by one, the women filed into the hut with their children. Yet more weary women arrived with each passing hour so that there was a constant line standing, or sitting, on the dry earth outside as the sun began to climb and the desert heat rose steadily.

Inside, a white woman sat at a desk in the corner of the hut. She was auditing the drugs and monitoring attendance that morning, as she did regularly at each of a dozen mobile field clinics that were operated across the region by her team.

Hannah Johnson looked up from her laptop, alerted by raised voices and the concern among the team following the arrival of a sick child, now the centre of attention of her

SUnV6nRXLd

UnV6nRXLd/-1 of 1-/premium-uk/0 A3

Thank
you for
shopping
at
Amazon.co.uk!

Packing slip for
Your order of 20 May 2024
Order ID 206-8295332-3246769

Packing slip number UnV6nRXLd
Shipping date 21 May 2024

Qty.	Order Summary	Bin
1	**Cold Coffee in Asmara** Paperback. Andrew Goss. 1916668305 : 1916668305: 9781916668300	

We hope you enjoy your gift, and we'd love to see you soon at www.amazon.co.uk

0/UnV6nRXLd/-1 of 1-//AMZL-DPO1-ND/premium-uk/0/0521-23:45/0521-20:46 Pack Type : A3

nursing colleagues. The infant was clearly dehydrated, its stunted body and feverish eyes a cause for alarm. Johnson rose from her desk and approached. As the senior nurse and programme manager, she held responsibility for confirming the diagnosis and judging what action to take.

For her, there was no doubt. The child was suffering from malaria, a potentially fatal condition for a child so young. She would decide whether to evacuate the infant and its mother to the nearest hospital in the hope a life could be saved. Or to send them back into the desert with what medication they had and let nature take its course. She acted calmly and decisively.

"The child will receive good care at the hospital," she said, looking into the mother's eyes. "It will be OK." Johnson's was a kind and compassionate face which, when she smiled, brought dimples to her cheeks. For a moment, she held the child's tiny hand in hers, then raised her head and swept a strand of brown hair from her face.

"Ask for Kidane to come inside immediately," she added, turning to the nurse beside her. The driver entered the hut a few moments later. The child should be driven by Land Cruiser across the desert to the hospital at Tessenei near the Sudanese border, where the infant had every chance of survival. The dark-skinned African nodded in understanding.

"Yes, ma'am," he replied. It was a two-hour drive, but he knew he could be back in time to transport the team back to base camp when their work was done.

Malaria: it was a common hazard. Not just during the prolonged monsoon period. Mosquitoes swarmed above the water points and isolated oases across the landscape, even in the heat of the dry season. The disease claimed the lives of hundreds. Needlessly. Nets were distributed to families by the British aid agency that operated across the region. It was a simple, but effective, solution. But all too often, the nets were sold on by poor families or simply went unused. It was not the custom for locals to sleep under nets, and changing age-old habits was slow in parts of the world where other, more pressing, issues dictated daily survival.

Johnson stepped from the hut and watched as the woman and child were led out to the Land Cruiser and the vehicle sped off, kicking up a trail of dust as it headed out across the desert. She gazed up at the bright, cloudless sky and wondered just how much suffering could be endured by a people under one sun.

It was the same sun which shone down so much more benevolently upon her own world and the rolling green hills of the southern counties in England, where she'd been raised. Suddenly the safety and security of her own country seemed a million miles away, though she'd left it barely six months ago. She hoped the youngster could be saved. The mother had already lost a little girl, killed by an exploding landmine. It was an ongoing, persistent threat. Scores of deadly minefields still lay beneath the parched earth across the borderlands. Always it was the children who went for the water, or the firewood, that fell victim. She cursed silently under her breath and headed back into the hut to rejoin her team.

———❧———

The road east was long in the shimmering heat that beat down relentlessly on the desert track in the early afternoon sun. Cutting through the heart of the country's Gash-Barka region, the terrain was harsh and unforgiving as the medical team made its weary return to base camp which lay within the small town of Barentu on the dry slopes west of the highland capital Asmara.

They passed through small villages along the way, connected by the single track which ran straight and narrow through rocky landscape dotted with low scrub. A solitary baobab tree in the distance, raising its twisted branches forlornly to the sky, might signal there was water. But there was little sign of other life at a time of day when the heat reached scorching temperatures. No other traffic could be seen travelling the route, except the occasional donkey, or camel, led by a figure wrapped entirely in loose cotton garments and bent against the searing heat. Or sometimes there was a child with a plastic water cannister.

Occasionally, though, there were unexpected treats along the way; sometimes they pulled in at a small roadside shop in one of the hamlets advertising cold colas from an icebox powered by generator. It was the ultimate oasis along the unforgiving route home. Home? Johnson smiled at the thought. Home was currently a flat-roofed bungalow which offered shade and ceiling fans. And sleep while the heat of the afternoon beat down relentlessly.

At least the mother and child had been transported safely to the hospital in Tessenei, and Kidane reported the toddler had received almost immediate attention.

Johnson felt the infant had every chance of survival with the right care. She was in no doubt she had made the right decision as she closed her eyes and allowed herself to doze to the sound of the engine as the vehicle sped along the dusty track.

Usually, the team would arrive in Barentu parched and exhausted late in the afternoon, following an hour, or two, on the road, when the sun was high and temperatures topped forty degrees Celsius at the height of the dry season. And they would drag themselves from their vehicles and retire to the shade offered by their rooms to rest.

Sometimes, Johnson would make herself a tea, or coffee, and reflect upon the activities at the field clinic. More often, though, she was too fatigued by the sapping heat and would slump onto her bed, draw the mosquito net closed and sleep until the day began to cool with the setting of the sun. Later, the day would then begin anew, with a shower followed by an evening meal – and coffee, as only the Eritreans know how.

CHAPTER TWO

"TAKE SOME TIME for yourself, Hannah," he said in a voice that was calm and measured. "You're working too hard," he told her.

"Doctor's orders?" she replied, smiling, and shot him a sideways glance as they stood on the veranda, gazing out along the dusty road, watching the sun begin to rise.

"No," he said, with a hint of impatience. "The advice of a friend." Then he paused, taking in the cool morning air before continuing: "I worry about how hard you drive yourself. I've seen how hard you work." He paused again. "First rule," he reminded her.

"I know," she said. "If you go down, you're no good to anyone…" she duly recited.

"Which is why you should take yourself to Asmara for the weekend," he said, turning towards her once more. She looked tired. Yet hers was a beautiful face, he thought, though he would never dream to say so. "Switch off!"

"And what would I do there?"

"Relax!" he said simply. "Drink sweet tea in the shade."

She knew he was right, as they fell silent, watching the glow of the morning sky above the small desert town. But she had come to care for the peoples of Eritrea. And like all those who cared, she felt the misery of those she saw suffer. There was never enough time. Another busy day was in prospect. The need she had seen was so very great. But her work also helped her. Distracted her.

It was a new, all-consuming life away from the memories which still haunted her. A world distant from the disappointments of London and the horrors she had experienced in Bosnia, which were still so raw.

Doctor David Walters knew that too. But he also saw the effects of her long hours in the field. There was an underlying weariness about her, despite her outward cheerfulness. There were shadows of fatigue beginning to form beneath her eyes. That wasn't good either. She was no newcomer to working in difficult conditions overseas and should know better. That was also true. She had worked much tougher duty stations.

Bosnia had been the hardest. She'd seen the impact of war upon civilian populations close up. The women and children were at the heart of it. She had followed in the wake of ethnic cleansing, seen the mass graves and bodies lying unclaimed in the streets of Pristina city. Worse still was the hunger and despair. And the fear which came with every bombardment, every shell that exploded somewhere across the city with a dull thud that shook the earth. Sometimes the shells landed close enough to rattle the windows, and one had once exploded at the end of the street and blown the windows out of the UN mission.

That had been her first overseas assignment, driven to seek new experience away from the emotional turmoil that had left her feeling numb, empty and worthless. Julian had not loved her. Not enough to marry. So, she had asked to join her father, at that time part of a multi-agency peace mission in Sarajevo. And, though Clive Horatio Johnson, OBE, had misgivings, he was sufficiently concerned by his daughter's emotional distress to agree, perhaps against his better judgment. She might volunteer with one of the medical NGOs. Just for a few weeks. She was, after all, a nurse. It would give her time to reflect upon her life. Besides, most of the fighting had subsided, and he would welcome the company.

What her father didn't foresee was how quickly his daughter would find work of her own. Sitting in a quiet café in Livno town, as these things happen, a German aid worker was drinking coffee at the next table. Curious to see a young woman clearly of Western-European appearance, she struck up a conversation.

The German woman worked for a medical aid agency. They could use an extra pair of hands, especially a qualified nurse. Would she care to meet the head of the organisation? That was the first time she heard the name Seamus O'Connor, who was to play such a pivotal role in her life. An eccentric, shaggy-haired Irishman driven by danger and compassion in equal measure, it was he who set her on a path she could not have imagined.

O'Connor took one look at the young English nurse and offered her a job. He liked the look of her and admired her courage.

So, when her father left, she stayed to care for the sick and diseased, the homeless and the heartbroken, bearing witness to that terrible ethnic conflict which had put murder in the hearts of a people who had co-existed side by side for centuries. She saw the violence escalate with each new atrocity between peoples so alike, so suddenly divided. By what?! A line on the map. A different faith. A national fervour which had lain dormant for decades, if not centuries? A drive for independence? The violence didn't make any sense to her. It was shocking in its savagery.

It haunted her still sometimes as she lay awake at night, or if she awoke plagued by bad dreams, uncertain at first of where she was. And she would remember; wake to painful images she had tried so hard to forget. Memories of death and destruction in a part of the world seized by madness.

The bloody incident at the checkpoint had shaken her to the core; made her doubt all she had come to believe. Traumatised her. She'd seen death on the streets of towns and cities across Bosnia in the weeks that had followed her appointment. She'd seen suffering.

But this was different. She and Gëzim had grown close, even though they had spoken little during the months they had known each other. He barely knew a word of English. But it was not necessary. It was the shared experience. She trusted him implicitly. He was a good driver. He knew the roads, and he knew his people. Always, he had managed to deliver her safely, no matter how dangerous the situation became or how treacherous the route. And always, there was a smile.

As their vehicle drew to a halt before the armed guards who blocked the road, she could feel the tension. Gëzim handed their papers across, and they were abruptly snatched from him. There was a heated exchange. He told them his passenger was a UK nurse. They were on their way south on urgent humanitarian business. But the soldiers were part of an elite guard known for their brutality. Though he denied sympathy to the Albanian cause, they ordered him out of the vehicle. He was the wrong ethnicity, and that was enough. They dragged him from the vehicle onto the road and shot him through the head.

The English nurse was free to go. Yet she could not move. It seemed a long time before she was able to slide across the driver's seat and raise trembling hands to the wheel. When, finally, she managed to turn the ignition and drive off, it was as if she was in a dream. Her actions were automatic. All she could hear was that gunshot which had killed Gëzim echoing through her mind. As soon as she had left the checkpoint behind her, she pulled over and burst into tears, shaking violently, trying to collect herself.

And there she sat in shock. It had been so sudden. So unexpected. So terrible. She was still sobbing when, at last, she was able to pull back onto the road which would take her to her field team, another hour away.

A complaint was lodged with the NATO-led Stabilisation Force in Bosnia and Herzegovina and the UN, but the rogue unit from the checkpoint had vanished. A week later, she was sent home on emergency leave. But what was home? She couldn't settle. She found no peace. She felt out of step. How to explain the horrors she had witnessed? And so, within the month, she had returned to Bosnia to see out her contract. But it was not the same. There was an underlying sadness in her she was unable to shake. When, finally, she left the country for the last time, it was with a sense of enormous relief.

The draw to help others less fortunate overseas, though, was strong. It's what they say of aid workers. Once you have seen suffering, you realise just how vast it is and that whatever you might have done is simply a drop in an ocean of need. It is never enough. There is a restlessness and a compulsion to return to living that much closer to the edge. Yet Bosnia had been a reminder of the fragility of life.

Eritrea was a different story. Here the war was over. And when the opportunity of work came, she took it. It was about assisting a people tired of conflict, impoverished and sick from its effects. The fighting was done. They wanted to rebuild their homes, their livelihoods and their country in peace. It was about healing. She found the people were generous and gentle in their poverty. After Bosnia, it was like a breath of fresh air. Yet the need was acute. It therefore also filled a need within her. It gave her life purpose and meaning. It was one of the reasons she had thrown herself into her work. Perhaps it might help heal her too.

Walters was a good man who worked as hard as anyone. But as they stood on the veranda, she realised he was right. Lately, she had been feeling very tired. Sad too. Perhaps she did need some time to herself in Asmara.

"You're right, David," she said, taking the cigarette he offered her and leaning towards him as he lit it for her before lighting his own. He watched her draw on the cigarette, noting the pout with which her lips held it, the contours of her face and her eyes which gazed into his. He thought they were beautiful eyes, deep and compassionate, and when she smiled, her eyes did too.

Yes, he liked her very much. There was no pretence with Hannah. Above all, she was honest, straight and true. He might even have been a little in love with her, he thought, as he watched her draw in the smoke and blow it out into the morning air.

"That's settled then," he said. "Time for coffee and a bite." She nodded as they turned and walked back into the building.

CHAPTER THREE

McKenzie came to Africa on a short-term assignment. And he stayed. In truth, he was seduced. It wasn't the shimmering Red Sea coastline, with its fishermen casting their nets under the brilliant sun across sparkling blue waters from their small wooden boats. Nor was it the warm breeze that blew across the mountains as shepherds watched their flocks grazing the timeless rocky landscape. Or the onset of the sudden monsoon rains that brought the arid plains sloping down towards the Sudanese desert to life in an explosion of greenery.

It was the people. It was their will to survive and thrive in the extremes of weather and terrain in a forgotten corner of north-east Africa that moved him. There seemed a passion for survival, for life itself and a recognition that its pleasures, when they came, should not be taken for granted. Perhaps because they came among such hardship for most, like the sudden blossoming of desert life when the rains hit. It made for celebration when they came. That had been lacking in his own world. Here it was a life closer to the edge. It sharpened the senses. It made him feel alive and grateful for every day.

He had felt empty, unfulfilled and that a change – complete change – would do him good; was in fact essential. He therefore took the job that was offered almost on a whim, and before he knew it, he was there. He was unfamiliar with its peoples and its landscapes. Perhaps that was the attraction. He wanted to escape what he knew. He wanted to lose himself. Yet Africa, the 'dark continent', embraced him like a brother. Here he felt accepted.

Not that he wasn't fond of his native Scotland and the raw beauty of the Highlands he had known as a child. But he needed change; a break from the past which was so painful to him. Therefore, he took the assignment in Eritrea and consigned his troubles in Scotland to the past, although that too had not been without anguish and sometimes a sense of regret.

At first, he thought he might have something in common with the long-suffering peoples of that forgotten, war-ravaged corner of north-east Africa in which he found himself almost by accident. But then he realised he hadn't lost as much as he thought. In a sense, Africa found him. Its people were welcoming and generous in their poverty. Loss and grief he came to see as relative. It depended on context and where you started from.

McKenzie started from a good point in Africa, without any trappings of emotional or material wealth, naked and vulnerable.

He was therefore open to new experience, and the intoxicating wave of exotic sights, sounds and smells that immersed him numbed the pain he felt. It seemed a rebirth.

As he sat on his porch within the compound, which lay on the south-western side of Asmara, sipping his gin and tonic, he wondered what the new arrival would be like and whether the Englishman would fit into the team. He took another sip from his glass. The drink was a habit he had acquired early in his career as an aid worker on the premise that the quinine in the tonic water and the alcohol in the gin might prevent the onset of malaria. He wasn't sure if it was true. But somehow it stuck and became his preferred tipple. Truth be known, he hated the taste of whisky.

John Cousins had boarded the aircraft at Heathrow determined to travel light. Yet, in a sense, he too was carrying excess baggage. Bitter experience and loss weighed heavily upon him. He had found no peace in the heart of England following his work in South Asia. Yes, it had been good to be back among the familiar surroundings of the Midlands. Its greenery, its safety, its wealth. At least at first. There were friends and family. But nothing seemed to quell the sense of restlessness he felt.

Peace and fulfilment within his own country eluded him, and he was not able to find the comfort he sought. He was therefore driven to immerse himself in the unfamiliar. He wanted to do some good for others that might bring a redeeming purpose to his life. He wanted to abandon himself to a cause as some people lose themselves to drugs, or alcohol. He wanted to forget.

He had arrived back in England stripped of all those things that had given his life value. A wife he had loved, a home, his little boy and a life that had seemed idyllic and full of hope for the future. In short, his happiness had been shattered in Pakistan by the loss of everything he held precious. He knew it was gone. But he struggled to take it in. It left him wondering how much of his life had been real. It seemed everything had so suddenly been torn away. Had it all been an illusion? A dream was over. Perhaps another was about to begin. Yet he seemed caught in a web of sorrow and loss, unsure how to break free from the past. He wasn't sure what his new mission in northeast Africa might offer. But he had grasped the opportunity as a man lost at sea seizes whatever floats his way. In desperation.

He didn't know much about the country for which he was bound and what would become his new life in the months ahead.

Eritrea lies tucked within the northernmost corner of the Horn of Africa, stretching a territorial limb southwards along the hot and humid Red Sea coastline. Up in the mountains, where the air is cooler, the swish art deco coffee houses in the capital are a reminder of the country's colonial past. But the Italians left little else after Mussolini's demise, when Asmara fell into British hands for 'safekeeping'. After the Second World War ended, they too were soon gone, supposedly handing power to its peoples. But peace did not come to the region. Instead, Eritrea's neighbours vied for its territory and the country was then ravaged by a thirty-year conflict with neighbouring Ethiopia before finally securing independence. The cost was high both in human lives and economic impact.

—— ❧ ——

It was still dark when the aircraft approached the Horn from the east and came in to land in the early hours. Cousins had slept only intermittently on the seven-hour flight from London to Dubai, where he had time during the short stopover to grab a cup of coffee and focus on the thought that soon he would touch down in Africa. Now the Airbus was sweeping towards Asmara city on its final descent, with only a sprinkling of lights beneath the aircraft to suggest there was land below. He braced himself for the imminent landing and said a silent prayer. He wasn't a religious man, but he felt it would do no harm. There was a sudden jolt, and the plane taxied along the runway towards the flat-roofed terminal building.

He wasn't looking forward to passing through customs and passport control. His experience of airports in distant lands suggested a long and protracted process following a tiring journey. And there was always a worry about the required visas and documentation. He finally emerged from passport control into the cool morning air, as the sky began to glow orange, to face an eager crowd of locals waiting in muted anticipation for family and loved ones. Then he was caught in a shower of popcorn thrown across their path and the shrill sound of jubilation from the native women, clacking their tongues as they shrieked their traditional welcome. Nothing can prepare an unsuspecting traveller for that raw and exuberant greeting. He laughed, brushing the popcorn from his hair and shoulders as he followed his porter towards the Land Cruiser that had been sent to collect him.

The driver climbed from the waiting vehicle and stood eagerly before him, smiling broadly as Cousins approached.

"Jamal. Jamal," he told the Englishman as he stepped towards him, slapping the palm of his hand against his chest.

He was tall and of Arab, rather than black African appearance, dressed in a white, flowing tunic and a cotton scarf wrapped around his head. He was sweating as he rubbed his close-cropped beard. He was nervous to meet the foreigner. Not many white men came to Eritrea these days.

"Hello, Jamal," the Westerner said. "I'm John. John," he repeated. He too laid a hand against his chest as he spoke. "John Cousins."

"John," the man replied in a thick accent, and Cousins nodded. Jamal took the bags from his countryman and loaded them carefully into the back of the vehicle, as Cousins fished out a few notes and pressed them into the grateful hand of the porter.

Then he slipped onto the front seat beside his driver, and they set off for the guesthouse where he was expected for breakfast. Coffee too, of course. He didn't know it then, but no welcome was complete in Eritrea without coffee. Lots of it. Nor could he guess how much a part of his life the man seated beside him at the wheel would become in the months ahead, as they travelled in silence as the new day began to dawn.

The airport lay a short drive outside the city. As they sped along the dusty road through the darkness, there was little sign of life. He tried to make out the landscape in the semi-darkness, but it seemed devoid of features except for craggy embankments dotted with low brush and an occasional ragged tree stretching into the glow of the imminent sunrise.

Soon they entered the suburbs of the city, its streets lined with low, flat-roofed buildings which gave way to shops and more elaborate structures as the sun burst over the horizon.

This, then, was Asmara, a city more European than African, with wide boulevards now bathed in brilliant early morning light, which painted long, crisp shadows across streets lined with palm trees. The city seemed almost out of place. It might have been a small Italian town in southern Tuscany, or Umbria, he mused, were it not for the mosques or the scattering of people he saw wrapped in flowing cotton, leading their camels and donkeys. But there were magnificent churches too. He also noted splendid Italian coffee houses and villas along the main thoroughfares.

Yet there were also strong echoes of the industry upon which the town had flourished in the 1930s to become the economic hub at the centre of Italy's African empire. Like the grandiose Fiat Tagliero Building still dominating one of the city's main roads, standing proud with clean, defiant lines of Art Deco splendour. Except that now it was a petrol station, perhaps one of the grandest anywhere in the world.

Finally, the Land Cruiser pulled up outside a flat-roofed, two-story, colonial-style guesthouse.

"This your place," said the driver.

Almost immediately, an Eritrean in white cotton tunic, narrow trousers and a shawl over his shoulders stepped from the building and hurried towards them as they climbed from the vehicle.

"Welcome, sir, welcome." He grinned, wringing his hands, as Cousins nodded. "Come. Please," added the man in the shawl as the Englishman followed him into the villa.

A fan was gently whirring as he entered his room on the first floor, which was tastefully furnished. There was a double bed, a table and two chairs, reminiscent of the thirties and distinctly European in style. There was no mosquito net, but he had brought his own. He noted a TV in the corner of the room. He checked the washroom, turned the taps and was happy to see the water flowing into the basin. He was even more relieved when the toilet flushed at his first attempt. It all looked clean and tidy. There was a small balcony too, overlooking the street, now bathed in sunshine. Not quite what he had expected. His first instinct was to flop onto the bed and sleep. But he was too excited to rest. Besides, he had ordered breakfast, despite the weariness from his journey. He was hungry and needed coffee.

He approached the small balcony, opened the glass-panelled doors. He stepped out into the warmth of the sunshine, then stood breathing deeply, gazing out across the street, taking in the new sights and sounds around him. He watched traders below setting up their stalls. There was no traffic, save a few cyclists, donkeys and carts. The city was quiet, still waking up to a new day.

Jamal the driver was set to return later in the afternoon, and he would head to the office across the city to meet the team. But for now, he would take a leisurely breakfast, then try to catch up on some sleep, if he could. New experience beckoned. He was looking forward to getting out into the 'field'. Already, he felt he had made the right decision to come. Perhaps he would be able to put the past behind him and look forward to a new beginning. He was yet to discover the delights of a country of three climates and a gentle, simple people craving peace after the long years of war.

CHAPTER FOUR

H<small>E SAT ALONE</small> in the golden light streaming through the window of the small dining room and raised the cup of rich, dark coffee to his lips, watching the activity in the palm-lined street outside intensify as the sun rose higher.

His gaze rested on a group of elderly women outside, bent forward in white, flowing shawls, sweeping the dust meticulously from the tiled pavement with brooms, their grey hair carefully plaited. Some carried the tattoo of the Coptic Cross upon foreheads etched with lines of long, hard experience. Two soldiers across the road stood casually in their fatigues and their black plastic sandals, chatting and smiling as they too watched the women work. And a man wrapped head to foot in white cotton led a donkey heavy with baggage slowly past the window.

Cousins was tired from his journey. But the lure of the unfamiliar and exotic in the street outside was too strong. He therefore did not return to his room immediately after breakfast to sleep. Instead, he would explore the immediate vicinity. He rose from his table, slung his canvas bag over his shoulder and headed for the door.

He stepped out into the sunshine and squinted into the bright light along the street, standing for a moment to allow his eyes to adjust and take in his bearings. The ladies with their brooms had moved along, but the soldiers still stood chatting. They glanced at him, but their attention was drawn to a young girl approaching with a plastic water cannister strapped upon her back. A bicycle passed, and one of the soldiers hailed the rider with a greeting. "Salaam! Salaam!"

But there were no cars; no traffic noise one might expect in uptown Asmara. The streets were eerily silent, save the chug of a solitary battered yellow taxi on its way to pick up an unknown fare. Then all was quiet, except for the low murmur of intimate conversation or the cry of a traditional greeting as the morning sun beat down. And the pace of life seemed slow.

A magnificent minaret rose above the rooftops in the distance, set against the blue sky which carried a light whisper of cloud. The Englishman decided it was a reasonable landmark to head for and struck out along the avenue in its direction to see if he could locate the mosque to which it belonged. It felt dreamlike as he walked slowly along the sun-drenched streets, his senses assaulted by unfamiliar sights, sounds and smells. He found the city was cool and pleasant as he strolled without any sense of urgency.

Along the way, street traders offered a scant selection of fresh fruit and vegetables from their stalls. Others presented rich fabrics, traditional shawls or scarves of white and cream spread out before them. Some would beckon to him to come and buy, and he would smile politely. But the smile was always returned as he moved along under the dappled shadow of the palms. And occasionally, the light spring breeze would carry the aroma of fresh breads being prepared for breakfast over a hot stove in homes all over the city.

The capital's rich and varied architecture was a surprise. He hadn't expected such a strong European influence. Much of the city had been built in the 1920s and 1930s when Asmara lay at the heart of Mussolini's dream of African empire, and it was a busy hub for trade across the region, packed with Italian bankers and merchants. The traditional wooden shacks of the old shanty towns gave way to a uniformed grid system of streets and plazas modelled along elegant Art Deco lines over two decades of feverish construction to create a new 'Rome' in Africa. Yet, occasionally, the grandeur of its wealthy colonial past stretching back to the nineteenth century could still be seen. A lavish traditional Tuscany villa might still surprise, nestling among neoclassical uptown Asmara. To Cousins, the city seemed a mesmerising fusion of European, African and Arab influences, which he had never encountered before.

He turned the corner from a side street, and there it was. He found himself staring across a vast plaza paved in black slab laid out before a majestic white mosque of three domes in a blend of neoclassical and Islamic styles, its magnificent fluted minaret stretching into the blue sky. Breathtaking. It was the Al Kulafah Al Rashidan, the Great Mosque of Asmara.

He lit a cigarette and stood for several minutes in awe, allowing his eyes to rest on the grandeur of the scene before him, taking the smoke deep into his lungs and blowing it into the morning air. He knew, though, time was limited, and he still had to retrace his steps. Besides, he was beginning to feel tired. When he had finished smoking, he dropped the butt onto the floor and extinguished it with his boot. But he bent forward and picked it up, slipping the dogend into his side pocket. It felt almost sacrilegious to leave it there. He would visit again another day. He might even see if he could offer his prayers here. And so, he turned away, happy to have discovered the beautiful mosque.

When, finally, his guesthouse came into view and he approached the front door, he was almost reluctant to step out of the sunshine. Yet he was suddenly overcome by fatigue. He went up to his room and flopped onto his bed, before falling into a restless sleep. His driver was due to collect him after midday, when he would meet the team at the office.

He had a couple of hours. But now the need for sleep had become the overriding priority.

The British NGO was based across the city, one of just a handful of international organisations working in Eritrea.

It had set up office within a compound which comprised several flat-roofed white buildings on the west side of the capital. That was after the long war with Ethiopia was over, when food was scarce and the people first began to return from the refugee camps across the border in their thousands, hoping to reclaim the land of their ancestors. The country was broken after decades of conflict. It was a time to rebuild from the devastation. Homes and livelihoods, food and medical support were immediate priorities.

The new left-wing nationalist government that had finally triumphed against its larger neighbour knew it needed outside help. But it was wary of international aid organisations and the motives of foreign powers who had stood by and allowed conflict to continue over three decades. And it treasured its hard-won independence. Therefore, the numbers of those allowed to operate within the country were limited. The Italians were also based in Asmara, as was the Red Cross, Catholic Relief Services, Care International, several UN agencies and a small number of medical NGOs which underpinned a health system that was shattered. When conflict flared once more along the Eritrean border with its old adversary in 1998, most aid agencies stayed, operating from the relative safety of the capital, only to see much of their work in the south destroyed in the brutal fighting which cost the two bitter rivals a further seventy thousand dead and set the region's recovery back decades. An uneasy truce was negotiated with the advent of the new millennium and monitored by the UN, remaining in place in the years that followed.

BritAid was an international aid agency engaged in advocacy for the poorest across Africa and Asia, headed in-country by Scotsman James McKenzie. He was a veteran aid worker with decades of experience across Sub-Saharan Africa. But when he came to Eritrea after the long war, he found something in the people and culture he liked.

The British NGO's main focus from its national office in the highland capital lay in rebuilding livelihoods to alleviate poverty. With many of the men conscripted from their villages to bolster Eritrea's armed forces for indefinite periods, a major focus lay in empowering the country's women. And the organisation had seen some success in enabling female-headed households to boost their meagre incomes.

The aid agency also implemented health and hygiene programmes. They included the large-scale distribution of free mosquito nets to poor communities to the west and to the coastal regions in the east, where malaria and dengue fever were rampant. Education of a population which still practised behaviours stretching back centuries was also part of its work.

It was simply not enough to make the nets available. Villagers also needed to be shown the benefits of using them to safeguard themselves and their children. No small challenge in a part of the world in which other acute aspects of daily survival took priority and disease was accepted as a part of life. Communities had lived without sleeping under nets since the beginning of time. Therefore, it was not unknown to find the nets used for fishing, chicken coops or even curtains. It was one aspect that Cousins had been brought out to work on. Communications, advocacy and behavioural change.

It was a relatively broad brief. As a communications officer, he was required to be something of a generalist. His work would include reporting back to McKenzie and to head office back in London, providing case studies which could feed into the organisation's global marketing and fundraising campaigns. Media work, both locally and internationally, was also part of the job. Donors too had to be informed of the need on the ground – and how that need was being met. The organisation was required to show that it was making an impact; that it was changing lives for the better. And yes, he would also support the ongoing campaign to encourage villagers to sleep under the nets.

In essence, the work would not be unlike what he had delivered in Pakistan on his previous mission. Many of the issues were similar, their causes sadly familiar: harsh environments, extreme poverty, poor education and ineffective government. Natural disaster and war could so easily tilt the balance towards widescale human suffering when the margins between survival and humanitarian crisis were so narrow.

Would Eritrea be so very different? He didn't know. The culture was alien to him; the landscape different; and the people unfamiliar. Yet his travels had taught him people the world over were pretty much the same. They shared the same basic needs, the same fears, the same dreams. It was about survival. Putting a roof over your head and food on the table.

It was about protecting family and security for those one

cared about. So far, he liked what he had seen of Eritrea, so different to what he had expected.

Cousins was therefore unphased by what he might yet encounter. The language might provide some challenges. For although English and Arabic were widely understood, locally the language of the people was predominantly Tigrinya. There were other regional languages and dialects too. Almost a dozen. He would work with an interpreter, as he had in South Asia.

Therefore, as his vehicle sped across the city, his overriding emotion was one of excitement. He was a little anxious at the prospect of meeting new people, perhaps. That was to be expected. In some ways, it was the international aid workers themselves that were potentially more challenging than the locals, experience had taught him.

There were egos and agendas. No, at least he had arrived safely and was minutes away from the office where he would meet his new colleagues. He had felt an instant liking for his new boss during the Skype interview, though he was yet to meet McKenzie in person. Perhaps they had more in common than either knew.

A large roadside sign with 'BritAid' hand-painted in large blue letters signalled they had reached their destination. The Land Cruiser slowed and turned into a sweeping driveway, before pulling up outside a large white bungalow in a small cloud of dust. Cousins stepped from the vehicle, threw his bag over his shoulder and stood for a moment, staring at the building. He took a deep breath and walked towards the main entrance. He felt a new adventure was about to begin.

James Miller McKenzie was an experienced aid worker of almost two decades in the 'field'. At almost six feet tall, with wild, greying red hair and a ragged full moustache, he cut an imposing figure. The Scot prided himself on his Celtic roots. Sometimes he played on it. There was a natural rebelliousness to his nature. In truth, he was something of a maverick; a risk-taker. But he always seemed to win through. His uncle was a Scottish earl, and it was said there was a family castle somewhere in the Highlands. Despite, or perhaps because of, his own aristocratic background, he shunned, even despised, positions of wealth and privilege. And authority. McKenzie was seen as the proverbial 'black sheep' of the family. But he seemed to revel in his rebellion.

Yet, despite his daunting physical appearance and a direct, no-nonsense manner, he was a man driven by a sense of social justice. Therefore, he might have been forgiven his eccentricities, which included plain speaking to those in authority to the point of rudeness. Usually delivered with a wry smile and a sense of fun, which sometimes disguised his passion. He had charisma and was a force to be reckoned with.

He stretched out his palm to Cousins and grasped his hand firmly as the two men met for the first time.

"Welcome to the castle, John," McKenzie said jovially with a Scottish lilt. "Glad you made it."

"Happy to be here," Cousins replied as the two men eyed each other.

In truth, McKenzie had not initially been convinced about the communications role within his organisation which was now filled by the Englishman. He was himself a man of action, rather than words, and would have preferred another manager for his field team. But it was an essential head office requirement, and Cousins was better than nothing. Besides, international staff were few and far between, and he might be useful yet as an additional member of the management team which he would be required to support.

Yet the Scot could understand the benefits of giving a voice to those who often are not heard and of feeding head office with positive examples to highlight his team's work.

McKenzie turned towards the petite Eritrean receptionist sitting behind the front desk. "This is Kedija. Runs the place. John Cousins, our new communications guy from England."

She smiled at Cousins, who nodded politely towards her as they walked past.

"We'll be in my office, Kedija," McKenzie told her. Then, almost as an afterthought, added: "I'm expecting Doctor Walters. Show him in when he arrives. And do please organise some sweet tea!"

McKenzie's office was what one might expect. Simple and functional. Paperwork was stacked high upon the solitary desk, a couple of chairs, filing cabinets. There were maps of Eritrea's six administration regions on the walls, with coloured pins marking areas of the organisation's work. There were framed posters too, showing aspects of Eritrean life: camels being led across arid terrain; a shepherd with a flock of mountain sheep; a group of children happily splashing water at a village well.

"It's a fine country," McKenzie said as he watched the Englishman eye the images on the wall. "The people are gentle and friendly," he added. "Generally educated. But very poor. Still not much in the way of government infrastructure and services." He paused. "We've got our work cut out."

CHAPTER FIVE

T HE CALL FROM McKenzie came as a surprise that morning. David Walters was the senior programme manager with Medics International. The organisation held the compound adjacent to the British and shared some of their respective facilities in the interests of efficiency. It was a practical arrangement which also occasionally allowed them to cooperate on aspects of programming. So, the two men knew each other well. One might even have said they were friends, though they were very different in temperament. Perhaps that's why it worked so well.

He took the call from the Scotsman, expecting confirmation of the evening's social arrangements. There was a barbecue at the UN compound across the city and word had gone around the expat community. Instead, McKenzie was calling about the Englishman who was due to arrive later that day. It was the eagerly awaited communications expert. He wanted to invite the doctor to come and say 'hello'.

Walters had been a general practitioner from Christchurch,

New Zealand. But he had given up his suburban practice on the comfortable outskirts of the city following the death of his wife through ovarian cancer. The couple didn't have any children and, still in his mid-thirties, he had felt the need to abandon his grief and work overseas. There were too many reminders of the happiness he had known which had so suddenly been taken from him. He felt a calling to put his skills to use for those less fortunate. It helped to bring some purpose to life.

Quiet and considered – some might have said still preoccupied with loss – he was unlike McKenzie in almost every aspect, though the two men enjoyed each other's company. There was something funereal about Walters. Perhaps it was his height, his slight physique and the stoop with which he carried himself, uncharacteristic in one still relatively young. There was a seriousness about the face too, emphasised by his sallow complexion and the thick-rimmed glasses he wore. Yet sometimes the doctor's subtle humour, which seemed buried, would surface and surprise the Scot. And he would roar with laughter. Walters too seemed to shed years when he smiled, bringing a warmth to an otherwise plain and sombre countenance. The two men understood each other, though they found themselves in Eritrea for different reasons.

The doctor first laid eyes on Cousins that lunchtime in McKenzie's office. He was what one might have expected. Tall, rugged, unshaven. Firm handshake. Friendly. Yet with all new staff there was a degree of suspicion. Would he fit in? Would he complement the set-up? Was he any good? Walters would reserve his judgement. Yet first impressions were relatively neutral. That was a plus. Already, he knew that McKenzie had his own ideas on how the newcomer might fit in. He shared the Scotsman's view that any additional expat was essentially to be welcomed. They did, indeed, have their work cut out. There was a view too that, in time, Cousins might support joint communications initiatives between the two NGOs. The UN barbecue planned for that evening would provide a perfect introduction. Mancini, the Italian, was certain to be there and Siobhan Cullen too to keep everyone in check. Not to mention Sir Charles.

"I understand James has mentioned the event over at the UN compound this evening?" the doctor said.

"Yes," Cousins replied. "Looking forward to it."

"It's a good chance to meet a few people, eat well and have a few beers," McKenzie added. "Is Hannah going?"

"Yes, came back from the field yesterday," said Walters.

"Good! Now there's a girl," McKenzie told Cousins with a smile. "If I were twenty years younger, she'd be the one for me. Bloody good nurse!"

"She is," the doctor said, before adding soberly, "but I'm not sure any woman has been the girl for you in twenty years!"

And McKenzie roared with laughter. "Aye, maybe so. Maybe so, David."

The UN compound lay among the warehouses that lined the road to the airport on the south-western side of Asmara, in what was still the city's commercial hub. It was an imposing complex of grey concrete buildings surrounded by a high wall topped with razor wire. There was a checkpoint on entry with armed sentries of varying nationality, depending on which force was in town. Officially designated the United Nations Mission in Ethiopia and Eritrea (UNMEE), the complex had been set up in 2000 to monitor the peace and was headquarters to half a dozen agencies, including the World Food Programme

(WFP) and UNICEF. But it was dominated by the personnel of the UN Mine Action Coordination Center, largely cynical ex-services people.

In essence, the strong UN presence provided a reminder of the fragility of peace between Eritrea and its southern neighbour and the impact of the conflict still felt acutely across the region. Not least in clearing the millions of mines that still lay beneath the hard, dry earth. Yet it provided a hub of social activity for the international community. It was a secure haven; an oasis of plenty in a country still desperately food insecure.

Cousins had spent the afternoon meeting staff and moving his gear into his new quarters, a flat-roofed bungalow shared with two others he had yet to meet. Two of the four bedrooms were still vacant, and the Englishman was therefore able to choose which of the empty rooms he preferred. He took the one furthest from the makeshift generator backup of a dozen car batteries grouped in a corner of the shared central living room.

The good-sized room he moved into held a simple wooden double bed, a desk, chair, small chest of drawers and a battered wardrobe, all of similarly simple construction.

The words 'Gonzales was here, 2002' was etched into the wood on the side panel, to which someone had added: 'So was Pieterson'. He smiled as he read the words. He wondered idly what had happened to them. He opened the wardrobe door to find a solitary plastic coat hanger. He sighed. Then he turned to gaze from the window which faced open, compacted ground with several lines of washing strung out to dry in the sun.

His luggage was sparse. A military backpack, laptop, a canvas shoulder bag, camara and tripod. But it was everything he needed. Anything else might be bought locally, he figured. Essentially, it was two sets of clothing, carefully rolled, spare pair of boots, plenty of socks and underwear. Several additional cotton T-shirts. Mosquito net. A washbag. And a few comforts from home, including ground coffee, a compact CD player and two paperback books. He'd brought several packs of batteries too. Within an inside pocket, there was a three-month supply of doxycycline tablets too for protection against malaria.

It didn't look much as he emptied his bags and methodically laid the contents out on the bed. He was meticulous in unpacking, almost obsessive. He wanted to find the right place in his room for each item. He liked to be organised. Finally, he had fixed the mosquito net from the hook on the ceiling and spread it across the four corners of the bed. After he had finished, he sat down on the plain wooden chair at the desk and realised he was sweating. He leaned forward towards his backpack and pulled a bottle of water from one of the side pockets, unscrewed the top and drank deeply.

He needed to freshen up. He felt hot and grubby. He rose and stepped into the adjoining washroom. It was tiled, with an open shower, wash basin and a basic toilet. There was a small, white towel lying at the side of the hand basin, and he noted there was half a roll of toilet paper on the window ledge. He turned the shower on full and watched a disappointing spray from its head cascade onto the tiled floor. The flow was adequate; the water was warm to the touch, heated by the sun from a tank on the roof. It would do. He went to fetch his washbag.

They sat outside on a thick blanket laid out upon the ground beneath the red sky as the sun began to slip from the horizon and the heat of the day gave way to the approaching chill of the Eritrean evening. The light across the UN compound was fading to reveal the first stars as Cousins stared absently into the heavens. He stayed close to McKenzie and his finance manager, a cheerful, easy-going Kenyan everyone called Joe. There were several Eritrean nationals too, who seemed part of the Scotsman's team. Two white women, with cotton shawls, had also come to sit close to join them at the barbecue.

There were others now gathering in small groups, plates and bottles of beer in hand, standing in the darkness which began to envelope the solitary figure standing over the half oil drum filled with hot coals balanced upon a stack of bricks.

"Chicken, anybody?" came a cry from the burley South African stooped and sweating over the task at hand. Then he would deftly transfer several pieces of meat onto a plate held out towards him. Occasionally, there was a burst of yellow flame lighting up faces as the fat from the meat dripped onto glowing embers and flared angrily. The man would curse and take a step back from the heat, steel tongues in hand, ready to lunge forward to rescue the meat threatened by incineration. And the faces of those who watched him would flicker in the light, their eyes reflecting the flames as darkness fell upon the group outside.

Every now and then, someone would tap McKenzie on the shoulder, and he would smile in acknowledgement or offer a jovial comment. He seemed popular and responded with equal enthusiasm to locals and expats alike.

The meat was good. A little chewy, perhaps, served with local flatbread. But the taste was smoky and magnificent. Cousins watched those around the barbecue as he ate.

"It's good," he said. "Very tasty! What is it?"

"Goat, or camel, I would expect," McKenzie replied. "I had the chicken." And he smiled to himself.

After he had finished eating, Cousins rose awkwardly to his feet. His knees were stiff. He wasn't used to sitting on the ground.

"Just going for a smoke," he told McKenzie, and the Scotsman nodded, still chewing his own food. He pointed across the yard towards a small brick hut opposite the corner of the main building. It lay bathed in the spotlight which shone away from them across the compound towards the parking area in which a variety of UN vehicles were lined up in rows. The structure provided refuge for smokers during the monsoon when they would dash from the social club building through the heavy rain to find cover outside for their cigarette break. A solitary UN soldier stood in fatigues, leaning against the outbuilding smoking, eyes fixed to the ground. He looked up and nodded as Cousins approached, then flicked his cigarette butt into an adjacent metal bucket and left. The Englishman took the man's place, reached for the battered pack of cigarettes from his pocket and lit up, blowing the smoke up at the mosquitos swarming overhead. Clouds of them railed against the nearby light, crackling as they fried in the heat from the lamp.

He saw the silhouette of a woman approach in the darkness from the main group. As she drew nearer, he could see that she too was dressed casually, her head and shoulders wrapped with a white cotton scarf, and he realised that she was European.

"Hello." She smiled as she stepped from the darkness into the light, and he saw her face for the first time. It was a pretty face that took on an additional beauty when she smiled.

"Hello," he replied.

"Got a light?"

He nodded, reaching into his pocket. He deftly flicked the Zippo with a practised thumb, offering the flame to her as she leaned towards him with her cigarette between her lips and puffed to get it alight.

"You look new," she said, stepping back to study him.

"What does 'new' look like?" He smiled.

"I've not seen you before..."

"I'm with McKenzie," he told her.

She nodded. "The writer..."

"That's me," he said. "And what do you do around here?"

"I'm a nurse."

"British?"

"Yup."

"John Cousins." He reached out a hand.

"Hannah."

"You work with Walters, the doctor..."

"I do, for my sins. We run the basic health units on the western side."

"I've heard about your work."

"I've heard about you too. You'll have to come out and take a look at what we do."

"I'd like that," he said.

And they both stood smiling at each other.

"Least the UN can organise a decent barbecue out here," he said, nodding towards the group gathered around the grill.

"I'm sorry?" She wasn't sure what he meant.

"Just saying," he continued. "The UN. Can't usually even schedule a meeting to organise the next meeting!"

"They do all right here," she told him, feeling slightly defensive.

"I'm sure they do," he said, sensing her indignance. "Would you like another drink?"

She nodded, and they headed back towards the main building to get a beer. Who was this guy?

CHAPTER SIX

T HE TALL AFRICAN stood shrouded in cotton at the centre of the village under the hot sun in front of the well, surrounded by a crowd of men, women and children. It seemed the entire community had gathered to support their elder and witness the moment. Cousins too stood in anticipation, camera in hand, flanked by Lorenzo Mancini and the Eritrean driver. There was a murmur of expectation as they stood and watched. All eyes were on the man at the well.

He glanced across at Mancini, who nodded for him to proceed, and two powerful hands extended from his white shawl to grasp the iron handle before him to work the pump, cranking it up and down. Suddenly, a burst of clear water gushed from the spout, shining silver in the strong sunlight, and splashed to the ground. Cousins raised his camera to capture the source of wonder as the crowd cheered.

"*Bene. Magnifico!*" Mancini exclaimed, for whom the magic was never lost. Children rushed forward as the man continued to pump the well, splashing in a frenzy of spray and laughter in the water which split the brilliant light into an exploding rainbow of transient colour. It represented a turning point. There was now clean water for an entire community; a life-changing intervention for more than two hundred villagers. At a cost of four hundred pounds. That covered drilling down fifty metres into the sun-baked earth and hitting the cool, clear groundwater. It included fitting a simple hand pump and its basic filters.

Not a bad way to spend your first day in the 'field', Cousins mused. He had risen early and headed out across the courtyard towards the waiting Land Cruiser as the sun had broken over the mountain, casting its shadow long across the ground. The Eritrean driver Jamal had smiled a welcoming salaam to the Englishman as he had approached. He was one of four drivers working for the British NGO and was to cut across Asmara to pick up the Italian from his team house before making for the village. It lay some five hours to the south-west, along the road to Barentu, where the rocky mountain landscape sloped towards the arid plains of the Gash-Barka region, scattered with isolated villages and small nomadic settlements.

The drilling of wells was part of a shared water and sanitation programme between the Italian aid agency Cesvi and the British, which cross-cut into health and hygiene initiatives. Clean water could save countless lives from preventable waterborne disease and dysentery. The central well would spare the children of the village from trekking across the parched landscape to the waterholes that had been used by the community and its animals for generations.

The women of the village would be trained in hand-washing and hygiene promotion to further safeguard their families; basic knowledge that could also protect health. But it meant change and engagement with the people, empowering them to better their lives. It was the same when it came to disease. So often, the obstacle was a lack of knowledge and traditional practices that stretched back to Biblical times. The advance of technology might have brought mobile phones in abundance across the developing world, but when it came to changing behaviours, progress was often achingly slow, hampered by ignorance, poverty and ancient practices. Yet the provision of clean water was a practical change whose benefits were obvious to all.

Jamal the driver watched the exuberance of the community and smiled. His family came from a village not unlike the one in which he now stood. For him, the coming of the aid workers had meant steady employment that provided a decent income for his family and relative security. There was food and shelter for his loved ones, which included his parents, his brothers and sisters and their extended family. For he was not yet married. Neither had he spoken to the family of the girl who had caught his eye. One of the reasons was the doubt he, like many young Eritreans, had for their future. He had not yet been called for military service, which had already taken many of his friends from their families. Some had fled across the border to escape and seek their fortunes in wealthier countries. But for now, he was happy. He was very pleased to work for a foreign aid agency helping his people.

Cousins was standing with the village elder, making notes. The chieftain stood proud in his loosely wrapped turban. He was satisfied. It was a big day for the village. The well provided a degree of security. It lifted a burden from families whose children laboured under the tedious daily chore of fetching the water. Yes, it was a good day. He was very grateful to the foreigners for helping his people. And where was the Westerner from? the elder enquired. He smiled. Ah, English. He had a cousin in London. May Allah bless the British. And the Italians. They would surely join the village to celebrate the occasion by feasting with them. Then there would be football with the children. What team did Cousins support? Chelsea? Liverpool? Manchester United, perhaps. Here there were many followers of the English game.

"My tribe is Leicester City," Cousins replied. At which the African smiled at him politely and said no more.

The long drive back to Asmara took them along the narrow road which led back towards the hills. Mancini slept most of the way, and the driver was silent, keeping his eyes fixed ahead as the track before him stretched into the distance as the vehicle sped along, kicking up a cloud of dust as it skirted the hills north-eastwards across the dry and desolate landscape in the searing heat of the relentless afternoon sun.

Occasionally, there was a figure across the plains in the distance, driving a small flock of goats, or a small group of nomads with their camels in the vast expanses which lay between the settlements of flat-roofed mud houses strung out along 150 miles of road. Or there might be a couple of small children carrying plastic containers for water, tiny splashes of colour on the landscape on the horizon under the clear blue sky. There was no traffic, except for a battered Coca-Cola truck making its deliveries.

Mancini opened his eyes, raised himself and signalled for the driver to pull over. It was the only stop they made, as the vehicle slowly began to climb into the first folds of the hill country. The Italian, still bleary-eyed, staggered from the vehicle to disappear behind the rocks and relieve himself. Cousins took the opportunity to smoke, squinting into the distance. Climbing from the air-conditioned vehicle was like stepping into a wall of heat. The sun was high, and the temperature had reached its greatest intensity. They would not make Asmara until late afternoon, when the sun would turn orange and begin to sink in the blazing sky before slipping beyond the mountain peaks.

As the Italian settled back into the vehicle and closed his eyes, Cousins thought about the nurse he had met the previous evening. She was young and pretty, and he wondered what had brought her to Eritrea. McKenzie was right. She was a smasher. That was when he had first met Mancini too, who was now happily dozing next to him on the back seat, gently snoring as the vehicle continued its journey. The middle-aged Italian seemed a decent sort. Experienced. Passionate about the people. He'd met Charlotte at the barbecue too. A mature woman of advancing years who had reminded him of a public schoolteacher. Well spoken, well mannered, with a reassuring smile and a wry sense of humour. She worked for one of the UN agencies, he thought someone had said.

It was only after they had finally reached the capital, and when they had dropped the Italian at his team house, that Cousins struck up a conversation with the driver.

"Nearly home," the Englishman said.

"Yes, sir," he replied, concentrating on the flow of vehicles he was now forced to contend with, after hours on the open road.

"Is your family from Asmara?"

"No, sir," said the driver. "Small place in Gash-Barka."

"Where we have just been?"

"Yes."

"But you live in the city now?"

"Yes. Very good for work."

"Yes," said Cousins absently.

And they fell silent once more.

"Are you married?" the driver asked abruptly, drawing

confidence from their initial exchange. Cousins was not unprepared. He was accustomed to such sudden personal questions from his time in Pakistan.

"No," Cousins replied, "but I have loved a woman." It was the easiest answer. "Are you married?"

The driver grinned awkwardly. "No, sir," he said, "but there is a woman I would like to marry," the Eritrean added.

"I am sure she is very beautiful," Cousins said.

"Oh yes. Most beautiful."

"Will you marry soon?"

The driver sighed. Then he considered his reply. "Is difficult…"

"It always is when the girl is beautiful," smiled Cousins.

"There is problem with military service."

"You have to join the Army?"

"Everyone join Army. It is the law of Eritrea."

"National service?"

"Yes, sir. I do not know when I will go. Or when I come back."

Cousins had read something about the conscription of young Eritreans into the forces. Usually for indefinite periods which could last many years. Even decades. It was a major factor in young people seeking to leave the country. Often through people smugglers across the border into the Sudan.

"Does the girl love you?"

"Oh yes, sir. Very much."

"That's nice. What is her name?"

"Name is Ayana."

"That's lovely. Does it have a meaning?"

"All names in Eritrea have meaning. It means 'God answers her," the driver told him. "I hope God does answer her," the Englishman said.

"If it is written…" And there was a sadness that seemed to fill the driver's eyes.

The Land Cruiser pulled into the BritAid courtyard and swept to a halt as the sun began to set and a soft breeze gently stirred the jacaranda blossom.

"Thank you, Jamal," Cousins said, and the driver nodded as the Englishman climbed from the vehicle. He reached into the back seat to grab his camera bag, threw it across his shoulder and walked towards the main house as the Land Cruiser pulled away.

—⁂—

McKenzie glanced up and smiled from behind his desk as the Englishman walked in. His office door was open, and he rose to greet Cousins. "How was the first day?" he asked.

"Good," he responded. Cousins told him about the village and the well, as the Scotsman nodded and smiled.

"Ah, water. It's a big issue here," he said. "A well like that can change the lives of an entire community. It's a good partnership initiative. Then we follow up with health and hygiene, mobilise the women. They're more reliable." There was involvement from the medics too on a range of overarching health programming.

Cousins nodded. But he was dead beat. And he had a raging thirst. The heat and the journey had been exhausting. It had been quite a day.

"Go take a rest, John. Relax. Freshen up. I'll see you over dinner."

"Thanks."

"Tomorrow I'd like you to head back into the field. Stay over at the office at Tessenei for a few days. That's past Barentu towards the Sudanese border. Get something on the mosquito

44

nets being distributed. We're getting some pressure to show results on the programme, and it would be good to have a story out there. Head office will like that. Driver will pick you up in the morning. He's a good man."

"Sure, Jim."

"That's a long drive," the Scotsman added. He paused, as if he was going to say something more. "I'll fill you in later. Well done. By the way, it's James, or Mac, if you prefer." Cousins nodded. Then McKenzie turned and headed back into his office. He still had some paperwork to complete. The demands of head office and the donors seemed never-ending. There were still the financial issues he needed to speak to the Kenyan about.

He sighed, rubbing his fingers to smooth his ragged moustache. There was always something. Corruption was a constant niggle. If it wasn't the fuel, it was the cooking oil. Or vehicle parts. Even the mosquito nets. He didn't really blame the locals. He knew they were desperately poor. It was an occupational hazard in developing countries, a game. As long as it was contained within acceptable margins. It was collateral damage. He thought about Cousins. He would brief him about the minefields over dinner. He was pleased. Perhaps things would work out with the Englishman after all.

CHAPTER SEVEN

T HE FRONTIER TOWN lay on the road west from Barentu close to the Sudanese border. Tessenei was essentially a hub for the movement of goods and people, a bustling hive of activity, some legal, some not, much fought over during the long war with Ethiopia. Its untidy collection of flat-roofed buildings lay sprawling beneath the hills on the flood plains of the Gash River.

The river bubbled forth from the mountains of central Eritrea, ran south-west to form the border with Ethiopia for several hundred miles, before flowing lazily north-west, up towards the town and into the Sudan in its bid to reach the Nile, where it dissipated and sank into hot desert sands. For many months, large stretches of the waterway flowing through the border settlement ran dry and were then suddenly swollen by the monsoon rains, when the parched landscape dotted with acacia scrub and doum palm burst into a temporary sea of greenery. But during the long dry season, its stagnant waters were a breeding ground for mosquitos, with malaria and dengue rampant.

The town's buildings still carried the scars of protracted conflict, peppered with bullet holes or showing gaping shell damage. Some districts comprised clusters of traditional tribal dwellings, round mud-bricked homes with conical thatched roofs. And there were tented settlements everywhere. But there were signs of new building too in an effort to support the influx of those returning from the Sudan to homes they had abandoned during the conflict. It was a melting pot of peoples whose business was daily survival and a bid to construct a better future. The town saw a constant flow of those from across the nearby border who knew hunger and disease.

But growth outwards was restricted. Eritrea's economy and its infrastructure was broken. Besides, the town was still surrounded by minefields from the war, a constant menace which lay beneath the scorched landscape scattered with outlying villages. Traffic in and out of the town was therefore careful to follow the roads and narrow dirt tracks known to be safe, their edges marked by skull and crossbones painted in white letters onto large red signs to warn of the hidden danger. Occasionally, a bus, or a truck, would hit an anti-tank mine. Sometimes it might be a village farmer out on the land. Yet life went on. It seemed an occupational hazard. And the people went about their business. Dubious traders worked alongside government and military agents, sometimes in tandem. The American dollar, the Saudi riyal or Sudanese pound were hotly exchanged for goods and services. Most lucrative of all was the trafficking of human beings.

This was where BritAid operated one of its field offices. Essentially, it was a flat-roofed guesthouse on the outskirts of the town with some office space and accommodation for up to half a dozen staff. But it formed a frontline for the NGO's battle against malaria. And at the heart of its programme was the distribution of the nets.

"Don't leave the compound unless you're with one of the locals," McKenzie told Cousins, breaking off a piece of *injera* flatbread with his fingers and scooping the *tsebhi* stew. "It's a den of thieves," he added, pushing the parcel of food into his mouth, as Cousins nodded. "Farjad will be your main man," the Scotsman continued, still chewing on the meat. "He's a good guy. As is Jamal, the driver. Stick to them like glue."

"I will," the Englishman replied, reaching for the bottle of cold beer as the heat of the spices began to burn his palate.

"You'll be all right," McKenzie said, almost as if he was trying to convince himself. In truth, he was a little worried. Tessenei was a dangerous place, especially for those new to the country.

Cousins would be taken to a settlement where the distribution of the mosquito nets was due to take place. He was to gather stories, using Farjad as his interpreter.

"Take lots of pictures," McKenzie told him. "Show our engagement with the community. That's what donors want to see. We need to show that the programme is working." He took a swig of his own beer, then laid a hand on Cousins' shoulder. "Aye, you'll be all right," he repeated. Then he chuckled to himself, as the alcohol began to take hold. He wished he could have spared the time to visit the Tessenei office himself.

It was his smile that first struck Cousins when he met the Eritrean field coordinator. Broad and sincere. He was smaller than the Englishman had imagined, with fine features common to the peoples of the region. He had expected a more rugged, solid man. Perhaps because of the way in which McKenzie had described his character and his achievements in Tessenei. Farjad knew his people and their ways, good and bad. He was streetwise.

Beneath the smile lay an experienced, hardened practitioner who deftly straddled two worlds: that of his own countryfolk and that of his British employer. Often, they were at odds. Sometimes that required juggling. In short, Farjad was a BritAid legend, who had learned to take the challenges of the job in his stride. Always with a smile.

He didn't think Cousins would present a problem, nor the task the Englishman was sent to complete. He understood what McKenzie needed. He grasped what was expected of him. That was primarily to ensure the safety of Cousins, while enabling access to the distribution. And he knew exactly where to direct the communications man to ensure he would leave with what he required. It would not be a difficult distribution. The people welcomed the nets. They were in truth something of a sideshow. They weren't going to change lives. The people accepted them because they already knew the aid agency, which had been working with the community for many months. They knew the medics too and were grateful. There was therefore already a degree of knowledge and trust. So, they took the nets. They were still to be convinced of their value, other than the many weird and wonderful uses that could be found for them.

The woman was sitting, staring absently at the ground, only lifting her face as they approached. In the sling across her stomach, she cradled an infant, while a toddler ran towards her and leaned against the woman's shoulder, having seen the men move towards her. The child stared up at them with dark, enquiring eyes as it clung to the folds of its mother's shawl. The woman was one of many sitting in a long line in the dirt, waiting to receive a neatly packaged mosquito net in the morning sun.

Farjad leaned towards the mother and addressed her in her native language. To Cousins, it sounded like Arabic. She nodded to the Eritrean team leader, and he crouched down on his haunches so that he might explain to her what was being requested. Again, she nodded, shooting a sideways glance at the Englishman who stood beside them.

"She is very happy to talk with you," Farjad told him, and Cousins sat beside them on the parched earth, notebook in hand. He would translate.

Her name was Rahwa. She had no husband. He was gone. The family had fled the fighting and lived for several years in one of the many tented encampments across the border. They were long, hard years, she said.

But last year, after the rains, her husband had left and crossed back into Eritrea to find work in Tessenei. He would work for their return. But he had not come back for them. Weeks turned into months, and she had finally decided she must make the trek back into her homeland alone with her daughter and baby son to try to find him. Again, she found herself living in a tent with her children in one of the camps supported by the UN. And she gestured with her arm the general direction of the encampment which lay on the outskirts of the town.

Once more, she was waiting for better days. Still, she hoped she would be reunited with her husband. Farjad asked about the aid she received. She had access to food. But it was not always enough. Sometimes the children were hungry. She was very happy when the medics came. The nurses would weigh and check the children for illness. And then she would receive more food.

Cousins smiled. For he knew she spoke of the mobile health clinics operated by Walters, and he thought of the nurse he had met at the barbecue a few days ago on the evening of his arrival. And the nets? The mother was pleased to have them. Farjad told the Englishman it was good because they kept her children safe from disease, especially in the dry season, when the region was plagued by swarms of mosquitos spawning over stagnant water. Cousins nodded, taking down the words relayed to him by his Eritrean colleague. He smiled to himself. Farjad was a slick operator.

He had what he needed, though he realised the nets were not seen as important. The people wanted food, shelter and medicine. Above all, they wanted a normal, peaceful life and the means to provide for their families. That required more than an insecticide-treated net. Besides, he knew it was common practice for people to sleep unprotected out in the open air in the stifling heat and humidity of the night. But he realised too the nets were a necessary tool in the fight against malaria, even if their distribution required a supplementary educational programme to encourage behavioural change. However, it made for strengthening relationships with the community, which allowed other initiatives to be introduced. It was not for him to judge the value of any intervention. How could he even begin to comprehend the many issues facing thousands of women just like the mother who now sat beside him? It was about the necessary means for daily survival for her and her young children in a world broken by conflict and poverty.

What was her hope for the future, he asked her.

"A better life," she said simply.

Could he take a picture of her with her children?

Once more she agreed, adjusting the shawl across her shoulders and holding her little girl close to her as she stared directly into the camera lens, lifting her face almost defiantly. It was an image that was to haunt Cousins later, when he viewed the pictures he had taken that day. Her features were typical of the region. Her hair was pulled back, framing a bronze face with a high forehead and delicate features. But it was her gaze that struck him. Her dark eyes seemed unflinching in their resignation of her situation and her determination to survive. The woman was one of several he spoke to with Farjad that morning. All had similar stories. All said they welcomed and would use the nets.

He was surprised by the marked absence of husbands. Many women had lost their men. Either in the fighting during the long years of conflict or to the military for compulsory national service. He was staggered too by the numbers of people still displaced. After all, the fighting had ended years ago. The UN estimated more than a million had been displaced within Eritrea during the fighting in 2000 and a further hundred thousand forced to flee their homes across into the Sudan. Many thousands still languished in camps either side of the border. The majority were women, children and the elderly. Such was the scale of the catastrophe from which the country was struggling to recover. And today he had started to understand the challenges facing its people.

It had a profound impact on him as he reviewed his notes that evening back at the team house in Tessenei. He was pleased with the pictures he had taken. It was impossible not to be moved. That was what he liked about work in the 'field'. It was what inspired and haunted him in equal measure.

But he was tired and emotionally drained. Though the heat of the day was beginning to cool, it was still hot inside. Yet he wouldn't be anywhere else. He felt alive and that he was doing something valuable. He hoped he would be able to sleep. He took comfort in the green tea he sipped as he sat and reflected. He found it was more refreshing than any cold drink. It was a habit he had acquired in Pakistan.

—∞—

At the tented refugee camp across the town, the woman known as Rahwa was reflecting on her own circumstances. Her children were crying. But that was not unusual. Outside, a dog was barking. She felt sorry for the old man coughing in the tent beside hers, for whom she sometimes did the washing. He deserved some peace.

They said he was not long for this world and had been calling for his family, though they had long since been lost. No one knew where they were or if they still lived. But Aiysha Begum was with him, wiping his brow as once more the fever took hold. The Imam had been summoned and would surely come before the breaking of the new day.

Rahwa sighed deeply. The children's cries would soon subside as they tired. And they would sleep beneath the net she had received earlier that day. Among the heat and the noise, she took the time to lean forward in the flickering light of the oil lamp. She would pray to her God in thanks and to ask that she and her children be delivered to a better life. Her faith brought her comfort and was a hope she could cling to. She would pray for the old man too, that peace would finally come to him.

CHAPTER EIGHT

H E FIRST ENCOUNTERED the girl early on the morning of his second day in Tessenei, when the sun kissed the rooftops as it rose above the town. Cousins was returning from the main house after a light breakfast when he saw the small figure bent under the weight of a laundry bag upon her back, scuttling towards him across the dirt. She didn't see him until she was almost upon him, such was her haste as she hurried along, her eyes fixed to the ground.

"Good morning! Salaam!" said the Englishman. The girl stopped in her tracks just a few paces from him, raising her dark eyes to stare at the foreigner. She wore a ragged printed cotton skirt and a grubby oversized T-shirt with a Batman motif and could be no older than nine, or ten, he judged. For a moment, she stared directly at Cousins. Then she smiled awkwardly before dropping her gaze nervously to her feet, which were without shoes or sandals.

"Hello," Cousins ventured again, still facing the girl standing before him in the early morning light. Her skin was chestnut brown, and she looked more African than Arab. Sudanese rather than Eritrean, he would have guessed.

"Salaam," came the hesitant response in a small voice from the girl, still rooted to the spot as she raised herself upright, drawing the ties of her sling more tightly across her tummy with small, brown hands as she gazed curiously at the Westerner before her.

"My name is John." He smiled. "You must be Batman?"

The child made no reply as she continued to stare at the white man, unsure of her next action. She smiled faintly. Then she bowed her head once more under the weight of her laundry and hurried past him towards the small hut to the rear of the main building on the opposite side of the yard. He watched her until she had turned the corner out of sight. Then it suddenly occurred to him she probably didn't even know who Batman was.

―∞―

"Who's the little girl?"

Farjad returned a quizzical look. "Girl?"

"Yes. The girl running around the compound with the laundry," Cousins said.

"Ah, you mean Lula! That girl is the daughter of the Christian woman who works for us here," replied the Eritrean. "Everybody like Lula," he added, beaming.

"I saw her this morning," the Englishman told him.

"Mother does not have husband and works here. Girl is helping."

"I see," said Cousins thoughtfully. "Does the girl go to school?"

Again the African smiled. "Sometimes she is in school."

"That's good," said Cousins. "Do we help her?"

Farjad shrugged his shoulders. "Mother is very poor. But she has an income from her work here. Also, she receives food from the kitchen. This is a powerful help. The girl goes to school when she can."

He said nothing more. Farjad was well aware what the Englishman's view might be. In an ideal world, the girl should receive a proper education. But this was Eritrea. And the country was broken. So often it was a question of survival, rather than ideals. The issue was not as simple as the Westerner might think. The mother was on her own and very poor; the girl helped her mother. Not just with the laundry but with other daily chores too. Ultimately, she lived within an area whose culture did not view the education of girls as a priority. She was Christian too, a minority in the region.

Best leave the foreigner to make enquiries and gain a better understanding of the world in which many Eritreans were living. He was new. Perhaps Cousins should speak to the girl's mother, he suggested. Maybe to McKenzie too on his return to Asmara. Farjad was a wise man. He would take the Westerner to see the mother before he embarked upon the long drive to the capital later that day.

The Christian woman known as Mariam was sitting outside the hut behind the main house, watching over a pot simmering upon an open fire.

"Good morning," said Cousins, and the woman rose to her feet, while the smoke from the fire billowed and twisted into the air beyond and was carried away by the light breeze.

Farjad explained that the Englishman wanted to talk to her about Lula and the woman looked at Cousins with a hint of suspicion. The girl was on an errand collecting fuel for the fire, gathering any kindling wood she might find. If she was lucky, she might come back with some dried animal dung too. It was a daily chore, for although the family had access to the kitchen stove and oil for the lamps at night, the mother cooked mostly outside on the flames of an open fire.

Yes, she told them, her daughter sometimes attended school. She would like her to go more regularly. But the uniform was expensive and besides, the mother had work for her. What was she to do? She was without a husband to support her, and life was hard.

Cousins nodded as Farjad translated her words. He could understand the mother's situation. He asked if she was happy in her work for BritAid. She told him she was grateful to God, and she didn't know how she would survive without it. Work in the compound was good and allowed life to go on. It provided a degree of security.

Again, Cousins nodded and smiled. He said he was happy to meet her and thankful for the services she provided before he and Farjad left her to her cooking.

"She works well for us," Farjad said. "She and the girl are no trouble. They are lucky," he added. "I can show you a thousand women in the town whose children go hungry."

It set Cousins thinking. Though he knew little about the country and its culture, Lula's situation and future troubled him. But he also knew that Farjad was right. How many countless thousands struggled for survival every day in a country racked by war and poverty, whose infrastructure was broken? He wondered what sort of future Lula would have. Though she was one of the 'lucky ones', her life prospects were limited. There must be something that could be done. He would speak to McKenzie on his return.

It was the same feeling he had experienced in Pakistan. As a privileged Westerner, there was the pull for personal involvement. A sense of guilt? Conscience? Compassion, perhaps. In the meantime, the long journey back to the office lay in prospect. Already the sun was high, and the heat of a spring day was beating down upon the desert town.

The men had checked in by radio. All was well. For two weeks, the pair had been camping out in the remoteness of the desert landscape in Gash-Barka's north-west. The field clinic drew the nomadic people of the plains from far and wide and often they would begin to gather around the two tents before the sun had risen. Mainly they were women with their children who had walked many miles. Some were sick. Some were malnourished. Others came for reassurance and the prospect of the fortified food for their children.

The two Eritrean nurses had worked for the Western NGO for more than a year. They were experienced and trusted members of the team, were well liked, good at what they did. No one could have guessed. They had kept their plan secret. Told no one. Not even their closest family members. It was too dangerous and best people didn't know. It was the surest way of protecting them. Besides, perhaps they might have tried to talk them out of it. Lord knows, it was hard enough as it was.

As the light faded, the men fastened the canvas tents securely from the outside. They looked at each other and, without exchanging a word, they picked up their backpacks and headed out across the parched landscape towards the setting sun. Inside their packs, food and water for three days and a wad of Sudanese pounds and US dollars.

It was Daniel who spoke first as they trekked towards the agreed rendezvous point.

"Do you think they will be there?" he asked his Muslim companion.

"They will be there," Juba replied with certainty. He knew the Rashaida were a people of their word. It was the bond upon which they did business. And for money they could be trusted. The tribesmen would be there. Of that, he was sure.

From the settlement they would be taken to the border. By bus, by pickup. Perhaps even by mule, or camel. He hoped not on foot. For it was surely twenty miles, or more. Then, at the border, they would pass into the Sudan. Of that he was also sure. For the Rashaida had a reputation to deliver what they promised. They were known smugglers and traffickers of goods, guns and people, with their established contacts that would allow safe passage from Eritrea. For a price.

Most likely they would then be taken westwards to the town of Kassala and from there negotiate their onwards journey. Perhaps to Khartoum. Then northwards – the hazardous route to Cairo, if they were lucky, or the Libyan port cities of Derna, or Benghazi. Europe beckoned across the Mediterranean. Then freedom. The freedom to live. To work. To be safe. It was surely a dream. But others had gone before, through Greece, Turkey, Italy or Israel.

Earlier, the men had prayed in silence before their departure, each to their respective gods. They prayed for safety and success of the epic adventure they were set to undertake. They asked for deliverance. It would be a journey fraught with risk, danger and hardship. And uncertainty. But the prize made the risk worth taking.

It was a bid for life itself; a future of hope to join those who had already made the journey and settled in Europe. Therefore, as they prayed, they committed their souls into the hands of a higher power in the hope that providence would deliver them safely to a new life. Each man thought of his family and what they were leaving behind. It was everything they had known.

Now every silent footfall upon the parched earth was taking them towards the first stage of their journey, the meeting with the Rashaida.

As the sun threw out its last rays across the desert, the glow of a campfire could be seen, and the first tents of the encampment came into view. The two men stopped and looked uncertainly at each other.

"May Allah protect us," Juba muttered.

"Amen," whispered Daniel, trying to appear confident before whispering a silent prayer to his own God. He drew a deep breath, adjusted his backpack and started forward towards the camp, followed by his companion.

Within a few paces, they were spotted by the Rashaida, who now rose from where they had been squatting around the fire against the desert chill to stand in silhouette against its orange glow. There could be no going back now, as the two men approached from the darkness that began to envelope the desert like a blanket.

CHAPTER NINE

T HE RIDERS CAME from the arid plains when the silver crescent of the moon was barely visible in the night sky and crossed the border into Eritrea undetected. It was not difficult. The Rashaida, the nomadic 'children of the desert', knew the terrain as if they were part of the sweeping landscape. They were familiar with the points at which to cross unseen in the darkness. Besides, they had their contacts. There wasn't much cash couldn't buy.

The Rashaida tribe was known for moving arms and people across the border, no questions asked. They were proud, independent Bedouin, and they were armed. To see a group approach in their Toyota pickups was always a moment of trepidation, their warriors wrapped in traditional Arab headscarves, against the heat and the dust, often with only their dark eyes visible.

Essentially, they were beyond the law, such as it was. Except for their own tribal code, which was based on the pillars of Islam. Yet they held no allegiance to any political force and considered themselves as free as the sirocco might blow across the landscape. They lived as nomads independently from the machinery of government, relying on their camel herds and the lucrative smuggling of goods across the region. Like all Arab peoples, they revered their camels, upon which their lives depended. For milk, for meat and the finest traded with their 'cousins' across the Red Sea for racing.

They had no interest in the aid workers operating in the area, whom they viewed as passing through, as the wind might blow across the parched earth. Except sometimes to offer a service, for a price.

The group of riders crossing the border were travelling from the Sudan this night by traditional means, by camel, which the coolness of the dark desert sky and the relative shortness of their journey comfortably allowed. They were on their way from a business meeting with local agents. Aside from allowing them to travel the plains 'off-road', they were enjoying their journey, and there was a real sense among the men of reaching back to their roots, as they trotted with their steeds rapidly across the barren plains.

The chieftain, his senior captains and their bodyguards were engaged in the trafficking of people. It was a lucrative trade, with many young Eritreans seeking passage to the safety of the Sudan to escape years of enforced national service with the military. From the bustling town of Kassala across the border, overlooking the banks of the Gash River, they might make their way north and possibly even cross the Mediterranean to seek asylum in Europe. If they were able to pay top dollar. If they were lucky.

It was from the Sudanese town from which the riders were returning. In Kassala they had made arrangements for a small group of migrants to be 'stored' within a safe house on the edge of the town controlled by their tribal 'brothers'. Societal shielding by local communities was a common feature on which their operations relied.

The riders approached the camp almost without sound from the darkness and, as they brought their animals to a halt and dismounted, were welcomed by the man from Tessenei flanked by his accomplice and a driver. He and his men had pitched two tents the day before in readiness. A Hilux was parked up, as agreed, the man told the arrivals. He was short and stocky and clearly subservient to the chieftain to whom he reported.

The Rashaida leader who stood before him was an imposing figure, a little taller than the others and entirely draped in dark cotton robes, with a headdress that only allowed his eyes to be seen. The camels were led away and tied, and the chieftain and his captains entered the larger of the two low tents, followed by the stocky man from Tessenei. Inside, there was sweet tea and bread prepared by a local woman who was heavily veiled according to traditional custom.

The men sat on the ground in a circle on the carpets that had been laid out, as the tea was served, and the chieftain removed the covering from his face. He was dark-skinned with a close-cropped beard. His features were more Arabic than African. And from the corner of one eye, a jagged scar ran across his cheek to his upper lip. He spoke as someone to be obeyed. When he did, it was in a Bedouin Arab dialect prevalent in the nomadic people of the region.

He was, ironically perhaps, known as Abu. It was term of endearment commonly taken to mean father. But always it was spoken with respect. Yet he was a man who was feared like no other in the group of men which had assembled in the remote corner of Gash-Barka to do business. He and his men reported everything was in order in Kassala; he expected to hear the same from the man from Tessenei. He was not disappointed.

The small group of migrants had arrived at the camp after sunset, as agreed, and handed over the first instalment of their cash. Now they sat anxiously in the second tent, out of sight. Later that night, they would be taken across the nearby border. By that time, the Rashaida leader Abu Khattab would be gone. He would leave two of his men to accompany them on their journey by pickup to meet a further guide on the Sudanese side. It was a short drive of no more than half an hour. Then they would take up the road to Kassala. They were unlikely to be stopped en route. And if they were, they knew what to do. It was the best time of the month to travel undetected, particularly as the moon was still on the wane and the desert sky at its darkest.

The riders inside the tent talked and drank and ate until they were satisfied, attended by the woman who moved as if unseen. After coffee had been served, and a short blessing said, his men took their leave and went outside to sit at the fire to talk and smoke under the stars. Only the Rashaida leader remained with the man from Tessenei.

"Good," said Khattab to his agent. "Then we are ready."

The second man nodded. The cash had been paid, and he had already received his cut.

Several additional bands of Eritreans were to be delivered across the border in the nights to follow. It was a busy time. But no problems were foreseen. For the Rashaida, it was a regular trade. Many hundreds of desperate people had been ferried into the Sudan over the last few years. Sometimes with weapons, still plentiful in Eritrea. They were part of an established smuggling network, which included arms and other contraband. And everyone, including officials and security personnel, as necessary, took their cut. Bribery was the best means of securing safe passage.

Among the group set to leave the country that night were the two nurses from Medics International, a young engineer and his woman, who seemed to be married, and a mysterious dark-skinned man who claimed to be Somali. But then no questions were asked. It was irrelevant. It was about having the cash required by the Rashaida for safe transit over the border and a place to stay in Kassala. That was all. Then they would negotiate their own way.

They were anxious moments for the group of migrants as they sat silently in the flickering light of a solitary oil lamp. None were sure what would happen next. But all knew if they were caught by the Eritrean authorities, they and their families would be punished severely. That would mean lengthy spells in jail and hefty fines for their families. They might even be shot by border forces. Perhaps attacked by bandits and sold into slavery, or worse.

Few words were spoken. It was the young engineer who spoke first. "What will happen to us?" he asked. "I have heard sometimes there is kidnapping."

It was the voice of the dark-skinned African that answered from the corner of the tent which lay in shadow.

"Not from this band of Rashaida. They will deliver us," he said with certainty. And he paused. "The danger is in Kassala. That is where we must be careful. For there is no agreement for our journey beyond the town. We must make new deals and take our chances."

The two nurses had a guarantee of safe passage onwards, through extended family who agreed to pay for the two men to travel up towards Khartoum, then to be smuggled once more into Egypt, where they would make for Cairo or Alexandria. And perhaps a fishing boat to Greece. But for now, they said nothing. Each party would have to make their own way. It was almost too much to contemplate, to hope for.

"It will be all right. We must place our faith in God," Juba said. "God is great!"

The dark-skinned African chuckled. "Which god is that, brother?"

In the low light of the tent, the engineer took the hand of his wife under the fabric of her shawl and squeezed gently as she turned towards him. So many thoughts were racing through her mind. She was a schoolteacher in the Kunama village that had been their home. She wondered what the children would say when they learned she had gone. She thought of her mother. And the small farm that was now lost. She felt like crying. But no tears would come. So, she said a silent prayer of her own to draw comfort. It was a hope of deliverance. Outside, they could hear voices. The tent flap lifted, and a man with heavy headscarf peered in. "Come," he said in Arabic. "It is time."

The night was cool and dark as they emerged from the tent into the desert air with their bags and were ushered by the man in the turban towards the pickup parked a few yards from the tent. They saw he carried an AK47 in his right hand which he used to wave them towards the vehicle. The driver stood waiting for them to climb onto the back of the truck.

When they were aboard, the man from Tessenei came to see them off. "Salaam. Safe journey," he shouted as the driver climbed behind the wheel and fired the Toyota into life. The armed Rashaida tribesman sat in the passenger seat, while a second climbed up behind to sit with the group of migrants.

Daniel and Juba looked at each other anxiously as the vehicle moved off at speed towards the west, where the border lay half an hour across through the darkness.

CHAPTER TEN

T HERE WAS NO warning. When the phone call came, it took Walters completely by surprise. He didn't recognise the voice at first. The line was bad, and there seemed to be a good deal of shouting in the background.

"We are here in Kassala. But we are safe! So sorry, Mr Walters," the voice said with urgency.

"In Kassala?" Walters repeated.

"It is Daniel. I am with Juba."

"Daniel and Juba. In Kassala," Walters said. "Well, what are you doing there?" he added, before he understood what had happened.

"Please tell everyone we are safe," the voice insisted. "So sorry!" Daniel repeated and the line went dead. For a moment, Walters stared at the phone. His first reaction was shock, as the news sank in. Then a sense of alarm. Two of his best nurses had just absconded across the border. When, finally, he rose to step from his office, he was smiling faintly.

"I'll be damned!" he uttered. The truth was, he didn't

really blame them. The news spread like wildfire. Within the hour, the entire staff of Medics International and BritAid had heard. The overwhelming feeling was one of jubilation. It was every young Eritrean's dream to escape the country for a better life. And Daniel and Juba were on their way. They had crossed the border and made it to Kassala. From there, they had every chance.

The abandoned field unit was a side issue. It was collateral damage. But the loss of two qualified nurses was a nuisance. No. The prevailing sentiment across the organisation was one of happiness for the two men. Their families would have to be informed immediately. A report would also need to go to the authorities. But the truth was that the two men had kept their plans secret and taken everyone by surprise. No one could have known. Therefore, there was no one to blame. That was the very best protection for all concerned, for life to go on as before.

"And you really had no idea?" McKenzie asked.

"None at all," Walters replied truthfully, staring at his desk.

"And Hannah?"

Walters shook his head.

"Best that way," said the Scotsman. "Seen it before with some of my people. Good for them," he added. Walters looked unconvinced.

"So, what do I tell the authorities?"

"The truth. What can they do? Hundreds head across to Sudan every day of the week." McKenzie paused, drawing a deep breath, looking directly at his friend. "Best start looking for two new nurses!"

The doctor nodded sombrely in his funereal way.

"Guess this calls for a drink," McKenzie said, and the two men grinned at each other.

———⌘———

When Cousins arrived at the compound, there was an undeniable buzz at the office. The local staff were milling around reception, chatting excitedly, and the aroma of coffee beans being roasted in the back kitchen was apparent. McKenzie was out on urgent business next door with the medics, the receptionist told him with the broadest smile.

"Anything happening?" he asked.

"You not heard?" she said, still smiling. "The two nurses at the Medics gone across the border. And they not gonna come back anytime soon!"

There was a general murmur of approval from the assembled national staff. Cousins wasn't sure what to say.

"Are they going to be in trouble?" he asked naively.

"Only if they be caught. But they're gone from the country now... to *Kassala*." She said the name with emphasis, almost in reverence, as if it represented life's ultimate goal.

"You seem happy they crossed the border," said Cousins.

"Oh, we are. Ain't no future for people here," the receptionist said. "That's why we are happy for them. There's coffee coming."

"Smells great! I could use a cup," he replied.

"You're invited. Mr McKenzie, he'll be back soon enough and will drink a cup with us too. And Mr Walters from the Medics."

Preparations for the coffee ceremony were underway. It was a way the peoples of the region had of socialising and celebrating. At every opportunity. It bonded the people, and it was beautifully ceremonial. Already, the green coffee beans were being roasted over an open flame by the women. Meanwhile, rugs and grasses were being spread on the ground outside, scattered with small yellow flowers by many hands under the fading sun of the late summer afternoon. After roasting, the beans would be ground by hand in mortar and pestle before being added to boiling water.

There was time for Cousins to freshen up before the thick brew would be served out communally in the yard as the afternoon sun hung low and shadows grew long.

It was good to strip down in his room and step into the shower, even though the jet was weak and the water tepid. Washing away the sweat and the dust of the day was like a renewal. He threw on a fresh cotton shirt and jeans and sat for a few minutes on the edge of his bed. Then he slipped his socks over his feet and pulled his boots on. He wasn't quite sure what to expect when he returned to the office. Though he had read about them, he had not yet attended a local coffee ceremony.

When he returned to the office, the scene was already set. He'd not seen so many staff at the compound before. It seemed the medics team had been invited too. He saw McKenzie was back, standing to one side in conversation with Walters, watching the flurry of activity as food was being ferried outside. The easy-going Kenyan was there too.

Johnson emerged from the kitchen, basket of popcorn in hand, with several of the Eritrean nurses. On the reception desk was a tray of small cups, ready to receive the coffee still brewing in the kitchen out back. Cousins went to join McKenzie and Walters, who smiled and nodded on his approach.

"How was the trip back, John?" McKenzie asked.

"Good. All went well," smiled Cousins. "This is great," he said, eying the scene. "You've not experienced the coffee ceremony before..." said the Scotsman.

"No, but I've read about it."

"It's the local way of socialising. Of celebration. Just enjoy. The coffee is out of this world."

"Sorry to hear about your nurses," Cousins said, addressing Walters.

"You've heard then. *C'est la vie*," he said stoically, shrugging his shoulders.

"Has it happened before?" the Englishman asked.

"Not while I've been here. Not in eighteen months," the doctor replied sombrely.

"I've seen it," McKenzie said. "It's what you call an occupational hazard here. Happens now and again. You can't blame them." He paused. "And if you can't blame them, join them," he added with a sweeping gesture of his arm.

"The staff seem happy," said Cousins.

"They are," the Scotsman told him. "They don't talk about it to us. But the nurses getting across the border represents a small victory against the oppression the people feel. It's a successful bid for freedom."

As they spoke, the Eritrean cook emerged from the kitchen carrying a large ceramic *jebena* jug, accompanied by Kedija, the receptionist. Johnson was there too, this time carrying a basket of the sweet *ambasha* bread. Another woman lit a small bowl of crystalised incense, the sweetness of frankincense mingling with the aroma of the coffee which hung heavy in the air.

Cousins watched in fascination as the woman with the black earthenware jug poured the dark, steaming coffee from a few inches above into the small cups in one, elegant action. There must have been almost two dozen tiny, handle-less vessels lined up neatly in rows on the tray.

"They pour the coffee in one," McKenzie said above the growing murmur of anticipation, leaning towards the Englishman. "So the grinds are not disturbed. This first round is the strongest brew. It's what coffee should be!" Cousins nodded, watching the practised, graceful movements of the woman as she finished pouring.

"They always pour an extra cup," McKenzie told him. "Some say it's for absent friends; others that it is for departed souls." The receptionist then lifted the tray of coffee carefully and they followed her into the courtyard.

Outside was a blanket of rugs, grasses and flowers, scattered with floor cushions. Some staff were already sitting on the ground, passing snacks of popcorn and peanuts. The tray of coffee was offered around the group, with each person taking a cup into their hands. The Westerners too lowered themselves onto the ground to join the others.

McKenzie was right. The coffee was strong and good, with a hint of spice. Not as bitter as Cousins had expected. Even so, he helped himself to sugar placed for those who required it. That was usually the foreigners. The Englishman half expected an announcement by McKenzie, or Walters, about the two nurses. But none was forthcoming. It was not necessary. All those present knew what had happened. And they wished the two men well. The ceremony was in effect a statement in itself.

There were three servings of coffee. Then the coffee grinds went back into boiling water, each time becoming less intense, more diluted. The first serving was known as the *awel*, McKenzie explained. The second the *kale-i*. The third and final serving, known as the *beraka*, was effectively a blessing. Sometimes the ceremony might go onto five servings, McKenzie told him. Always it was performed with great ritual and respect. Often over the course of several hours. But always it was a relaxed social affair, at least for the guests.

It was as Cousins separated himself from the group to smoke a cigarette under the tall palm, as the sun began to set and people were beginning to disperse, that she approached and they finally found themselves alone. He had watched her earlier, as she helped the women during the ceremony. He was impressed by the easiness with which she mixed with the locals. And always with a smile. It was the English nurse.

"Hello," he said, smiling as she gratefully accepted a cigarette from him. "How's it going?"

"Good," she said. "Quite a day!"

"Too bad about your nurses," he said.

"Yes," she replied. "They are good nurses. Not that I blame them."

"That's what everyone says."

"Well, there's not much of a future for young people here."

"You mean the national service," said Cousins.

"People receive their papers and have to go. Sometimes for decades. Some don't come back at all." He nodded and they fell silent. "Don't you sometimes feel like running away?" she asked him.

"I thought I already had," he said absently as they watched the group from a distance, sipping their cups of coffee in the failing light of the day.

"I mean somewhere you've always longed to be," she said, looking directly into his eyes. "You know, following the dream."

He considered for a moment before replying. "I thought I had found it," he replied. "Once. In Pakistan. So, I guess I'm still looking."

"Is that why you're here?" she asked him. He nodded. "Me too," she added with a hint of sadness.

"Well, perhaps we can look for our respective dreams together," he said.

And suddenly she blushed.

Realising he had embarrassed her, he suddenly felt clumsy and foolish. "I didn't mean it to sound quite that way," he stammered.

"It's OK," she replied. Now they were both smiling.

"Let's hope your nurses make it to safety," he said.

"Yes, I hope so too!"

"Aren't you worried about losing your staff across the border?" he asked her.

"No," she said. "It's not for us to judge, or to interfere. We're merely observers, aren't we? We're just passing through."

They extinguished their cigarettes and began walking slowly back towards the main building as the final rays of the sun slipped beyond the skyline. The Eritrean staff who lingered long over their coffee were still chatting and smiling with an easy ambience as the evening shadows gently enveloped them. They seemed oblivious to the couple's approach as they took their place beside them on the ground. Then, as they sat and watched, sipping the last of the coffee and eating the bread, he realised that perhaps she was right. They were just passing through.

CHAPTER ELEVEN

IN THE DAYS that followed, there was no news of the runaway nurses. As time passed, the two men began to fade from consciousness as new priorities gained focus as surely as the hot North African sun beat down and scorched the earth dry. Life went on. Clinics continued in the field; boreholes were drilled in villages, bringing the prospect of clean water to communities for the first time; and nets were distributed as before. Daniel and Juba were not spoken about. The hope was they had made it. No one wanted to hear otherwise.

Occasionally, there were reports of gunfire and skirmishes on the border with Ethiopia. But they were rare. Sometimes landmine explosions and their fatalities made the local news, a reminder that thousands of mines still lay beneath the soil following the country's distant conflict. But it too was receding from memory as the people sought to rebuild their lives and move on. The UN mine-clearing operation continued. Always in the relentless, draining heat that beat down upon the plains.

You never really grew accustomed to the harshness of the climate. You just learned how to cope and tried to avoid disease. Mainly dysentery and malaria. Typhoid, perhaps. Dehydration. Exhaustion too. For it was easy to work additional hours to offset long periods of boredom and loneliness which come with prolonged postings in foreign lands, many miles from home.

Cousins learned the value of a shady tree on the western plains and an afternoon nap back at the compound when the heat was at its fiercest. As he continued to work within communities, gathering his stories, he came to respect the quiet dignity and resilience of the people, who carried on regardless in the face of ongoing hardship.

In the hills, the climate was cooler and kinder. He looked forward to his days in Asmara, where he was able to relax every other week. Then he would enjoy the sights and sounds of the city and the coffee shops. Sometimes he would see Johnson, either at the compound or at social events, such as they were, at the Blue Nile Bar and Restaurant or at the UN base. The bar and the barbecue were still popular with expats. It was a rare chance to socialise and exchange stories over a beer. It was a reminder of the familiar from back home. Then it was back into the ferocious heat of Gash-Barka in the west. But soon the rains would come, they said. That would be a time of celebration.

He had spoken to McKenzie about Lula, the little girl at the field base in Tessenei. The Scot had no objection if Cousins wanted to help in some small way.

As long as he was careful not to overpromise. The organisation operated a no child sponsorship scheme. But could he maintain the required long-term commitment? That would surely be the worst thing, to begin support to raise hopes and then withdraw it. He should think about it, McKenzie told him. And he did. He wanted to help. Every time he travelled to Tessenei, he was reminded that he was one of the lucky ones. He saw it in the faces of the people. It lay at the heart of every story he covered in the weeks since his arrival. In the poverty, the disease and the hardship that existed.

It was still on his mind when he found himself back in Asmara one scorching day in May. He'd seen Johnson that weekend, meeting unexpectedly at the BritAid house when she had come over with Walters to discuss a programme issue with McKenzie. She looked even better than he remembered, dressed in khaki shorts, a loose cotton top and those heavy NGO boots that seemed to be standard issue for aid workers. And when they suddenly found themselves alone in the shade of the veranda, he had finally popped the question: would she meet him for coffee?

She had initially blushed. He had taken her by surprise. She'd liked him from the very first time they had met. That had been at the UN barbecue, back in March when he had arrived. But somehow, they hadn't seen much of each other in the weeks that followed, although she sometimes heard Walters and McKenzie talk about him. He was a good writer, they said. Committed. Popular with the locals. But she too had been busy in the field, rarely back in the capital, though he had often enquired about her. Sometimes she heard about the work she undertook with her teams out west, past Barentu, on the plains of Gash-Barka or further north, to provide basic health provision where otherwise there was none. And he wondered about her.

Now he had asked her to meet at one of the Italian coffee houses. "Is it a date?" Cousins had asked her with a smile.

"Why not?!" she replied. "If you're sure…"

"I'd like it very much," he told her. "It doesn't mean we're engaged," he added.

And she laughed. "Well thank goodness for that!"

They met on the Sunday afternoon as the heat of the day began to subside and a light breeze blew through the feathered leaves of the palms which lined the main avenue. They walked casually, weaving among the locals, out on the streets to enjoy the cooler temperature of the early evening and go about their business. Nobody paid them any attention, for in Asmara it was not unusual to see Westerners.

They took a table in the shaded courtyard at the Dolce Vita Café, just off the main avenue near the Mai Jah water fountain, and picked up a menu.

"So, how's it going?" she asked him.

"Good," he replied. "I think I could get used to being here."

"Me too. I should spend more time in Asmara. That's what Walters keeps telling me," she said and swept the hair from her face. It was a nice face, with a complexion that tanned easily in the sun, which had brought out light freckles across the bridge of her nose. Her lips were full and, when she smiled, she showed a dimple in her cheeks above the corners of her mouth. And when she smiled her eyes did too, showing a warmth and compassion that seemed to shine from them. They were the lightest shade of brown and held a sense of experience beyond her years, he thought.

"The Americano is good," she added, as the Eritrean waiter approached to take their order.

"Then I'll have an Americano, with a little hot milk on the side," he said as she watched him turn towards the African to order.

"Me too," she said, and the waiter nodded politely and withdrew.

"No, I mean I'm really enjoying the work and the country," he said. "I think I'd like to stay in Eritrea for a while."

"I think they're very pleased with you," she told him, lifting the coffee cup to her lips. "That's good then."

She studied him over the rim of her cup.

"What about you? How long have you been out here?" he asked her.

"Nearly a year," she told him.

"Impressive. What brought you to Eritrea?"

"Long story!" She paused. "We all seem to be running away from something."

"Perhaps that's true of most aid workers." He smiled. "So, what are you running from?"

"From Bosnia, I guess..." Then she fell silent.

"I'm sure that was pretty rough."

"It was." She paused. "It really was." And he saw a look of sadness in her face.

"What about McKenzie?" he said, sensing she was not comfortable talking about it.

"Oh, he's been here forever. Came over not long after the war, when things were really desperate. Has a place outside town. Have you been?"

"No. Not yet."

"He has a woman there," she added.

"A woman! You mean a local woman?"

She nodded. "Somalian, we think. It's sort of an open secret. But I think he keeps her pretty much out of sight."

"Interesting. I had no idea. What about Walters?"

She laughed. "No. No secrets there. He keeps his own company. But I think he's been out to McKenzie's place a few times. They're pretty close, you know."

"Seems fond of you!"

"Walters?! God, no!" she said. "You're terrible!"

"It's the journalist in me." He smiled. They leaned back to allow the waiter to place their coffee on the table before them.

"Actually, Hannah, I was going to ask your advice."

She stared at him, wondering what he was going to say.

"There's a girl in Tessenei." She raised her eyebrows. "I mean a little girl. At the camp. Name's Lula. Her mother works there. The family is very poor..."

She watched him over the rim of her coffee cup as he continued.

"Well, I'd like to help in some way. You know, financially."

"What does McKenzie say?"

"He says it's OK. But I have to be careful. Be sure of the commitment, once I start. I guess he doesn't want me to raise long-term hopes if I can't deliver."

"I think he's right," she said.

"I understand that. Thing is, I feel I should do something. I've thought about it a lot. We're so very lucky. We get paid well for what we do."

She nodded. "I've had the same thoughts too," she told him.

"I'm not sure how to pitch this. But will you help me?" he asked.

"How do you mean?"

"Would you come and meet Lula and her mother sometime? Make up your own mind. Besides, I think it would be better if you were involved. Being a woman. I think she is a bit suspicious of accepting any help from a man. What do you think?" He watched her as she considered.

Since she had arrived in Eritrea, she had never really thought about a direct personal involvement. But she was open to the prospect of helping. During the course of her work, she too had developed a respect and fondness for the people she worked with. Often, she had wanted to offer more. She admired his desire to do the same.

"Yes. I'd like to meet the little girl," she answered. "It's possible, next time I am out that way. But I'd need to clear it with Walters," she said, as if thinking aloud. "But yes. It would be a good thing to do. It's true, we are the lucky ones. By accident of birth."

"That's brilliant! Let's see if we can set something up in the weeks ahead."

"I'd be willing to contribute. Financially, I mean."

"You're a good woman," he said.

"Am I?"

"You are. And it's not just me who thinks so," he said, draining the last of his coffee.

———— ✿ ————

Later that evening, as she sat on her bed, she reflected on their meeting and the idea of helping the little girl. The more she thought about it, the more it appealed to her. It was a purpose, a goal. Something positive. That had seemed lacking in her personal life. The thought of Cousins warmed her too. He seemed a good man. That he was tall, dark and ruggedly handsome scared her a little. For she had not felt an attraction for any man for a very long time.

There had been a moment as they had parted when they had leaned towards each other, and she thought he might kiss her. The same thought had occurred to him. But he had refrained. He too was a little afraid. He didn't want to risk the friendship that was developing between them.

She sipped the last of her sweet tea. Then she slipped beneath her mosquito net and switched out the light. And as she lay there, she realised she was smiling.

CHAPTER TWELVE

H E AWOKE WITH a pounding head and stared up through narrowed, bleary eyes at the white mosquito net stretched out like a veil above him in the early morning light. He'd had a troubled, restless sleep. His body too was aching.

For a few moments he lay there, taking in his surroundings, conscious of his own heartbeat and his breathing in the silence of the new day. He had woken before his alarm clock had sounded. And it was light. He therefore figured it must be sometime between 6am and 7am.

He decided to make an effort to climb from his bed and rolled over to unpeg the net with clumsy fingers. His senses were blurred, his head searing with pain, his limbs heavy and fatigued as he swung his legs out. He sat on the edge of the bed, hunched forward, his breathing laboured, slightly disorientated and uncertain of his next action.

Often, he awoke with a heavy head and had become accustomed to taking regular painkillers to stave off blinding headaches. But this was different. He felt cold. Yet he realised he was sweating.

"Bugger!" he muttered. He felt weak and tired. Then he began to feel nauseous. He was still sitting on his bed when the alarm clock began to bleep, and he stretched out an arm to silence it. The effort seemed too much, and he slumped backwards onto the mattress. He lay there, staring up at the net, and began to shiver. He was thirsty too but now seemed unable to raise himself. He closed his eyes as his grip on reality diminished and he sank into a feverish state of light and shadow.

Cousins was still lying there when he became vaguely aware of the knocking on his door. Yet he seemed unable to respond from the dreamlike state somewhere between sleep and consciousness in which he now found himself. He heard African voices. He felt the touch of cool fingers upon his forehead. More voices. This time female. Then it seemed he was falling, dropping into a deep, dark and bottomless chasm...

Hannah Johnson was bent over Cousins as he lay in his bed. She sat on the edge of the mattress watching him, listening to the laboured sound of his breathing. His eyes were closed but seemed to flicker as if perhaps he was dreaming. It was a handsome face, she mused as she studied its features, though clearly the man was ill. There were dark rings beneath his eyes. His cheeks were gaunt and already there was the shadow of several days' beard growth. His skin was pallid, and there were small beads of sweat upon his forehead.

He slept for long periods of time during the day. Sometimes he had spoken in his sleep; anxious, meandering mutterings of fear or deep sadness as the fever and the shivers persisted. But there had been moments of lucidity too, when he was able to raise his body to sit up in bed to drink. Slowly and with assistance. Then he would feel the need to rest again, and he would sink back into a troubled sleep. The fever had not yet broken.

Johnson had been a regular visitor. She sighed before reaching forward and dabbing his forehead with the cool cloth in her hand. Then she looked up at the figure standing beside her. Walters watched her pensively, with knitted brow, a look of concern upon his face.

"He seems better," she said.

The doctor took a deep breath. "But we can't leave it much longer," he said. "Another day, perhaps... if the fever and delirium continue, we're going to have to get him to hospital. We can't take the risk. Most likely they'll want to play safe," he added.

"I know," she replied absently and wiped Cousins' forehead again. She knew Walters was right. Perhaps they had been wrong to delay. Malaria was one of the biggest killers in Eritrea. Though the illness was less severe in adults, it killed children in their thousands. It remained a dangerous hazard for the Westerners who came to work, not just in Eritrea but across sub-Saharan Africa. They had no immunity to the parasite. It hit those who developed symptoms hard. Often, they would need to be hospitalised. Some were repatriated; the severest cases could cause complications that were fatal. But they were rare.

There was no real protection. The side effects of anti-malarial medication were too harsh for many. Prolonged usage could damage the nervous and immune systems. The skin would break down, or the eyes would become oversensitive to light. Sometimes the effects were long-term. So, you took your chance. The best protection was a mosquito net, repellents and scanning your room day and night for any sign of the insects. And, of course, keeping your skin covered. But it was something of a gamble.

The blood tests indicated Cousins had contracted what was termed 'uncomplicated malaria'. It was not the severest form of the disease. That was a relief. Emergency treatment had started immediately with artemisinin tablets.

The fever should break within the next day or so. He might then slowly regain his strength over the next few days, if he rested. That was the hope. But there was always a small element of doubt.

So far, his raging temperature had fluctuated. The delirium too had been intermittent. There was no coma. That was good. The patient had even seemed cheerful at times, sitting up in bed when his fever subsided a little. He was adamant he did not want to leave Eritrea. Yet in reality, it was out of his hands. That would be for the head of mission to decide. If he was no better within the next twenty-four hours, the decision would be made for him. He'd be admitted to the nearby hospital. There was still a vague possibility of complications. No one would want to take that chance. Even McKenzie had stood at his bedside, shaking his head. But he had made no decision.

For now, Cousins was being attended by Walters and Johnson at the request of the British NGO he was working for. The international medics shared a compound in Asmara adjacent to the British and their staff had agreed with McKenzie to keep a close eye on the 'patient'. And the Englishman dutifully took the large blue and white capsules offered with water that would cleanse his blood of the parasites that had infected his blood.

"I'll sit with him for a while," Johnson said.

Walters nodded. "I'll see you later," he replied and turned to leave the room. He paused at the door. "But if he is no better in the morning, we'll have to take him to the hospital."

"Yes, David," she replied absently, watching Cousins, whose eyes were still closed. He seemed unaware of her presence. She rose from his bed, pulled the net across and then drew up a wicker chair. Outside, the sun was beginning to set. She'd stay with him until darkness fell.

Cousins was far away. In his dreamlike state, he was back in Pakistan, reliving the loss that had led him to Eritrea. It was his worst nightmare. Yet he rarely dreamed about it now, even though it still haunted him.

He'd loved her. Afsa Ali had been his life. He hadn't seen the signs. He was working away in the Punjab when the message came to him. She needed him. Yet in his dream, he was unable to reach her. When, finally, he arrived at the family home in Islamabad, she had seemed different. Distant.

"I need you here," Ali had told him. She too was working, spending long hours away in the 'field', often writing her reports until the early hours. It was taking its toll. He decided to step back from his own work which took him away from the family home to help care for their little boy. She could also give up her own work, he suggested, if it was too demanding. They didn't need the money.

She had insisted she continue. He knew it was only work that took her away from him, in Peshawar and the north-west alongside the UN to support the many refugees who crossed the border from neighbouring Afghanistan. She would return to Islamabad at the weekends exhausted. Even then she continued to work. It was like a spiralling obsession. It was an opportunity she could not give up, even though it was pushing her to the brink of a 'burnout'. He'd seen it before in others, and he was worried.

She became cold, emotionally distant; secretive, even. It was as though she was becoming a different person, almost unrecognisable. The intimacy they had known together was gone. At times, she even seemed to despise him. Yet he felt powerless. The more he tried to help her, the more she seemed to push him away. In her head, he had become the enemy. Then one day, she told him.

"I don't think I love you anymore; you add nothing to my life." It was a statement that lacked any emotion or compassion. Then she smiled awkwardly. Inappropriately, as some people do on the announcement of an unexpected death. He was stunned and hurt. What did she mean? They had argued. But she maintained her distance. She told him he had failed her. He didn't understand. Her work seemed the only thing of value to her. Not even their little boy seemed important. And he, least of all. The woman he loved so deeply was disappearing before his very eyes, tottering on the brink of breakdown.

They were still sleeping together, though the physical and emotional intimacy had gone. Sometimes, though, as she lay sleeping, he would watch her in the early morning light. It was only in those moments that her face relaxed and some of its softness would return. In her sleep, she might lean towards him, or even reach out to him. But it would sadden him, for even in his dream, he knew the closeness would pass. The hardness would return in the cold light of day. It was a look which broke his heart. Once more, the distance would be there, which was a gap he was unable to bridge.

Then, one night, he found himself sleeping alone. In the darkness, he could see a rectangle of burning light which framed the adjoining bathroom door. For a while, he lay there, unable to move, his heart filled with a sense of dread. When she did not return, he was finally able to force himself to rise from his bed and approach the light framing the bathroom door. Yet, as he stood there, he could hear nothing. He knocked, but there was no response. He knocked again, a little louder. Nothing.

Now worried, he forced the door, pushing all his weight against it until it gave way. And suddenly, he was presented with the terrible scene he had feared most of all. She lay in the bath, eyes closed, slumped within the blood-red water in which her naked body lay, her head to one side, her life ebbing slowly from the deep cuts to her wrists.

"Oh my God," he heard himself utter in despair as he found himself watching the scene play out like a detached, out-of-body observer. He saw himself rush forward. His one overpowering thought: *God, please let me not be too late.*

He watched himself stoop over the bath and lift her from the water into his arms. The wounds were deep. He watched his desperate self clutch frantically for towels and press them over the lacerations, cradling her to him. Her eyes fluttered open for a moment, and she gazed up at him. "I'm sorry," she murmured. The coldness was gone, and he felt an overwhelming rush of love for the woman in his arms.

"It's all right, baby," he heard himself say with mounting despair. "Hold on. Please. Hold on!"

"So very sorry," she repeated, gazing into his eyes as he held her.

"It's OK," he told her. "It's going to be OK."

She smiled faintly. But the life was draining from her. "Sorry I couldn't love you better..." she said, almost in a whisper.

His mind was racing, his heart pounding. He felt the tears begin to blur his eyes. "I know you loved me as well as you were able," he heard himself say, his voice trembling with emotion as she closed her eyes for the last time and slipped into unconsciousness.

"It's all right... my darling, it will be all right..." he told her. But the life had gone from her body which lay limp in his arms. Then he began to sob and shake uncontrollably. His heart was breaking.

—⚬⚬—

He cried out loud as he awoke. And as he lay under the net, blinking in the soft light, he realised he was crying. Hannah Johnson awoke too with a start, still sitting in the wicker chair where she had fallen asleep.

In the light of the lamp, she could see Cousins, although his eyes still seemed to be closed. She pulled back the net to see his face was wet with tears. Then he opened his eyes and gazed up at her. "Are you all right?" she asked him.

"Bad dream," he answered. "Painful memories."

"I'm sorry," she said, reaching across to put her hand gently upon his forehead, which was cool to her touch. The fever had broken. "Welcome back, John." She smiled.

CHAPTER THIRTEEN

"Hannah," he muttered in recognition. She nodded and smiled at him. "How are you feeling now?" she asked him.

"Exhausted. Like a bag of crap!" He struggled to raise himself in his bed, and she leaned forward to help him. "How long was I out for?" he asked her.

"Long enough for us to worry," she told him, wedging a thermometer under his arm as he sat up propped against his pillows.

"You kept an eye on me…"

"We did. David and I," she replied.

"Was I babbling?"

Again, she nodded. "Wildly," she told him. "But your secrets are safe with me," she added with a playful smile.

"Secrets? I must have been raving…"

"Just a bit," she said simply. "But you came through it."

He was thankful she didn't dwell on the subject. "Thank you, nurse," he said. "All part of the service."

"Service?" he repeated.

"Put it this way, it was either that or sending you straight to the hospital. David thought we'd give you a day or two. As a favour to James, who says you're a good writer. But it was close. You can't always be sure with malaria. If your fever hadn't broken when it did, we would have had to take you to the hospital."

"Malaria," he said absently. "Well, I'm very grateful to you," he added, looking directly at her.

"My pleasure."

"Sure could use a drink," he said.

"Alcohol?" And she smiled again.

"I can see I'll have to watch you!" he said. Now he was smiling too. A little weakly, perhaps. But he was feeling much better.

"I'll get you a drink. You must be parched."

He watched her as she rose to fetch a bottle of water from a small cabinet in the corner of the room. "Thanks again," he said, as she walked back towards him, unscrewed the top, then handed him the bottle. When he had taken a few sips, she retrieved the thermometer from under his arm and raised it towards her, squinting to check the reading in the light from the window.

"That's good. Pretty much back to normal," she told him. "Looks like you'll live to tell the tale."

"I'll drink to that." He grinned, raising the water to his lips once more and drinking deeply.

"I'm so glad," she said. "But you'll still have to take it easy for a few days."

He nodded. "Will there be any lasting effects?" he asked her.

She shook her head. "Shouldn't be. If you behave! But you'll feel weak for a while. You've been quite poorly."

"Yes, nurse."

"Hungry?"

Again, he nodded.

"I'll ask Farooq to bring you some of his delicious soup. David will drop by later to check you're OK. But he's stricter than I am."

"I'll look forward to that," he said, as she unpegged the mosquito net and let it fall back into place.

"And don't forget to take your tablets," she reminded him as she turned to leave. She paused at the door. "Do try to get some sleep," she told him. Then she was gone, leaving him propped up in bed.

But he was smiling as he thought about her. He felt lucky. Lucky to have recovered. He wondered idly about Johnson, how grateful he felt for her friendship and above all for her nursing him. He wondered when he might see her again as he drifted into a satisfying sleep.

———

Time passed slowly as he lay in his bed, and he would lose track of time as he stared up at the mosquito net that stretched out above him, drifting in and out of sleep as he continued to recover. He would hear indistinct voices outside, invading his dreams. Sometimes they were African, or South Asian, or he was back in England as his subconscious gave shape to memories, real or imagined. And sometimes she came to him in his sleep. Then he would be immersed in what it had been to love her.

In his dream, Afsa Ali stood motionless on the marble walkway framed by the grandeur of the white mosque, set against its dramatic mountain backdrop. Her face was turned towards the cool air blowing from the north in contemplation, and the flowing fabric of her gown fluttered in the soothing breeze like a delicate flame.

Conspicuous by her lack of movement, she was like a fixed point in a kaleidoscope of motion and colour as worshippers passed by, seemingly oblivious to all around her. A flush of crimson light still outlined the dark peaks on which her eyes rested, and she felt the wind caress her face as she watched the last remnants of the day slip away.

She seemed at peace as he observed her from a distance. And he was reluctant to approach and thereby cause the moment to pass. It was the first time he realised he had fallen in love with the Pakistani aid worker, and the scene was forever etched in his mind. It was not one he wanted to let go.

He opened his eyes and found himself gazing at the white net above him. Then, as the reality of where he lay took hold of his senses, his eyes began to blur with tears. It was that dream again, from which he woke reluctantly, in which she came to him. He sighed deeply. Then he raised himself, pulled the net back and grimaced as he swung his legs out of bed with effort. He leaned forward to reach for the pack of cigarettes on the bedside table, took one from the carton and lit up, drawing the smoke deep into his lungs as he sat on the edge of the mattress.

Outside, the sun was setting, and its last rays fell through his window against the wall beyond him, bathing his room in its last glory of golden light. He observed the tiny specs of dust that hung within its brilliance.

Must get up, he thought. His gaze fell upon the pile of clothes lying on the wicker chair, just beyond his reach. But he still felt weak. It was while he contemplated whether to try and raise himself to his feet that he heard a gentle rap on his bedroom door.

"Yeah! Come in." His voice sounded fatigued.

It was Farooq who stood in the doorway, a bowl of steaming soup upon a tray. "Please, you must be in bed," he told Cousins with a sense of alarm. "Nurse Hannah is coming," he added to emphasise his point.

Cousins smiled wearily. "It's all right, Farooq," he said, pulling his legs back onto the bed with his hands as the Eritrean approached.

"Nurse Hannah says you must rest," he repeated, resting the bowl upon the bedside table, then plumping the pillows up as the Englishman leaned forward. He then handed him the soup, which Cousins took in his cupped hands.

"Thank you, Farooq. You make a wonderful nurse yourself," he said, and the African smiled.

He remained standing at the bedside, as if to make sure Cousins ate the soup dutifully. It was his own recipe. A soup for all ailments. And it was good. Just the right consistency. Not too thick. A little meat, an assortment of local vegetables and a hint of spice.

Johnson watched him from the doorway as he spooned up the last of the broth.

"The patient's not giving you any trouble, is he, Farooq?"

"No, madam."

She approached the bed. "Thank you, Farooq," she said, and the Eritrean cook withdrew, leaving them alone. "Medication time." She smiled.

"Well, it's lovely to see you too!"

"Another day or two, and you should be well enough to get up."

"That's good. Gets lonely in here," he said.

"That's why I've come to keep you company for a while." She moved his clothes to the foot of the bed and sat in the wicker chair. "And I have news," she told him.

"You do?"

She nodded. "You should make a full recovery. James is very happy about that. And so am I." She paused. "I've also spoken to James and David about Lula, the little girl you told me about. They have agreed we can both go to visit and talk to the mother when you are well enough."

"That's great!"

"But first you have to rest and recover."

He finished the last of his soup and placed the empty bowl on the bedside table.

"That means taking the tablets," Johnson said.

He held out his hand mechanically, and she placed two of the large blue and white capsules into his palm. Then she handed him a bottle of water.

"Thank you, nurse."

"My pleasure," she replied. "Oh, and I have something." She fished out a small, battered paperback book from the side pocket of her cargo pants.

"What is it?" he asked as she handed it to him. It was a book of poetry. *The Essential Rumi.* "I know this." He smiled as if welcoming an old friend. "It's wonderful!"

"I've had it with me for a while. I found it helpful. It's yours now!"

"Thank you," he said. "You are lovely…"

But before he could say any more, she had popped a thermometer into his mouth and raised a forefinger to her lips. "You really have been lucky," she told him. "Looks like you got away with the malaria."

"I know," he replied, taking the thermometer from his mouth. "Nine lives!" he added, sliding it back beneath his tongue.

"You might even be well enough to get up tomorrow, David says." He nodded, then gave her the thumbs up.

———— ∞ ————

Cousins stood in front of the mirror and grimaced at his image. He still looked rough, there was no denying. But some of the greyness in his face was gone, though there were still dark rings beneath his eyes. Yet he felt better and steady on his feet.

"Just take it easy, John," McKenzie told him. He was relieved to hold onto his communications man. Not least because head office was pleased to see the stories flowing in from Eritrea, as they had. The donors were happy too. The Scot knew his man was still recovering. But he'd be all right. That's why he had agreed to the trip to Tessenei.

It was just the long drive he was concerned about. But then Hannah would be with him. They seemed good together. Even Walters had commented.

Outside in the compound, she waited with the two men for the Englishman.

"Keep an eye on him, Hannah," the New Zealander said, and the nurse nodded. Cousins ran a hand over his head to ruffle his hair. It was a habit he had. Then he grabbed his bag and headed out into the courtyard. Jamal had already brought the Land Cruiser round and waited in readiness as Cousins emerged and approached the group standing in the early morning sun. He still felt a little weak on his legs.

"Got everything?" McKenzie asked, and the Englishman nodded. "Remember," the Scotsman added, "take it steady."

"You too," said Walters, addressing Johnson, and she shot him a sideways glance as she too climbed into the vehicle. The two men waved as the Land Cruiser pulled away.

"They make a handsome couple, you have to admit," McKenzie said to his friend with a hint of mischief. And the doctor grimaced sourly.

They pair were on their way to the BritAid field base on the outskirts of the frontier town on the border, where Farjad was expecting them. The field programme coordinator would facilitate the visit. They would be in good hands. He had already spoken to the Christian woman. He wasn't quite sure what would come of it. But he too was pleased the mother and child might receive some support. None deserved it more. For that, he was thankful to McKenzie too. He was a good man.

CHAPTER FOURTEEN

For Lula, it was as if all Christmases had come at once. There was food to eat. Even meat to chew on. Best of all, there was sometimes chocolate that would be delivered when the Englishman came. Oh, how she loved to put a piece in her mouth and let it slowly melt across her tongue, enjoying the sweetness of it. He had stopped her one morning and given her a ball, which he produced from his canvas shoulder bag. A tennis ball, he called it. She wasn't sure what tennis was. But that's the kind of ball it was. It was light green and bounced high, almost up to her shoulder, when she threw it hard against the ground. And she treasured it.

A greater miracle still seemed in prospect. Regular school, just like the other boys and girls her age. A new uniform too. She thought she might like to be a teacher when she grew up so that she could share the things she would surely learn with other children of the village who were not as lucky as her.

Or perhaps an airline pilot so that she might fly away. Often, she watched jets passing overhead, high in the blue sky above, leaving a silver white trail behind them. *It must be wonderful to look down on the world below,* she thought. To be free. Free as a bird. No doubt she would be rich, being an airline pilot. And she wondered idly how she might spend that much money. Never would she, or her mother, have to go hungry again.

It was therefore with a sense of happiness and a skip in her step that she made her way to fetch the laundry that morning. Later, as she watched her mother work the washing to beat it clean, she just had to ask again.

"Mama, am I really going to school?"

"Sure, you are," her mother replied, wringing the water from the wet clothing as her daughter sat beside her. It was true, though she could scarcely believe it herself. Life had already changed since the day Cousins and Johnson had arrived. She knew from Farjad that the two aid workers wanted to see her. But she never dreamed what was to follow.

"We'd like to help with Lula's schooling," Cousins had said. He had cleared it with his boss Mr McKenzie in Asmara, he told the mother. She should look at it as a way of securing a future for her girl. It was important to them, her working for the field base; a way of saying 'thank you'. It was only right. Besides, Cousins had become fond of the little girl during his visits.

Johnson too told her that, as a woman, she felt obliged to support Lula in her schooling. After all, her own mother had been a schoolteacher and would expect it. It wasn't wholly the truth. A white lie. And so, the Christian woman known as Mariam had accepted the help. What else could she do? It was surely her God looking down and answering her prayers. So, it was agreed.

The couple had brought cash with them. They had thought a hundred dollars each to start. In Eritrean nakfa, the local currency. That would allow for some much-needed essentials. Some provisions too. That would also enable the mother to purchase the school uniform her daughter needed. The whitest new blouse, navy blue skirt, red socks. A pair of sandals too! Pens, pencils and books as well. The mother was to let them know as and when any school fees were necessary. It was a deal.

"Everything will be just fine," her mother told her. Mr McKenzie says so too. He's the big boss. In Asmara. Lula's eyes widened. Asmara! It had a magical ring to it. It was a distant, enchanting place in the mountains, she had heard. It was the centre for all things. Sometimes, when she was alone, she would speak the name slowly as if she might evoke the magic. Therefore, for the first time in her young life, Lula had a new feeling. It was happiness, for sure.

"Everything will be just fine," she would repeat, if she ever doubted it. Just like the mountain capital: "As-ma-ra!" She liked the sound of it.

Perhaps it was hope. It was security. Maybe it was being liked. Cared for. Even loved. That was something she had not really known from anyone except her mother. Her father had never been a part of her life. She didn't even know him. Mariam said he had died in the war. Maybe he just didn't want to come home when the fighting stopped. It was what some folks said. It had happened to other men. The fighting changed them.

But it made Lula sad. She wondered if it was her fault. Because sometimes her mother said she was bad; a difficult child that caused her nothing but worry. Perhaps that's why her papa had not returned. There were times too when her mother would cry. Then she would embrace her daughter so tenderly, so lovingly. So desperately. As if it was all she had to cling to. She would then embrace her daughter and stroke her hair and her face. They were the times when Lula would feel safe in the love of her mother's embrace.

———∞———

"Mister John, he's coming to see us," her mother told her one hot day in early June, and Lula's eyes lit up. That would mean chocolate, for sure. Perhaps other surprises too.

"And he's bringing his lady. Miss Hannah!"

Double joy! Her two favourite people in the world.

"You make sure you tell them how good you doin' in school now," the mother told her. "Show them your books." The girl nodded obediently. But she had to ask.

"Are they married, Mama?"

"Sure oughta be," she said. "Seems to me they always together anyhow. And a man needs lookin' after, and she bein' a nurse..."

The little girl's eyes widened.

"Meant to be, if you ask me," the mother continued as she leaned towards the cooking pot simmering over the open fire, wooden spoon in hand. "You can see it in their eyes when they're together." Lula nodded, for she thought so too. "But don't you go sayin' anythin', girl." The girl shook her head. "Man needs to figure these things out himself!"

Again, the little girl nodded in agreement. But she didn't really understand. Was it really so hard to say what you felt?

"Sure hope they work it out," her mother added, stirring the pot with her spoon vigorously, then leaning back as she sat on the ground. Then she sighed. And Lula sighed too.

They came that day in two Land Cruisers, arriving in the afternoon, when the sun hung low in the sky. Sure enough, there were gifts. Chocolate for Lula, of course. There was a box of coloured pencils. Reading books too. Cousins said he would read them to her. There was a lion and a witch and a magic wardrobe, he said. But she particularly liked the story of the tiger who came to tea at the home of a white girl with red hair. And the tiger, of course. She wondered if it really was that hot where the white girl lived. Hot enough for tigers. She would ask the Englishman.

Just like the tiger, they stayed for tea and later for something to eat too, when the day began to cool. Even the drivers, sitting out back, ate of the stew Mariam had prepared and the flatbread. Then Miss Hannah announced she had to leave to go onwards to the field camp before the sun set. Something about new babies, Lula overheard.

In truth, Johnson was to spend several days in the field overseeing an initiative for safe birthing. Medics International helped coordinate the community midwives trained and mobilised to educate and support women in remote areas. It was part of an ongoing programme to reduce mother and infant mortality through simple, safer practice. Infant death from tetanus and infection was a major concern, due to age-old practices. Health outcomes could be dramatically improved simply through the use of a clean, sharp blade when the umbilical cord was cut.

Then there were the 'old ways' of smearing dung over the child's bleeding naval stump to ensure it healed. The availability of cheap medication, including antibiotics, was another major factor. An ignorance of basic health and hygiene practices was an ongoing challenge. As was the lack of access to clean water. But these issues were commonplace in remote parts, where ancient traditions held sway, education was limited and resources were scarce.

They all waved as Johnson climbed into her vehicle. Even Farjad came to say goodbye. Only Cousins and Lula lingered, the little girl standing close beside the Englishman. They watched in silence as the vehicle turned out from the drive onto the main road until the dust had settled. It would make its way across the town to pick up the track heading out towards the north-west.

"I like Miss Hannah," the girl said.

"Me too," Cousins replied. Then they turned to walk slowly back to the main house.

She was bursting to ask him all about tigers and how they came to visit white folks.

—❧—

Cousins visited the field office in Tessenei frequently. There were always stories for him to cover and pictures to take. It might be a distribution. A health and hygiene activity in the camps. Sometimes there was a new well in an outlying village. And when he was in camp, Lula was his shadow. For Cousins, it was welcome company. Perhaps it was a distraction from his work, which was sometimes distressing. He was certainly pleased by the little girl's progress at school.

For her, he seemed more than a kindly stranger. More than a favourite uncle, even. Not just for the compassion he showed towards her. He represented a world beyond hers. Of course, she welcomed the gifts. She knew too he had helped her mother, making it possible for her to attend school. But above all, it was his kindness and patience. Those fabulous stories. He read to her, and she would listen and imagine what he related from the pages of the books he brought to her. He came from Asmara. But she also knew he came from somewhere beyond the mountains which lay to the east. And she wanted to know about the world from which he came.

"What is Asmara like?" she asked one day as he stood smoking a cigarette in the yard.

"It's in the mountains," he told her. "One of the highest cities in the world."

"Is there snow there?"

He smiled. "No, there's no snow, but it is much cooler in Asmara than it is here."

"What's snow?"

"Snow? Ah… well…" he said as he considered. "Snow happens in places where it is very cold, like an icebox. Like in the mountains of Scotland, where my boss Mr McKenzie comes from," he added. "It is so cold there that the rain freezes high up in the clouds. Then it falls from the sky like frozen white feathers."

She fixed her wide brown eyes on him in wonder, almost in disbelief.

"It's true," he said. "Then, when the snow falls for a long time, it covers the ground like a thick white blanket. If you study hard, you might get to see it one day. It's a miracle." Then she smiled, contemplating the miracle he had just described.

CHAPTER FIFTEEN

"WHAT DID HAPPEN in Pakistan?" She had been afraid to ask him before. But now that they were alone, the question had come. Particularly as they were spending time together and were becoming more than colleagues, more than friends even. Two lonely people a world away from home and drawn to each other in a way that had surprised them both.

As soon as she had asked the question, she could see that it pained him. There was an awkward pause, as if he was reluctant to speak about that which he had been trying to forget. He hesitated as they looked into each other's eyes.

"Lost everything." He smiled. "Well, almost everything," he added, and suddenly his face was overcome with sadness. "It's hard for me to talk about," he said. And she felt she had made a mistake. Almost as if she was trespassing. "It's... painful." He sighed.

"I'm sorry..." she said in almost a whisper.

"It's OK. I wanted to tell you." He took a deep breath. "I... erm..." He paused. "I have a little boy in Pakistan..."

"With a local woman?"

He nodded. "She was my wife." He paused. "My life."

As Johnson looked at him, a hundred questions ran through her mind.

"I lost her. In Pakistan," he added, then fell silent, suddenly unable to meet her gaze.

"So sorry, John." Then, with a sense of hesitancy, "What happened?"

"Her name was Afsa. She... um... she..." But words would not come.

Instinctively, Johnson took his hand in hers. "You don't have to tell me."

But he wanted to. He wanted the sadness out of his heart that had troubled him for so long. He wanted to share the burden of pain he had been carrying. And he wanted to share it with her. When he spoke again, there were tears in his eyes, as images of the woman he had loved returned to him.

"I wasn't able to help her..." he said finally, his voice trembling with emotion. "She died."

It was a moment of heartbreaking intimacy. It was a moment when Johnson felt for the first time that she cared for him. Perhaps even loved him.

"I didn't realise what was happening at the time," he said. He fell silent again. He had wanted to say more, but he was not able to.

"Come," she said softly. "Let's take a walk outside."

He nodded. They rose from where they had been sitting on the veranda. Stepping out into the sunshine helped him compose himself and, as they made their way past the palms and flowering jacaranda along the driveway, she slipped her hand into his.

"Coffee?" she asked.

"That would be good," he replied, and they walked from

the compound towards the coffee shops which lined the main road just a few minutes away. They took an outside table at Guiseppe's and both ordered a cappuccino. And he decided to tell her about the terrible trauma which had led him to leave Pakistan, and which haunted him still.

Afsa Ali had been blessed with every advantage. Born to a wealthy, privileged family in Karachi, her parents seemed a model young couple representing all that Pakistan celebrated in the late 1970s: a secular, liberal Islamic republic that was still in awe of the West.

Her father Mohammed Raheem Ali was a rising star within the Pakistani civil service. He was considered a 'self-made' man, whose modest family in Lahore had fallen on hard times. Yet his keen intellect and burning ambition had allowed him to escape his relatively humble circumstances through scholarship and sponsorship. Unknown benefactors financed his university education. He even won a postgraduate placement overseas at Harvard, and a junior finance position within the civil service in Karachi was offered upon his return. He was part of the new order in Pakistan, a new hope. And he rose rapidly.

His wife was a society beauty from Rawalpindi. She too was well educated and strong-minded. She had resisted all marriage proposals and was working as a schoolteacher, against the expectations of her parents, who worried about her future.

To her prospective husband, she represented something of a 'catch', though when the dashing young civil servant with a love for poetry expressed his interest, the family breathed a sigh of relief and gave their blessing to the marriage. After all, their daughter was already twenty-eight. She had fallen in love with the young man's intellect and ambition. It was what they called a 'love match'.

In Karachi, the couple enjoyed the leisured lifestyle befitting the husband's upwardly mobile success. Two beautiful little girls followed in quick succession. First Afsa, then her sister Samina, after which the mother fell into depression following several miscarriages. The couple should continue to try for a boy. But she felt she had done her duty. Intellectually, she was also bored when her husband began to spend longer days at the office. It was the start of a decline. It wasn't even when her husband took his first mistress. There was an unspoken acceptance, particularly as she was no longer a willing bed partner. It was the move from Karachi to Islamabad, the country's shining new capital, away from her own family and friends. That was when the distance grew, a loneliness within marriage along with a rising sense of resentment.

It was about the time her little girl was singled out by her 'uncle'. He was a longstanding and trusted friend of the family whom they knew well. They might have even been related by blood, such was the bond that existed between them. Afsa was just six years old when she was first abused. Not that she understood what was happening. He was kind and he was gentle when he came to visit. And he would bring her gifts. He would stroke her intimately when they were alone. It was their special secret. Then one day he hurt her, and afterwards she could barely walk, such was the searing pain between her legs.

When the daughter came to her, the mother knew and did her best to comfort her little girl. Such things happened, she knew, but were not to be talked about. They were borne with an acceptance. Afsa was never to speak of it. It therefore remained a dark secret. It could never be openly acknowledged.

When the girl hit her teens, her abuser returned and, once more, she submitted. What else could she do? Her 'uncle' was an influential and trusted friend of the family. He brought sweets and gifts for the girls. But there were threats too. She should never tell. Or she and her family would suffer. She might be the target of an acid attack and lose her looks. She was afraid. She was angry too. Again, she felt violated. But she blamed herself for allowing it to happen. That's when she began to despise herself. Then she started to self-harm. Deep lacerations carved into her left arm in front of a mirror.

"Suffer, you dirty bitch," she would mutter, as she watched herself with complete detachment, and the blood flowed from the deep cuts she made. She felt no physical pain. But the sense of emotional release was intoxicating. Was addictive. Opening her wounds took away the emotional pain for a while. It was her only coping mechanism. Her mother wrung her hands in despair, while her father spent longer hours at the office.

It was only later, as she grew older and struggled to make sense of the world, that Afsa first attempted suicide. It was a cry for help. Yet still, she was expected to keep her secret from the outside world. What would people say? How could the family live with the shame? What about her father's government career? Or the girl's own marriage prospects? No, it never happened. She must never tell her future husband such things, her mother warned. So, she continued to suffer in silence as her inner turmoil grew.

Finally, escape was at hand. Following her A levels, she was expected to attend university. But a decline in her academic achievement limited her options. A degree course overseas was offered. Her father had gathered sufficient wealth and influence through his position beyond his government salary. Those he helped satisfy the demands of the state revenue department were grateful. And he was rewarded in kind. He was therefore able to make provision for his Afsa and her younger sister's education.

An overseas university was convenient – a perfect solution – and it represented a new hope. Afsa left Pakistan for New Zealand without regret. It was about as far away as it was possible to be. She could detach herself further from a world she had come to despise. Hers was a culture of dark undercurrents, secrets and hypocrisy that had brought her nothing but pain and self-loathing. She wanted to be free of it.

It was in Auckland, away from the confines of her family and the constraints of Muslim society, that she began to experiment. It was like being in a candy store. Young, beautiful and intelligent, she was finally able to express herself. But she was damaged.

There was a succession of boyfriends. There was sex, but no love. There were drugs too. And music. She indulged in all things Western to excess. But it did not ease her pain and only led to further confusion. Then there were periods of dark depression when she was lost in sadness.

Yet she was able to obtain counselling for the very first time through the university. A sympathetic, fair-haired woman who watched her over thick-rimmed spectacles and listened. She was able to tell her secret. It was like laying down a heavy burden. Initially, it helped. The cutting stopped. At least for a while. Somehow, she was able to continue her studies in English literature: Austen, Dickens, Shakespeare. But she was particularly impressed by Orwell and Hemingway. They helped too. But her life became a series of distractions to escape the pain she endured. It haunted her. It stalked her like a beast that might suddenly overtake her.

So, she kept herself busy. She ran; she pumped iron at the gym. She volunteered; she socialised; she studied. She was searching. She explored Christianity, Buddhism and Hinduism. She read the world's greatest poets. She studied psychology and became familiar with Nietzsche and Freud. Yet answers were elusive.

There was no escaping herself and the deep chasm of emptiness she felt. Then she would be overcome by periods of deep sadness and despair, when she withdrew from everything. Sometimes for many days.

When salvation finally came, it was in the form of her God. It was a god she had abandoned as a teenager. She still remembered the comfort in Allah as a child. A child that had not yet been corrupted. A child that had once felt happy and loved. A long time ago. The realisation she could return to her faith and have all sin wiped away was a eureka moment.

She knew her mother would support her; that the family would welcome her return. It coincided with the completion of her degree. Against all odds, she had managed to finish her studies. She had passed. It was a miracle. Perhaps it was divine intervention.

Her therapist told her she was an amazing young woman. She should be proud of her achievements. She should learn to love herself. For the first time, she tried to. Perhaps she succeeded. After years in the wilderness, she decided to return to Pakistan, land of the pure. Allah be praised! She would seek a life of service, of devotion to others. Maybe she could redeem herself and find a sense of peace through humanitarian work. She knew there was much to do in Pakistan. Despite her privileged background, she also knew what it was to suffer. Not materially, perhaps. But spiritually and emotionally. Yet that was surely the greatest suffering of all.

Therefore, when she returned to her family in Islamabad, she felt she had overcome her 'demons'. But in reality, she had just buried them deeper, where they simmered, waiting to surface should her new resolve begin to weaken, if her faith should falter.

Initially, she helped the less fortunate within her own community and through the local *jamaat*. But she also applied to several child-focused Western NGOs working within Pakistan.

Then, when a powerful earthquake struck the north-west that morning in October 2005, she felt ready to answer the call when it came. She found herself among the first teams ferried by helicopter into the devastated township of Balakot, which lay close to the epicentre of the disaster. And among the acute suffering she saw, she began to forget her own sorrow.

That was how they had met. Cousins had flown out from England to cover the story for his newspaper as the international relief effort gathered pace. After his initial ten-day assignment, he had been asked to return to support media and communications work with the same Western NGO Ali was working for. He had felt compelled to return following the terrible scenes of human misery he had witnessed in the mountains, which had moved him so profoundly.

Then something remarkable happened Ali could not have foreseen. She fell in love with someone who would understand and accept her, despite her past. It was another miracle.

———— ❧ ————

"So you met her in the earthquake zone." Johnson had listened to his story attentively as he had spoken, watching him over the rim of her coffee cup as he talked.

"Yes," he said. "She was the most beautiful and mysterious woman I had ever seen." It was true. But it had been something in her aloofness and unobtainability too he found alluring. For her initial disinterest in him was unmistakable.

Yet he had never imagined a romantic liaison in his wildest dreams. He too was hurting emotionally, following the failure of his marriage. Besides, their cultures were alien and the region in which they worked a highly conservative Muslim area. That aside, he too had travelled to the disaster area for humanitarian work. It was emotionally and physically relentless. A romantic involvement had been the last thing on his mind, he told Johnson. That was also true. But it happened. Slowly. Inevitably, perhaps. Maybe it was written.

Cousins smiled wryly.

"It's a wonderful love story," Johnson said, still gazing at him. "I'm sorry it turned out so badly."

"She... she took her own life."

"Oh my God!" Johnson was visibly moved.

"I found her one evening..." He paused to gather himself. "It was something I didn't see coming. I knew about her past. She was open about that. I admired her for her strength and courage. I loved her..."

"And your son? Where is he now?"

"He lives with his grandmother in Pakistan and is cared for by the family."

Johnson raised her eyebrows but said nothing.

"I just wasn't able to provide him with a home," he continued. "Emotionally, I was devastated. I just couldn't..." He fell silent. "I felt I needed to leave Pakistan. At least for a while. It seemed for the best," he told her.

"So sad. I'm sorry," she repeated.

"It's why I came to Africa. I had to get away. Needed to heal; get myself together." She understood better than he might have guessed. "It's good therapy. Helping others," she said, and he nodded.

"Thank you," he said finally. "For listening."

"Welcome," she told him. "Comes with the territory. We all

have our stories," she added. "Especially aid workers." Then she paused. "I'll tell you mine next time."

"Sure," he replied. "I'd like to hear them."

It seemed a moment of understanding had passed between them, which had surprised them both.

"We'd better head back," he said.

She nodded, and he reached for his wallet. He fished out a small photograph and reached it across for her to see. It was his little boy.

"Gorgeous," she said, taking the snapshot from his fingers to examine the image of the young child more closely. "I can see you in him."

"He has his mother's looks!"

"He's lovely," she said, handing the photograph back to him, and they rose to leave.

Later at the compound, as he sat alone in his room, his mind was back in Pakistan. Thoughts of Ali were never far from his mind, even now. He thought too about his little boy. He missed him. Had he done the right thing? Maybe he should step back from the aid work and raise his son. Perhaps they should return to England to be with his own family.

He picked up his watch from the bedside table and squinted at the dial. It was approaching 10pm, when the generator would shut down. He reached out from under the mosquito net to switch the lamp off and lay back onto his bed, staring up into the darkness, sweating under his mosquito net in the heat of the night. He was tired. He hoped he would sleep.

Outside, it was dark and silent. A warm breeze from the south was pushing the first bank of cloud across the continent towards the Horn, where it would build and gather in the coming days. The monsoon was approaching Eritrea when heavy rains would wash away the dust of the dry season and bring a sudden burst of greenery to the desert in the west and a respite from the heat on the coast. Storms would soon break over the mountains.

CHAPTER SIXTEEN

T HE TWO MEN breathed in the warm sea air as they gazed out across the shimmering water reflecting the brilliance of the early morning light. They squinted across the shining expanse towards the horizon, where the rising sun met the water with a renewed sense of hope. Somewhere out there lay their destination. Their destiny. Soon, the small fishing boat would cast off and navigate a course almost due north towards Greek waters and the rocky shores of Karpathos. It was a small island to the east of Crete. At the end of their voyage, they would literally step into Europe. They could scarcely believe it as they were ushered aboard and below deck.

"Allah be praised," the first man whispered as he drew the air deep into his lungs. Yet had his family and friends been there to see, they might not have recognised the emaciated figure led onto the vessel. His companion looked equally gaunt, with ragged clothing that seemed to hang from his undernourished frame. But at least Daniel and Juba had made it this far, against all odds. Many had perished along the route.

This was the day they were to set sail from the small Egyptian fishing port. Yet even when, God willing, they would step ashore upon the Greek island after two days at sea, if the weather was kind, they knew it would be the beginning of another journey, perhaps just as punishing. Still there were more countries to cross. More transport to be negotiated, more security forces to dodge, traffickers to pay. More risks to take. But what more horrors could they face?

It was hard to believe what they had already endured in the weeks since they had first crossed the border by night from Eritrea into the Sudan with the Rashaida, now almost two weeks ago. They had travelled along the road in darkness and reached the town of Kassala before sunrise, where they had been led into a boarding house, rank with decay. Here the two men languished in a darkened room with only the most basic facilities, sleeping on old mattresses on the floor for three days and nights. Occasionally, they were brought food. Or they would offer cash to their Rashaida minders for additional provisions. The young Kunama couple decided to remain in Kassala and negotiated to be taken to one of the camps still operated by the UN around the town. They would work the farms and hope to raise the additional funds they needed. They knew there were risks in staying. Risks of being detained by the authorities, or worse still, the danger of kidnap from the fields by traffickers.

Within a few days, Daniel and Juba were on the move again. Transport to Khartoum had been arranged. It was here, following the long, dusty trek by minibus, that the dark-skinned Somali left them to make his bid to the Libyan border. He aimed to make for Italy. They were sad to see him go. His had been a calm and steady voice of assurance.

They were anxious hours that followed for Daniel and Juba. For the first time, they felt they were captives, at the mercy of the Rashaida, who would not hesitate to abandon them. Or sell them on to traffickers if there was no further cash for their onwards journey.

This was the point at which they were relying on their relatives in Europe and the deal they had made in the weeks before travel. It was they who were to pay the smugglers for safe passage of the two men onwards, all the way into Egypt and to one of the many ports along its Mediterranean coastline. It was, perhaps, the longest day for the two men, who languished and prayed while they awaited the arrival of further funds. And they hoped for salvation.

When the cash transfer had finally been paid into relevant bank accounts, they could scarcely believe it. The leader of the Sudanese smugglers grinned, showing rotting teeth.

"You are lucky today," he told them. "We have the money, and my men will take you onwards. It seems Allah smiles upon you." He laughed to see the men sob with relief.

"Let us hope God remains with you for your journey onwards, insh'allah," he added.

Within the hour, Daniel and Juba were herded onto the small truck at gunpoint with other migrants. Men and women. Some were Eritrean, others Sudanese, numbering about a dozen. All were desperate and afraid. The most dangerous part of their journey was yet to come. They would travel the long trek north-west through the low mountains of the Qoz Abu Dulu, skirting the eastern edge of the Sahara, up along the Nile towards the city of Dongola. Already, they had known hunger, deprivation and fear over many long days and nights. Yet worse might follow. The road ahead was fraught with danger.

They set out from the city of Khartoum under the cover of darkness. Daniel and Juba were led towards the back of the battered Hino truck and ordered to climb aboard, where others were already seated, facing each other. Improvised straps had been crudely fitted to the back of the open-topped truck, and they were told to wind them around their arms or upper body. The truck would be travelling out into the desert where it would thunder along the dusty track up towards the town of Dongola, then onwards towards the Egyptian border at Wadi Halfa.

They might stop at Dongola for a brief respite and to take on supplies, if the going was good. It was a six-hour breakneck journey, and they did not anticipate a stop before then. Speed was their best protection along the perilous route. The danger was not detection by Sudanese security forces, but by bandits. It was a road well known to traffickers, who would not hesitate to ambush the smugglers and kidnap the people they were transporting. They left the city and took the main route north, roaring onto the road which would take them through the rolling hills of the Qoz Abu Dulu range under the night sky. As the Hino sped along the bumpy desert road, the straps wrapped around their arms cut into Daniel and Juba. They would travel at high speed along the remote highway to outrun security forces and bandits alike in a desperate dash across the desert landscape. If they were lucky, they might make the border before sunrise. It would be a white-knuckle ride all the way. Initially, they braced themselves against the bumps and grinds of the vehicle as it roared along among the cries of human suffering. Limbs grew numb from the pain as the straps bit into them or from bruising as the old Hino bumped and rocked along the uneven highway, sometimes swerving to avoid potholes, or boulders, upon the carriageway.

But as the journey continued across the desert landscape, the migrants grew silent in their suffering. Only their faces betrayed their pain and their fear. Some had slipped into unconsciousness. Others clung desperately to their straps, bracing themselves each time the truck hit uneven ground. It seemed the nightmare might never end until, without warning, they suddenly slowed and stopped. It was time for the smugglers to check their cargo and pass the water. It was not in their interest to lose anyone along the way. That was bad business.

Daniel and Juba looked at each other, then watched as the water was passed from person to person, each waiting to take a few grateful sips to quench their burning thirst and rinse the dust from their mouths. Those who were bruised and bleeding were tended with wet rags.

"How long?" Juba asked the smuggler in Arabic who had climbed among them with the water cannister. "How long before we make Dongola?"

"Two more hours to Dongola," he replied gruffly and stared hard at the Eritrean before continuing to administer the water. "Two more hours! Then we stop again. Maybe." After he seemed satisfied all had received the water, he jumped from the back of the vehicle.

"Now we move again!" Then he climbed back into the cab to join the driver. The migrants wrapped the straps around them once more as the truck began to move and gather speed.

"Just two more hours," Daniel muttered as he felt the belt dig into the bruising on his arms.

The crack of the first shots rang out, signalling the start of the attack. The bandits seemed to come from nowhere, two pickups pursuing the battered Hino from behind, as it sped along. The migrants screamed and wailed. The Sudanese smuggler leaned from the front passenger window, aiming his AK47 at the pursuing vehicles. His assault rifle stuttered above the roar of the tuck and empty cartridge cases flew out into the night air as they sped along the highway. More shots came from the pickups, which seemed to be gaining on them, their flashes of gunfire visible though the darkness.

There was a sense of sheer terror in the back of the Hino, as the migrants fumbled to loosen themselves from the straps that held them in order to crouch low or lie on the bed of the vehicle. In the panic, a young Eritrean man was thrown off-balance backwards. Suddenly he was gone, his body tumbling over the tailgate of the Hino. He lay still in the road where he had fallen, watched in horror by those who clung onto each other on the flatbed of the truck as it raced onwards. They saw the first pickup swerve around the body and continue its pursuit, while the second vehicle slowed and came to a halt beside the figure in the road. Two bandits climbed out to examine the man's battered body. Dead or alive, his fate was sealed.

Still there were more gun flashes and the splatter of bullets peppering the bodywork of the Hino. The smuggler in the front passenger seat continued to return fire, loading clip after clip into his assault rifle and firing relentlessly at the vehicle behind them. The driver beside him was shouting as he stared intently ahead, pressing the accelerator flat to the floor, both hands on the wheel to maintain control as the truck bumped and clattered along at full speed, desperate to escape.

Then the gap between the truck and its pursuers seemed to widen. The shooting stopped. The pickup dropped back into the distance and was swallowed by the darkness. Still the truck roared onwards.

"I'm injured," the Sudanese gunman told the driver, almost casually, as he leaned back into his seat clutching his right arm, which was wet with blood. The man at the wheel glanced at his companion. In his side mirror, he could see no sign of the bandits.

"Shall I pull over?"

"Drive on. I'm OK," his companion replied, his AK47 now resting between his knees. "We've lost them," the driver said. "Allah be praised!"

"I think I hit them several times," the gunman muttered, grimacing in pain.

Certainly, there was no sign of their attackers as they continued their journey. Perhaps the pickup had been hit. A lucky burst of fire? Maybe the front tyres were shot out. Or the windscreen. Perhaps the resistance was simply too fierce for the bandits. Whatever the reason, they had given up the chase.

The gunman groaned. He was struggling to contain the flow of blood from his arm, despite pulling a tourniquet tight with his teeth and pressing his scarf against the wound. In the back, a woman had also been hit and was moaning in pain. Daniel and Juba were trying to stem the blood flow, but her condition was serious. And the migrants were now beating against the rear cab window.

"We should stop," the driver said, and the gunman nodded.

The vehicle came to a halt on a slight incline, where the road swept around a rocky mound and they were relatively concealed. Their position allowed the driver an unobstructed view of the empty road behind, where he stood watching through narrowed eyes for their attackers, smoking a cigarette with trembling fingers.

The injured woman had grown quiet on the back of the Hino where she lay, her head resting on a folded shawl. Juba was at her side, pressing against the wound in her abdomen with a makeshift dressing. Another man came with water and gently wiped her forehead as her breathing became shallow, and a blanket was offered by other hands.

Daniel climbed from the vehicle and approached the injured smuggler, who was leaning against the rocks, breathing heavily.

"I'm a trained nurse," the Eritrean told him.

"Good that you are here then," the smuggler replied with a wry smile.

"I think you'll be all right," Daniel told him as he examined the wound. "You're lucky. The bullet grazed you; a flesh wound," he added as he pressed a folded scarf into the injury to stem the bleeding. The smuggler grimaced in pain. "It will be all right," Daniel assured him, as he tied the fabric over the wound, watched by the smuggler.

On the back of the truck, the injured woman had fallen into shock and now lay unconscious. Juba knew she needed urgent medical attention. There was little he could do except try to stop the loss of blood and keep her warm. But they were still an hour from their destination. Their only option was to resume their journey and seek medical help on their arrival. He wasn't sure she would make it.

As they approached the outskirts of Dongola, the woman died. Her body had shuddered and was then still. At peace. They should pray for her, Juba said solemnly, wiping her blood from his hands. He didn't even know her name. Someone said they thought it was Niyat.

They buried her in a shallow grave by the roadside before they entered the town, and a Muslim prayer was whispered and carried away on the desert winds.

———

The ragged border town of Wadi Halfa came into view as the first glimmer of light in the east touched the night sky, bringing the promise of a new day. There, weary and fatigued, they made their camp on the edge of the town. The Sudanese gunman came to offer his thanks as Daniel bedded down on the hard earth. There was less pain now, he said. The Eritrean told him the wound would heal. But he should seek clean dressings and medicines against infection. The smuggler nodded in gratitude.

"I owe you one," he said and smiled grimly, as was his habit.

Later they would seek out what they needed. Then they would cross the border in the evening. It would not be difficult. Nothing was when enough cash was paid. They would make for the village where their Egyptian guide waited. There they would be safe and could obtain provisions. But for now, they would rest and recover as best they could before the final part of their journey north towards the coast. From there, the migrants hoped for a passage by boat to Greek, or even Turkish, waters.

CHAPTER SEVENTEEN

T HE RAINS CAME early that year. Southernly winds blew across the parched continent, pushing dark, billowing clouds up from Ethiopia inland towards the mountains. And by mid-June, the hot wind blew hard, the clouds reared, blocking out the sun, and the water fell through humid grey skies for three days. The sudden torrential downpours were relentless and took everyone by surprise.

Such was the intensity of the monsoon rain that the water ran down the dry, red earth too rapidly to be absorbed, cutting deep channels into the hillsides as it rushed towards the lower ground. Like many, the nursing teams at Medics International were caught out by the resulting flash flooding, which created vast rivers of fast-flowing water, washing away everything in their path. Communities found themselves cut off and isolated on small tracts of land, surrounded by torrents of brown water as the rain continued to fall.

Hannah Johnson breathed deeply, brushed a strand of hair from her face and wiped the sweat from her brow. Her cotton shirt was wet with perspiration. The humidity had been intense, sapping the energy from her. It was a sign that soon the rains would break. She had worked from the base camp at Barentu for the last few days, overseeing the community midwives with her team. She enjoyed being in the field. Her Eritrean nurses were dependable and jovial, and the midwives were enthusiastic in their work.

Primarily, the field programme targeted young mothers and their newborn babies in remote areas. It was a drive to protect mothers and bring down the high infant mortality rate. That meant the education of communities in basic hygiene procedures with minimal equipment. It involved travel to isolated settlements and working with the village matriarchs, supported by locally trained women who could pass on the knowledge which could save lives. Basic health and hygiene concepts were not known. For there was no understanding of bacteria, or the causes of infection.

Johnson enjoyed working within the remote communities. She liked the intimacy. The people were kind and gentle. Always welcoming. The conditions were sometimes harsh, living in tents, washing on the contents of a small plastic bottle of water and eating what could be cooked on a small gas stove. Sometimes there was a hut to work from. But it was basic living, and it was physically harsh, not least in desert temperatures.

The young woman she attended that afternoon had smiled and nodded. Earlier, she had screamed in pain, wet with perspiration as she went into labour.

"You got to push, or there's no way that baby's comin,'" Armana the midwife told her. There were no complications. The larger-than-life Eritrean delivered the baby, coaxing and assuring the mother, assisted by two older women from the village. She'd seen it a hundred times.

"*Shukri, shukri!*" the mother panted as the screaming child was lifted to her chest for her to cradle. The midwife's smile was as broad as it was infectious, and Johnson found herself smiling too. It was an intense and beautiful moment of relief as old as creation whose wonder never ebbed for the English nurse. It was a miracle.

When it came to cutting the cord, a clean, sharp blade was provided. The midwife showed the village women. There was a sterile dressing for the child's naval which Fiyori applied. Then the nurse had washed and wrapped the infant. That was progress. In the remote villages, Johnson knew it was common to use rusted knives and animal dung to cover wounds. A sure risk of tetanus or infection. But all had gone well, and the young mother's relief was clear to see.

Johnson stepped out of the tent in Hambok village and gazed up anxiously at the gathering storm clouds above the distant mountains. The air was hot and humid. *The team should be on its way,* she thought. They were in hill country to the north-west, and there was still the dirt track to the Barentu turn to negotiate. Then, from their base at Barentu, the long road into the highlands to Asmara. She could use a break in the capital.

The sky darkened, and a distant rumble could be heard across the hills as the first drops of rain began to patter onto the canvas. Hastily, the team loaded up the Land Cruiser aided by Samuel. The driver then checked in at base camp over the radio. They should set off without delay, he said. The rains were already falling across the mountains to the east. But the roads were still clear. They had just climbed into their Land Cruiser as the heavens opened, and the water began to drum upon the roof as the vehicle slowly moved off into the driving rain.

Onwards they drove, the wipers barely able to clear the volume of water lashing against the windscreen, with visibility down to less than twenty metres. The track too was awash with water, and Samuel was forced to switch to four-wheel drive to allow the wheels a better grip as the ground began to soften beneath them. Still the rain hammered down from leaden skies, splashing the water high as it kicked up from the sodden earth. The anxiety within the vehicle was beginning to rise.

They felt the Land Cruiser slide as it struggled to maintain momentum and direction on the dirt track, which was rapidly turning to mud, while its passengers clung tightly to the overhead handrails.

"What if we get stranded out here in the rain?" said the young Eritrean nurse with mounting panic.

"We can make it," Samuel told her calmly, his gaze fixed intently ahead.

"Course we're gonna make it through," Armana the midwife added.

"We can't be more than half an hour out from the Barentu turn," Johnson said. "We have the radio if we do get stuck."

"That's right, Miss Hannah. We can't be far from the main road now," Samuel said.

But conditions were deteriorating by the minute as they slowly pushed on. Then, suddenly, the driver brought the vehicle to a halt as they found themselves staring at a gushing river of mud cutting across the track ahead as the heavy rain continued to splash high around them.

"I dare not go into the water," Samuel announced. "I don't know how deep it is, Miss Hannah. Look how fast it flows. We might be swept away."

<hr />

Cousins was also caught in the sudden downpour just as he and his driver approached the outskirts of Barentu. He was on his return from Tessenei and also hoped to make a dash back to Asmara following his field trip to the frontier town. A weather warning had been issued but came too late for most. He now decided to divert to the Medics International base to see how the weather was before heading onwards to the capital. Besides, he knew Johnson had been operating from the compound and was likely still there.

But she and her team had not returned from the field and, given the extreme weather conditions, Dr David Walters was concerned. There had been no further word from the nursing team since they had radioed in to say they would be setting out shortly.

When Cousins pulled into the compound in Barentu, Johnson was still not back from the field. Then came the news that they had been cut off by flash floods on the road somewhere between the village of Hambok and the Barentu junction as the persistent rain continued to fall.

Joseph, the Medics International field coordinator, was distraught. Johnson had said they were unable to cross the flow of water which ran fast and deep across the track. She was asking for assistance. Then the signal had been lost, and he was not able to raise her again. And the weather alerts were grim, warning that the monsoon had begun, and the rain was likely to persist for the next few days.

Cousins decided to call McKenzie on the radio. Yes, he had heard. Walters was distraught.

"I'm in Barentu, and I'm with Jamal in Vehicle 22."

"Vehicle 22?"

"It has the winch at the front. I'd like to go out to Hannah and the others before the weather gets worse. I should be able to get them across and back to base."

"It's dangerous out there, John," McKenzie said.

"All the more reason to go. I repeat, I'm here with Jamal,

and he is confident we can get to them and bring them in."

"Let me check the situation with Walters. I'll get right back to you. Over."

"Copy, Mac. Standing by."

Yet Cousins had already made his decision.

———⚬⚬⚬———

Samuel the driver peered from the Land Cruiser through the driving rain across the fast-flowing water. He was sure he could see the glimmer of lights on the other side. He wiped the condensation from the windscreen and moved closer to the glass in order to see better.

"Headlights," he said.

Suddenly alert, the others leaned forward to see. Sure enough, there were lights shining directly at them through the heavy rain. Less distinct, the outline of what appeared to be a pickup facing them across the flow.

"I'm getting out," Johnson announced, and before Samuel could object, she was standing in the pouring rain. She could see figures beside the pickup, and she called out to them through the rain. The men seemed to be waving to her. They were shouting too, though she could not understand what they were saying. Then she saw it. The unmistakeable shape of a heavy digger beyond the first vehicle, moving slowly, purposefully forward, towards the water.

Now the others had joined her as all four stood in the pelting rain. It was a rescue. They began to shout and cheer. It was a small miracle. And Johnson found that she was laughing as the heavy rain continued to fall, drenching her to the skin.

They watched as the digger chugged forward into the water where it took up its position in the centre of the flow which covered its tracks almost entirely, just a few inches below the cab in which the driver sat. He extended the digger's hydraulic arm and swung it back towards the bank on which the pickup sat, resting its clawed bucket onto the earth.

One of the men climbed into the scoop, and the mechanical arm swung slowly in a 180-degree arc over the water to the other side. The arm slowly lowered the bucket to the ground, and the turbaned man climbed out, watched almost in disbelief by Johnson and her team. She was certain he was Rashaida as he approached.

"I am Abu Bashir from the nearby village," he said in perfect English. "We see you have trouble. Will you accept our help?"

For a moment Johnson wasn't quite sure how to react.

"Thank you." She smiled uncertainly.

"We are Rashaida," the man explained. "But there is no charge for the help. We know of your work with our people. You are the nurses that care for our women and our children."

"Thank you," Johnson repeated, trying to contain a rush of emotion. She wasn't sure whether to laugh or cry.

It seemed the elders were on urgent business and had found the track already barred by water. They had gone for help at a nearby settlement and returned with the digger in a bid to bridge the water. It was a case of pure chance. Not that the Rashaida believed in such things. It was surely written, and they would receive a reward from their God for helping the medical ladies, as they called them. It was a case of *maktub*.

One by one, the women were ferried across the wild torrent of water within the digger's scoop and gently set down upon the other side as the rain continued to fall. The young Eritrean nurse was first, screaming as she gazed down at the rushing water below, clinging desperately to the sides of the large metal bucket as the digger's arm swung her slowly across. Then it was Armana, the midwife who bore the ride across in silence. Lastly, it was Johnson's turn. She climbed into the scoop and was swung slowly across. The group whooped as she was set down.

Only Samuel remained. He was determined to stay with the vehicle. For he did not trust the Rashaida. Johnson had reluctantly agreed. He would watch to see if they could make a bridge. If not, he would head for the nearest village to find shelter and wait for the rain to pass.

As their vehicle drove along the road from Barentu through the rain, Cousins was consumed by worry. He realised he had come to care for Johnson. What if something happened to her? The weather was getting worse and, as they reached the turn from the main carriageway, Jamal brought the vehicle slowly to a halt.

"Do we go on, Mr John?" he asked as they stared at the waterlogged track before them.

"Let's do it," Cousins replied, grabbing the overhead handrail as Jamal slid the gear lever into four-wheel drive, and the Land Cruiser lurched forward. Already, parts of the track were softening as the water sank into the dry earth, turning large tracts to mud. It was slow, heavy going. But Jamal was an experienced driver in all conditions, and he was able to maintain the movement forward as the four wheels powered the vehicle onwards through the mud and the rain.

Then, as they topped a small rise, they suddenly saw the group ahead, standing in the rain. It was one of the most bizarre spectacles Cousins had ever seen: two vehicles facing off across a wild torrent of water in which a digger stood half submerged. On the nearest side, a group of figures huddled together in the torrential downpour; their faces now turned towards them as they approached. Then he saw her, and he was out of the vehicle almost before it had stopped.

"Hannah!" he called out through the rain, and she smiled as she recognised him.

"John," she said absently as she stepped forward, and he began to run towards her through the mud and the teeming rain, oblivious to everything except that she was there and she was safe. As he stood before her, there was no longer any doubt. They stepped towards each other and embraced. Then she lifted her face to his, and they kissed for the first time as the rain continued to fall.

CHAPTER EIGHTEEN

S IR CHARLES LAIDLAW fixed himself a drink and stared absently from his hotel room at the street beneath his window. He took a sip from the whiskey glass and felt it run down to the pit of his stomach. The 'meeting' had gone well, he thought as he watched the pedestrians walking below in the sunshine.

He wondered idly how his wife's shopping expedition was progressing and whether she had found herself a new outfit at the boutique. No doubt she would eat out with one of the women from the club. Or perhaps she was meeting a man, he mused. It might have eased his conscience a little, though he knew it was wishful thinking.

It was not yet eleven. He downed the remaining spirit from his glass. As yet, he was still sober. But the day was young. He caught sight of his reflection in the glass, standing casually in his underpants, a light cotton shirt still unbuttoned and hanging loose. Behind him, the woman still lay naked on the bed, her dark skin contrasting with the white linen. A fan whirring in the background was the only sound to be heard. He turned towards her and watched as she propped herself up, drawing the sheets around herself.

"Are we done?" she asked.

"Yes. Thank you," he replied. "That was good."

He was still sweating from his recent exertion with the woman, who was staring absently ahead. She was slim and dark, with delicate facial features common to the region. For a moment, he allowed his gaze to rest on her face. She had been passive when he had taken her, and he wondered if she had enjoyed their physical intimacy. That was vanity, for in reality, she was no stranger to selling herself to foreigners. But he did care for her.

Laidlaw wasn't a bad man. He was just desperately unhappy. Which is why he drank to excess, sometimes to the point of drunkenness. It helped. But his periods between drinking were growing shorter and his craving for alcohol becoming more intense.

Now he drank from necessity to stop his hands from shaking. And, of course, to stem the sense of panic whenever he found himself without access to drink. His reputation for extra-marital sex was exaggerated. It happened rarely, without any real sense of satisfaction or peace. It wasn't a power thing, he told himself. It was a need for distraction and a search for some fulfilment in his life. In reality, he still loved his wife.

The posting to the consulate in Eritrea had been timely, following the mission to West Africa, where he had first acquired a reputation for liaisons with local women. Certainly, it might have been less complicated, perhaps because there was no likelihood of emotional attachment. Then the new assignment beckoned. A fresh start? Perhaps, he had told himself. Yet he brought his vices with him.

His Venezuelan wife had expected more. She was sick of Africa. Why not a posting in Eastern Europe at least? Or back in South America? Even Bolivia would do. She had married an ambassador, after all, but life had fallen short of her expectations.

So, she busied herself arranging parties or hosting the bridge club on a Saturday afternoon. Or shopping. She also made time to take new arrivals under her wing, at least socially. Which is how she came to know McKenzie, Walters and Johnson. Walters was an excellent bridge partner. Of course, she enjoyed spending her husband's generous income too.

She suspected Sir Charles's indiscretions. In some ways, it was a relief. For there had never been love. For her, he had been a way out from Venezuela and access to higher social circles. Yes, she had married a British diplomat. At least she could say that. There was a UK passport too. So, she bore her husband's reputation with good grace as the wife of a senior government civil servant overseas should. In silence.

Outwardly, she looked stunning. Her long, dark hair was always immaculate, her make-up and nails perfect. She looked after herself, attending the city's exclusive gym, which came with Fabio, her own personal trainer.

The child was simply another trapping. An additional duty. Almost an inconvenience. Their daughter was still young. Spoiled, overindulged and expectant of the very best. Even at the age of nine. She was her mother's daughter in every sense. At least there was domestic help in abundance. It allowed Maria Christina Gonzales Laidlaw the independence she liked. Needed, perhaps. For there was not a maternal bone in her well-toned body. She had done her duty, though there would be no further children.

Eritrea was a far cry from her whirlwind romance in South America with the handsome, ambitious (some said ruthless)

British diplomat. Indeed, they made an attractive couple. Everybody said so. Yet, like many things, the romance was not all it seemed. She was strikingly beautiful, and he was smitten from the first. It was a case of lust at first sight. But there was no love.

In the hotel room in Asmara city, Sir Charles sighed. He buttoned his white shirt before reaching for the smartly pressed trousers he had carefully laid over the chair. He pulled them on, tucked his shirt in and fastened them at the waist.

He dug a hand into his jacket pocket, fished out a narrow white envelope and lay it on the bedside table without further dialogue with the girl. He slipped his shoes on, grabbed his jacket and left, zipping his fly on the way out. The girl stared vacantly, lost in thought, vaguely aware of the gently whirring fan.

∞

Johnson had initially found Laidlaw handsome, charming and somewhat intriguing. Yet he was never anything but polite and courteous towards her. He flirted outrageously, almost childishly, without ever signalling serious intent. He liked her. He teased her. Though he thought she was attractive, he admired and respected her for the dedication to her work. Besides, though they enjoyed each other's company whenever they met, she wasn't his type. They understood each other. So, they were able to be friends.

The first time she saw him drunk was at the UN bar one evening. He was deeply and suggestively in conversation with one of her Eritrean nurses and she had intervened, discretely. Later, he had chastised her for 'spoiling my fun'. Then they had laughed. It signalled the start of their friendship. She felt she had a measure of him and that he knew it. She also knew things he preferred to keep hidden. Not just his interest in other women. He was extraordinarily supportive to charitable causes and had, on occasions, made significant personal donations.

To many he appeared rakish, a little too well groomed, with a clipped upper-class English accent suggesting a public-school education. To some, he was superficially jovial, sometimes detached, which led to the view that he was shallow and insincere. The truth of it was that he was so often bored with the whole charade that went with the diplomacy expected of him that he liked to make his own entertainment.

He held no illusions of grandeur and was often self-effacing, poking fun at himself and his position as ambassador for the United Kingdom, a small group of islands in a cold climate with an impressive history. That was his private view. It was a world away from life in Eritrea. He knew it.

Still, outwardly, he represented Queen and country to the best of his ability and perhaps with a degree of embarrassment, considering its own shameful colonial past. Some might have said he was kind.

Certainly, he was an enthusiastic and generous supporter of local welfare initiatives. Some were supported by the British Government's UK aid programme. Less well known was his personal patronage to charitable causes, not least for Medics International, to which he had contributed sizeable donations from his own pocket.

He was also popular in his open support for the international NGO community in general. He was liked and respected in Eritrean Government circles too. He listened to their issues, and he treated them with respect. His fluent Arabic also impressed. Often, he had used his influence to help secure permissions and documentation for the small number of aid agencies that worked in the country, sometimes even backing individual visa applications that hit a 'snag' and had disappeared into a void of red tape bureaucracy. Usually, that meant pulling some unofficial strings or organising a cash payment to smooth the way. In short, he made himself available and was their 'go-to' person in times of trouble.

There was also a 'maverick' side to him he usually kept hidden. There were whispers he sometimes travelled incognito in local dress to remote tribal areas on the arid plains of Gash-Barka region close to the Sudanese border for undisclosed meetings. There were stories too that he would head for the humid Red Sea coast, staying effectively off-grid in small fishing villages for days at a time to sample local life and culture, which he loved. But no one knew for sure. In short, he was something of an enigma.

But most knew him from the 'garden parties' he hosted with his glamourous wife at their private residence in a fashionable district of Asmara, where they would entertain lavishly, inviting local groups to rub shoulders with the city's elite, usually in support of worthy causes. Particularly women's groups, which was, perhaps, an irony. Or maybe his conscience. Certainly, Sir Charles's events were quite the place to be seen. They were fun too, often featuring popular Eritrean entertainment. He was, by all accounts, an accomplished jazz musician. There was a story they told of the time during an independence party when he joined the local band, brandishing a trumpet, while an Eritrean minister picked up a *kebero* drum and McKenzie played the 'spoons'.

***

It was at the next UN barbecue that Sir Charles spotted her. There had been a break in the rain, and it was decided to go ahead, with the cooking taking place in one of the nearby outbuildings.

It proved to be a popular magnet for the expat community and local NGO staff fed up with the persistent downpours and the mud. So, they headed to the compound on the airport road in search of a release, including the ambassador. It was an opportunity to have a few drinks, a bite to eat and catch up with the gossip. Laidlaw made a beeline towards her at the bar, where he tapped her gently on the shoulder.

"It's the English rose," he said, grinning as she turned to face him.

"Why, if it's not Sir Charles." She smiled.

"How's the medical world?" he asked. "I've not seen you since… well, since I heard about your romantic entanglement in the rain."

Immediately, she felt herself blush.

"Who is the lucky young man? I'm madly jealous, darling…"

"Nothing happened, Charles."

"That's usually my line," he quipped, and they both laughed. "Seriously, though, I hear he's the writer chappy who works for McKenzie."

"John Cousins, if you must know."

"Quite handsome, I hear…"

Again, she felt herself blush. "He was there at the rescue when we were caught in the flash flooding. That's all."

"Heard all about it. Very romantic, kissing in the monsoon rain…"

"It wasn't quite like that," she said with a degree of agitation.

"Ah, what it is to be young and single!"

"You are awful, you know."

"I do hope so! You must tell me all about him. I want to know *everything*."

"You met him," she said. "At the last barbecue."

"I did?! Damned if I remember."

"That's because you were at the bar most of the evening!"
He feigned a look of emotional hurt. "So young, so callous.
But I'm sure you're right. And I love you too, sweetie!"

"Drink?" she asked.

"What a question."

"And a double scotch," she said to the barman as he slid a
beer towards her.

"Where is he tonight? Will I like him?"

"You'll love him!"

"As you do?" He chuckled.

"Yes, Charles, as I do. But he's not here. He's in the field."

"Then I have you to myself tonight."

"In your dreams," she said, and he laughed out loud.

"Not my type, darling, as you know!"

"He'll be at the party next week. I'll introduce you."

"Party?"

"*The* party. At McKenzie's place."

"Ah, *that* party! Yes, that should be jolly... have you met
his wife?"

"Wife? You mean McKenzie's married?"

"He is, my dear. I thought everybody knew. Quite the
story at the time."

"You are shocking."

"Oh, I hope so." He chuckled, reaching for the double
scotch from the bar. He raised a toast to her and downed it
in one.

CHAPTER NINETEEN

T HE GIRL WATCHED him in anticipation as he took the plastic carrier bag and passed it into her small, brown hands. Her eyes widened with excitement as she peered inside to see its contents. Then she looked up at him and beamed.

"Go on," he coaxed. "It's all yours." And the mother laughed to see the joy the foreigner brought to their lives as Lula lifted out each item.

There was a new paint set and an artist's pad with the cleanest white paper she'd ever seen. There was chocolate. He had brought a new book to read with her too. They had nearly finished *The Lion, the Witch and the Wardrobe*, and this was the second. For a moment, she held the volume like a coveted treasure, staring at the colourful image on its cover, rubbing her fingers slowly over the picture which showed an exotic young prince.

"Is there stories of magic in this one too?" she asked.

"Sure," he said. "The kind that's in all of us, if we believe," he told her.

She wanted a wardrobe just like the one in the story they were reading, that could take her to other worlds. Asmara would be a good start, she said.

For Mariam, the girl's mother, there was a sack of rice in the Land Cruiser and cooking oil. It made him happy to help. There had been joy too when he and Johnson had purchased the gifts together in the capital. He wished she could have been there to see the happiness on their faces.

The onset of the heavy rains had confined him to camp. He had been caught in Tessenei near the border as they hit with renewed intensity and travel was simply not possible. They were long days when torrential rain fell from darkened skies of billowing black cloud. It allowed him to spend time with Lula. Sometimes he would read to her. Or they would paint together. Or they would simply talk about his life in England, beyond the world she knew, and there would be an unending stream of questions. He was heartened that she was now attending school more regularly. She was hungry to learn.

When he was alone, Cousins would sit out on the porch reading his own book to the ever-present patter of the teeming rain upon the corrugated iron roof and the splashing of water upon the red earth within the compound, now a quagmire of mud. He felt he was in good company with Hemingway and Lawrence, two of his literary heroes. Sometimes he would gaze out at the sky in search of brightness, but the greyness seemed total, covering the land with an impenetrable blanket.

Thoughts of the past and of his young son in Pakistan were never far from his mind. He thought of Johnson too. Or he would conjure images of his family in England and leafy, green country lanes bathed in gentle sunshine.

Then he was back in Eritrea and always there was the sound of water falling from the heavens. To the east, torrents of brown water ran from the mountains onto the plains and dry riverbeds just days before were now flowing wild and full. For days, he had been laid up at the compound, waiting for a break in the monsoon rain. But there was none. There was nothing for it but to wait it out. The ground was now sodden, and although there was access to the frontier town over waterlogged roads, the tracks out to the villages had turned to mud, bringing too great a risk of becoming stranded, even with four-wheel drive.

In camp, an umbrella was an essential piece of kit to dash across the yard without becoming soaked to the skin within seconds. Plastic sandals too, for the mud was too deep, even for heavy boots. But you had to be careful. There were parasites to guard against and Cousins was careful to wash his feet after trudging through mud up to his ankles.

One might have thought the rain would bring respite from the heat, but the nights were hot and carried a stifling humidity as he lay naked, sweating under his net, the smallest movement adding to his discomfort. He must have drunk gallons of bottled water. He became accustomed to gravity-defying geckos which scurried along the whitewashed interior of his room, before coming to rest motionless on its walls and ceiling.

The army of black millipedes too that somehow found their way inside. Along with the mosquitoes. He lost count of the hours spent chasing the insects with a folded newspaper, or with spray, from the corners of his room. Sometimes his net was the only refuge.

Yet life went on. He enjoyed talking to Farjad and Jamal about their culture and the issues their people faced. Usually, they ate together. Simple fare, often rice or pulses with meat and bread Mariam prepared for them. Sometimes Cousins liked to be alone, when he missed his own space and privacy. It was a Western thing which the Eritreans could scarcely comprehend. For they preferred to be in company. Community was everything,

One day Farjad produced a chess set. Then they would drink coffee and play. He lacked practice these days, the Eritrean said, but the field coordinator was an accomplished master with the worn pieces on the battered wooden board. An Italian had once brought the set from Asmara, and it had been a useful distraction ever since, especially when the rains came. Several of the pawns were missing, but it didn't matter. They had been replaced with small pieces of wood, crudely fashioned as replacement counters. Lula would sit with Cousins and advise him. Jamal would take Farjad's side. Sometimes the games went deep into the night when the two men would battle it out alone to the patter of the relentless rain when the air was still and humid.

Then suddenly one morning the rain simply stopped, and there was total silence. The clouds parted, and the sun beat down onto the sodden earth which was steaming in the heat. It was what they had waited for. They needed to access the remote villages on the plains to the north-west, where Farjad would talk to communities about their livelihoods. They were pastoral, nomadic peoples, and BritAid had been working with the Eritrean Government on initiatives to support their fragile way of life, which was largely dependent on their animals. They would take the opportunity to distribute some mosquito nets too, for the insects were swarming over stagnant water following the rain.

He was naked from the waist up, leaning awkwardly against the solitary tree at the centre of the tented settlement, his shaved head slightly to one side. That itself seemed strange.

For the men usually wore the all-encompassing *jelabiya* and allowed their hair to grow long. The man appeared to be resting on his hands which were wedged between the small of his back and the stunted acacia tree behind him, its canopy casting a welcome shadow from the sun which now shone strongly from a break in the billowing cloud.

The man straightened his head and watched Cousins approach, accompanied by the local chief, Farjad and a throng of villagers who trailed them through a thin mist rising from the ground in the midday heat. He could not recall the last time he had seen a white man, though he spoke fluent English from the days he had worked for the British in Asmara. That was a long time ago. For a moment, he thought he might be dreaming. He gazed down at his bare feet resting in the mud in which he stood and at the shackle around his ankle, then looked up again as the group approached.

Cousins became increasingly disturbed as he drew closer. This couldn't be right. He was shocked to realise the man's leg was chained to the tree.

"I don't understand," he said, turning to Farjad, who looked uneasy.

"You must say nothing," the Eritrean muttered to his English companion.

They were being introduced to the one person in the village who could speak fluent English; an interpreter of the local language, which was sometimes difficult even for Farjad to follow. As they stood before the chained man, he gazed at them passively. The chief spoke in an Arabic dialect and gestured by way of introduction. Cousins guessed the man before them might be in his mid-thirties, though it was hard to tell. His name was Saleem.

He was to be their interpreter. Cousins glanced questioningly at Farjad, but the field coordinator shot him a warning look and spoke before the Englishman could voice any objection.

"*Asalaam-u-alaikum*," he said by way of universal Muslim greeting, and the chained man responded calmly in kind. Then he smiled. The village chief nodded. For a moment, there was an uneasy silence while the chief considered, rubbing a hand over his greying beard. Then he gave an instruction for the man to be released, and two villagers stepped forward to unchain him. He was to join them to talk and help with the language.

Inwardly, Farjad breathed a sigh of relief, for they were a long way from Tessenei, and the people of the plains had their own traditions and beliefs. Sometimes they were hostile to ideas that might challenge customs practised for centuries that lay somewhere between ancient tribal ritual and Islam. It was therefore a strange group that made its way across the muddy ground to the tent where they would talk, comprising the elderly clan chief, the Englishman, the Eritrean field coordinator and the half-naked interpreter the village kept chained to a tree. There they would sit, talk, discuss and negotiate over sweet tea, as was the custom.

The settlement consisted of a dozen or so families. They were members of the Hedareb tribe. Their core beliefs were loosely based upon the principles of Islam. As a pastoral community, they relied on their animals and a nomadic, migratory way of life, living essentially from the land and the produce of their animals. They were mainly goats, though there was a small number of camels too, which provided milk and meat. But the community was prone to drought and epidemic. Water was a determining factor for survival. That and the ability for their herds to feed off the land.

Inside the tent, Cousins was awed by Saleem's fluency, who spoke near-perfect English as the Westerner sat watching and listening. Restocking the goat herds had helped the community. The seasons were drier, the rains less predictable. The animals they received proved hardy and yielded more milk. The chieftain was grateful. A scheme to help harvest water had also improved the settlement's situation. But the idea of boring down to groundwater to create a new well had been rejected. They would move with the changing of the seasons to follow the water and better grazing as their forefathers before them. Besides, a well would only attract neighbouring groups to an area already sparse on resources, the chieftain explained, and the elders nodded in agreement.

The idea of a field dispensary was still being considered. Perhaps a team could visit with medicines one day before the time came for the settlement to break camp? Before they moved eastwards, towards the hills, where there was better foraging and grazing for their animals during the dry season. They were not farmers, their host told them with a sense of pride. They were a people free to roam the land like the wind. Farjad nodded in understanding.

Agreement had been reached that the BritAid water and sanitation team could return and would be made welcome. Additional containers for collecting and storing water, especially during the rainy season, would be useful. The community would take the mosquito nets too, as they had brought them, although Farjad was in some doubt about how they might be used. Permission was also forthcoming for Cousins to gather the pictures he needed and, before they left the village, he had taken shots of several villagers with their goat herds. Of course, no women were allowed to be seen, in line with Islamic principles of purdah.

The clan chief proved an enthusiastic subject for Cousins' pictures. He seemed ever ready to strike an impressive pose himself, standing proud with his wild shock of greying hair, his flowing *jelabiya* and magnificent waistcoat, gazing straight to camera. There were also pictures of villagers receiving their mosquito nets from Farjad and Jamal. The team had everything they needed and were ready for the long journey back to Tessenei, waved off by village children, who ran excitedly in pursuit of their Land Cruiser as it slowly moved off from the settlement through the mud.

Farjad had been able to establish the circumstances behind their interpreter's situation, which he shared with Cousins during their return journey. The man was prone to unexpected fits, when he would fall screaming to the ground, shaking uncontrollably and foaming at the mouth. It was, according to village belief, the work of a djinn; an evil spirit which entered the man's body. Then, after several minutes, he would lie still, exhausted by the experience. Sometimes the episodes were more frequent and prolonged, as they had been during the rains. The villagers were superstitious. The man needed to be kept safe; the djinn had to be contained. After the episodes, he was able to return to his family.

Cousins had been enthralled by the visit. There had been something surreal about sitting in the tent sipping tea with the man the village deemed to be mad, speaking perfect English, explaining a way of life that had essentially remained unchanged for centuries. Yet the people were willing to embrace new methods, if they would preserve the life they knew. He wondered what would become of the man known as Saleem as their vehicle pushed on along the muddy track that would take them to the Tessenei Road and back to camp.

CHAPTER TWENTY

T HEY SAID ANY party only really started with the arrival
of Sir Charles. He had the ability to draw a crowd to him
like a magnet. Yet he was different things to different people.
To some, he represented the British presence in Asmara. To
the locals, he was an unusual government official; a Westerner
who understood and embraced their culture.

To those who knew him best, he was reliable, a good sort,
always charming, ever gregarious and a useful chap to have
onside in a tight spot. Fewer still counted on him as a friend
and really knew what lay beneath. McKenzie was among them.
They had known each other since Sir Charles had first arrived
at the British residence in Maryam Gmbi Street. By then, the
Scot was already part of the established Asmara expat scene.
So, they had known each other more years than either man
cared to count. Walters too, along with several other long-
term aid workers, including Mancini, the Italian, were part
of his inner social circle. Indeed, the party was not an official
engagement.

It was why Sir Charles was due to arrive without his wife, when he was at his best and worst. Those who were close to him knew he was flawed. But he was fun. He was loyal to his closest friends, that small number of people he spoke to openly and took into his confidence. And they adored him. Johnson too had come to view the charismatic diplomat as more than an acquaintance. The feeling was mutual; he had taken quite a shine to the English nurse. Perhaps because there was no pretence. She was honest and open with all she met. He liked that, especially in the world in which he operated.

She and Cousins arrived together, sharing a vehicle which had brought them across the city under grey skies as the cloud began to gather and thicken once more. Neither were quite sure what to expect from the party. McKenzie rarely entertained, and it was the first social event at his private residence either had attended.

The old villa was grand, colonial in style, of the kind wealthy Italian merchants had built before the end of the nineteenth century, when Eritrea lay at the heart of trade with the outside world. The heavy wooden front door was ajar as they approached from the driveway on foot. Some blue and white balloons fixed beneath a sign on the house which proclaimed 'Dun Roamin' told them this must be the place. As they stepped inside, they were greeted by McKenzie's Eritrean housekeeper, who smiled faintly in welcome.

She wore a stunningly colourful full-length dress that was not untypical of the women from the city. Her dark, slightly greying hair was drawn back to frame a high forehead and delicate face with fine features that suggested a mixed Arab-African heritage. There was no denying she was a handsome woman.

"Welcome," she said. "You must be Hannah the nurse." Johnson nodded.

"And I'm John..."

"Ah yes, the writer."

"I guess," Cousins replied.

The woman smiled more broadly this time, showing perfect white teeth that contrasted attractively against the copper tone of her complexion, which was fair but not unusual by Eritrean standards.

"Please. You must come through. Drinks are being served in the garden," she said and led them into the main reception room, where the shutters were low, and the air was heavy with the sweet scent of incense. Cousins noted ornaments and trappings on the wall from across several continents, and there were bookcases with some handsomely bound collections of literary classics. Clearly, this was the home of a well-travelled, educated man who had experienced many different cultures.

Cousins and Johnson had arrived punctually and were among the first dozen or so expected guests. Most were expats already known to them both. The international aid community in Asmara was small. A scattering of people stood in small groups chatting, for it was early yet. They saw McKenzie in the far corner in lively discussion with Joe, the Kenyan and Mancini. The Scot waved jovially in acknowledgement as they entered, and they approached, followed by the housekeeper, who waited dutifully.

"I was just saying you can grow almost anything here in the hills," McKenzie said, clutching an empty spirit glass. "Take my potatoes..."

"That may hold good for the eastern slopes," Mancini countered, "but not for the plains. There's no irrigation."

"But that's my point exactly with the water," McKenzie insisted, before turning to the newly arrived pair. "Glad you could make it, you two. Welcome," he added, patting Cousins on the shoulder, then leaning towards Johnson, who kissed him on the cheek. "Drinks are outside," he added. "Tsibe will take you through," he said, addressing the Eritrean woman at their side. "Oh and be so good as to get a top-up for me, John, there's a good man," he said, thrusting his glass into Cousins' hand before resuming his conversation with Mancini. "As for the tomatoes..." they heard him continue, and they left him to it.

The woman known as Tsibe led them through the house and into an extensive walled garden at the rear with full-leafed banana trees and feathered date palms around its borders. In the centre of a perfectly kept lawn was a small marquee with drinks being served by a local barman. There was finger food too. They should help themselves, the housekeeper told them and withdrew to return to the house. In the corner of the lawn, a group of four young Eritreans sat at a table with drinks, chatting and laughing. All were dressed in identical *jelabiya*. Perhaps they were the local band that was due to play. A variety of musical equipment stood ready in a small area inside the tent, including guitars on stands, microphone, amplifiers and an assortment of African drums. It seemed McKenzie liked to entertain in style.

Two men were being served as they approached. They recognised them from the UN and nodded by way of 'hello'.

"Quite a place," said Cousins, turning to face her, and she nodded.

"You don't think McKenzie is going to perform?"

"Let's hope not," he replied. "There's a rumour he has a set of bagpipes!"

She raised her eyebrows. "God, no!"

The pair from the UN left with their drinks to head inside, and the barman came to them.

"Beer for me," said Johnson.

"Make that two beers, please. And a gin and tonic," Cousins added, and the barman nodded in acknowledgement.

He fished two bottles of dark Eritrean beer from a bucket of iced water and slid them across the table. Then he reached for a gin bottle and poured a generous measure. Cousins thanked him and turned towards his companion. "Cheers!" he exclaimed, clinking his bottle against hers and raising it to his lips.

More people were now heading out into the garden in twos and threes. They saw McKenzie walking with the team from Catholic Relief. They'd seen them around but hadn't met them before. The Scot was in deep conversation with Siobhan Cullen, the CR head of mission, trailed by two or three of her staff, heading towards them at the tent.

'Mother' Siobhan, as she was known, had a reputation. She stood for no nonsense. If aid workers were said to be either mercenaries, missionaries or misfits, she fell unmistakeably into the second category. She was driven by her faith and regarded as an austere and seasoned operator who knew Africa. She'd carried the Catholic Relief flag across the continent for nearly two decades and had pretty much seen it all. Therefore, she was revered and respected. Indeed, beneath an exterior which seemed rigid and reserved lay a driving passion for her fellow human beings.

She and McKenzie were unlikely friends. If she was conservative with a capital 'C', he was viewed by some as something of a maverick with a capital 'M'. Like the Scot, she too was a long-term fixture in Eritrea. She had first arrived in the early nineties, not long after the end of the thirty-year war. She'd worked through the carnage, driven by her faith. When hostilities flared again on the Ethiopian border, she refused to leave. For a while, she was forced to work in Kenya. But it wasn't long before she and her team were back in Asmara, and they saw it out until the peace was finally agreed with the onset of the new millennium.

Outwardly, McKenzie seemed to be everything she might disapprove of, and she would often chastise him playfully. But in fact, she liked him enormously, and they held a mutual respect for each other. Although their methods of delivery differed, their goals and their motivations were the same, which was recognised. Even so, she was known for her plain speaking and for running a tight ship. She watched over her staff like a reverend mother. Austere, certainly. Knowledgeable and experienced too. But also supportive. She looked after her team, and there was a softer side to her many people missed.

There had been a man once, it was said. Certainly, it might be true. You sensed there was a story behind those steady grey eyes. There was humour too when those eyes would soften, and the hardness of her face would melt into a girlish, mischievous smile. McKenzie knew how to draw it out. Which is why they considered themselves good friends. As it was, she cut an impressively composed figure, dressed in a full-length dress to her ankles, with her hair tied with a broad headband as she walked gracefully beside him. The contrast of the Scot's khaki knee-length shorts, sandals and Hawaiian shirt was perhaps the greatest visual indication of their respective characters.

McKenzie approached and introduced his companion. "I'd like you to meet my communications man, John Cousins."

Cousins nodded. "Pleasure," he said. He felt Cullen's grey eyes upon him. For a moment, he thought she might offer her hand to be kissed.

"And how are you finding Eritrea?" she asked, betraying a hint of her Irish roots in her accent.

"Hot and humid," he said. "But good, thank you."

"And you," she said, turning towards Johnson. "I've heard all about you from David."

Johnson felt herself flush. "Good things, I hope."

"Yes, only good things. We must meet for coffee," added the older woman. It sounded less of a request and more like an instruction.

"I'd like that," said the English nurse.

"Your drink," Cousins said and reached the glass of gin and tonic bottle towards McKenzie.

"Ah, that's grand!" he said and felt himself under Cullen's steely gaze.

"There's juice too," he heard himself say and gestured towards the tent which was now a flurry of activity. "Nice to meet you," Cousins said, though Cullen was now scanning the garden for her team as McKenzie led her to the bar.

Inside the house, Sir Charles breezed in fashionably late, followed by his man from the embassy with a crate of gin. It was McKenzie's favourite brand, no less. No doubt it had been secured through diplomatic channels from Kenya. Most of the alcohol, meat and cheese came from Nairobi. Sir Charles had picked up McKenzie's housekeeper on his way through, and they stepped into the garden arm in arm into the humid evening air.

"Charlie!" Johnson exclaimed, coming face to face with the pair. She was on her way towards the house to find Walters.

"Hannah, darling!" said Sir Charles, whose arm was still linked with the handsome woman at his side. "Where've you been all my life?" he quipped.

"I think that's my question, Charlie…"

"Have you two been introduced?" he asked.

"Not properly," Johnson said.

"Then allow me to do the formalities. Hannah Johnson. She's one of the Medics International team they're all raving about. Walters' outfit," he said, turning to the African woman beside him. "I'd like you to meet Mrs Tsibekti 'Capri' McKenzie."

Johnson was stunned. The woman wasn't the housekeeper. She was McKenzie's Eritrean wife.

"Delighted to meet you," said Mrs McKenzie. "Formally, that is," she added, smiling, and Johnson nodded in acknowledgement.

"And where is *Mr McKenzie?*" asked Sir Charles.

"Over at the tent," Johnson replied.

"Naturally!"

In fact, the Scot was organising the musicians, who were taking up their instruments, with McKenzie at the mic. He tapped it with his finger to check it was working.

"Greetings, everybody!" he announced over the PA system. There was a whine of feedback. "Thanks for coming. Without further ado, I'd like to introduce you to the band. Please welcome The Asmara Vagabonds! Enjoy!"

The up-tempo beat of a drum signalled the start of an accomplished set of jazz-fusion numbers with traditional Eritrean percussion, rising over the hubbub of conversation as more people came out from the house. Walters was among those drawn to the garden with the Asmara nursing team. They came to stand with Cousins and Johnson, and she mouthed a 'hello' to him, as all eyes turned towards the musicians.

An extended percussion break of bongos and traditional East African drums was irresistible. The Eritreans were the first to dance. They formed a circle and began to sway gently, rhythmically, from side to side as they moved around its wide circumference on McKenzie's lawn to the beat of the drums. Then the expats were there too, with McKenzie leading the way.

"Fancy a dance?" Cousins asked Johnson.

"Sure," she replied, and he led her to join the circle of dance, watched by Sir Charles with a mischievous grin. For a moment, she caught his gaze, and he winked at her. Then he spotted the young Eritrean nurse. He decided to move in.

As the evening sun threw lengthening shadows across the garden, the atmosphere was building, fuelled by the alcohol, the music and high spirits of the company that had been confined by the weather too long. There was a distant rumble of thunder, but it went unnoticed, drowned out by the music and the dance as the band played on. Even Cullen was seen dancing at one point, an achievement by any measure.

The patter of the first heavy drops of rain signalled the inevitable. The heavens opened, and the rain came down in sheets. The music stopped, and the partygoers scattered, running for cover. The musicians hastily brought their instruments under the safety of the marquee and packed them into cases.

Cousins and Johnson were the last to leave the lawn, reluctant to give up the intimacy they had been enjoying.

"Here we are again," he said as they stood facing each other, and the heavy rain continued to fall through the humid sky. He drew a protective arm around her as the downpour intensified, and they then dashed for shelter under the marquee, where they stood soaked to the skin, watching the water fall from the sky.

Sir Charles had watched them from inside the back doorway of the house. They looked good together, he thought. The Eritrean nurse had escaped from him once more. It was probably just as well. He stared at the empty glass in his hand, then out at the pouring rain. He wondered how he was going to get across the lawn to the tent for another drink. He turned to the group of people standing behind him. "Does anyone have an umbrella?" he asked.

CHAPTER TWENTY-ONE

H E LAY ON his back, staring up at the mosquito net in the semi-darkness of the early morning, listening to the sound of the persistent rain outside. He was the first to wake and had watched her as she slept, studying the contours of her face and body, noting the steady rise and fall of her breathing beneath the cotton sheet. Her face was relaxed, her eyes lightly closed, and she seemed totally at peace. Angelic even, he mused. He would let her sleep.

He hadn't foreseen the prospect of physical intimacy, naively, perhaps. Emotionally, he wasn't really ready for it. But after they had left the party together, he had invited her to his room for a drink. They enjoyed each other's company, and neither of them had really wanted the evening to end. He had made coffee on the gas stove in the communal kitchen in the Italian-style moka pot he had brought with him to Africa, and they had chatted by candlelight, still slightly intoxicated from the several bottles of Eritrean beer they had consumed. They talked about their experience of aid work, about England and the people they worked with. Not about anything too intimate. Certainly not about whether they wanted to make love.

It was a ritual, as old as creation. They had flirted in their conversation, teasing each other. They had moved closer; they had embraced and kissed, their breathing becoming heavy as the prospect of physical intimacy increased. That mixture of nervousness, excitement and carnal desire, with the latter almost inevitably winning out as the heart began to race, and the adrenalin took hold. Afterwards, they had lain breathless and naked, sweating in the stifling heat of the night as the rain outside continued to hammer down upon the tin roof. Finally, they had slept.

Now, as he lay beside her in the cold light of day, he began to feel a pang of guilt. She had been the first woman he had slept with since Pakistan. Not that he regretted what had happened. But he was still in love with Afsa Ali and had not yet processed her loss. The feelings he held for Johnson were intense. But it was different. He was essentially still grieving for the woman and the life he had lost. Yet he had found a closeness to Johnson that was comforting and fulfilling. Healing, even. She was a good woman, and he held no doubt that he could find happiness again; that in fact he had fallen in love with her.

He turned towards her and caught a hint of her perfume upon his pillow. It was a different scent. Sweet, light and refreshing, he thought. Distinctive to her. By a Japanese fashion designer, she had told him when he had asked. As he lay there, he wondered whether the fact that they had slept together would change anything between them. They had not discussed the idea of a future together, although they were clearly an 'item'.

There was something special in the closeness that had developed between them. Something natural. She felt they were friends first and foremost. That was something she had found lacking in her previous relationships, which she felt had been based on an initial physical attraction. Usually she had felt pursued, which had not been the case in her relationship with Cousins. In fact, he had seemed cautious. Even shy and distant at times. It was something she felt irresistibly drawn to. More importantly, perhaps, they shared a similar perspective on life. There was humour too. In short, she felt wanted for who she was, rather than how she looked. That was something she found exciting and refreshing. He felt it too.

Suddenly, the fan whirred into life, bringing a hint movement to the mosquito net as the air in his room began to circulate. *It must be seven*, he thought. The generator had been restarted for the day ahead.

"Good morning," he said as her eyes fluttered open.

"Hello," she replied sleepily, snuggling closer to him.

"It was lovely last night," he said.

"It was," she replied, closing her eyes again and smiling. "Thank you!"

"Thank *you*! Coffee?"

"Mmm... please," she muttered.

He kissed her on her cheek, then propped himself up. He unpegged the net and turned from her to sit on the edge of the bed, scanning the room for his trousers. He was naked and self-conscious. He tossed the sheet aside, then rose purposefully and somewhat shyly, with his back towards her. He picked up and pulled on his cargo pants quickly, awkwardly, almost losing his balance and falling. She chuckled as she watched his early morning clumsiness from the bed, and he turned sheepishly towards her.

"Nothing I haven't seen before," she said. "Besides, I am a nurse!"

"I'll get the coffee on," he replied with a grin, before heading out into the kitchen. He hoped the Kenyan was still sleeping.

———

No one was surprised when they announced they were seeing each other. In fact, the party and the fact that they had slept together afterwards *had* changed things between them. They felt closer than ever, and they were less cautious about being seen together. They had started to consider a future together and talked about the prospect of an engagement. Perhaps when she returned from her imminent trip to the UK to visit her family.

"Don't blame you," McKenzie had told him. "She's a great girl, John! Just be careful, though. I wouldn't wait too long. Don't let her get away. I wouldn't."

Walters was more considered. But then, Johnson was closer to him. She was one of his senior staff members, and they had worked together since her arrival in Eritrea. So, he felt doubly responsible, not least because he was fond of her himself.

"Do you think you have a future together?" he asked her.

"I do, David. We love each other. We're thinking of getting engaged when I'm back from England."

"Love? Isn't that rather sudden?" the doctor asked her. "What do you really know about him? You've told me about his loss in Pakistan. Is he ready?" He gazed at her over his glasses with that probing look of his.

"It feels right," she told him.

He sighed deeply, before he relented. "Well, you're over twenty-one. I guess you should know what you're doing." He said no more.

In his heart, he was sad. He had grown close to her during their time together through thick and thin. He might even have been a little bit in love with her himself. But he knew they could never be anything more than friends.

Sir Charles was genuinely excited when she joined him for coffee one day in the city, not least by the prospect of a love story within Asmara's expat community. He had met Cousins, and he liked him. He was genuinely pleased for Johnson.

"That's wonderful," he said. "I envy you. Happiness is a rare bird, as they say, and sometimes you have to seize the moment. It's always eluded me," he said with genuine sincerity that she found endearing.

"So, when's the wedding?" he asked. "You simply *must* allow me to be part of it. After all, you're both British subjects, and Her Majesty's Government has an interest in *all* domestic and foreign affairs, you know."

"You are awful, Charles…"

"No, no… I mean it. I'm sure I can pull some strings. We will have a society wedding in the city to remember, my dear!"

"That's very kind, Charles," she said.

"It will be my pleasure. Congratulations. Between you and I, I think he's quite a catch."

"Thank you." She smiled, and they hugged.

"Not only that, but I think he is a very lucky guy," he added. "And for that I'm jealous too!"

There was a real tenderness in his embrace, which touched her as they said goodbye.

"Safe travels," he called after her as he watched her disappear from view. Then she was gone. Next week she would be on her way back to the UK. He'd miss her.

Parting at the airport was difficult. She and Cousins were now officially a 'couple'. They spent time with each other whenever they could. They were also sleeping together regularly. Although they still had to be discreet, sneaking into each other's team houses. But it was different for expats. Even in Muslim parts of Eritrea. The locals viewed the personal relationships of international staff largely with indifference and as something very separate from their own world. As long as it did not cross cultural boundaries.

Theirs was indeed a world of privilege which seldom touched the lives of local people, even in more conservative areas. In reality, no one really cared what went on in the private lives of aid workers beyond closed doors. Within reason. In reality, the expat community was exempt from most of the real hardships and restrictions which governed the lives of most Eritreans. They both knew it. It wasn't about a lack of respect or not caring about the local culture. It was just the way it was.

Therefore, they were allowed a large degree of freedom in their relationship. Professionally, they worked independently, often in different parts of the country, sometimes separated for days. But at social events, particularly in the capital, they were always to be seen together. They had both been open and honest with their respective bosses, and they became accepted as a couple. Even Siobhan Cullen seemed to approve.

When Johnson finally met her at the UN club, Cullen had talked a great deal about her time in Eritrea and what it had been like immediately after the thirty-year war.

"In those days it was not unheard of for children to die of hunger in Tessenei, or Barentu, or Massawa, or Assab," she told Johnson. "It was hard enough in Asmara. We felt powerless. There simply wasn't enough food. Sometimes we went hungry ourselves." She paused. "No medicines either. They were the hardest of times," she recalled with a look of sadness.

She told Johnson how wonderful it was that she was supporting the health programme – so needed – and that she was a big fan of David Walters. "Now there's a man I respect," she had said. "A wonderful man who has put aside his personal grief to do good." Johnson knew it.

She had praise for McKenzie too. "A bit of a rogue, but a good man nevertheless," she had said. And she had said no more about him.

"Your writer seems a decent sort too. Nice looking. John... what's his name? How are you getting on with him?" Out it came, with a slight twinkle in those steely grey eyes.

Johnson laughed awkwardly. Then she felt a flush creep into her cheeks. "Good, thank you. In fact, we're thinking of getting engaged." There it was. It was out there.

"How wonderful,." Cullen smiled. Before the day was through, half of Asmara must have known.

He travelled out to the small airport with her that afternoon. It wasn't far from the city. Besides, it gave them a last opportunity to spend precious moments together before her departure.

"I'm going to miss you," he said.

"You too," she replied. "It will be strange to be back in England."

But she knew it was necessary. It wasn't just to have a break from Eritrea, which she needed. It was important to see her family too. She wanted to speak to her father about Cousins and to tell him they were planning to announce their engagement. She also had some unfinished business she hadn't mentioned. That is, she wanted to see Julian one last time. She had loved him so very much. He was the man responsible for her leaving England for Bosnia. For the first time, she felt she could put that part of her life behind her too.

It was therefore with mixed emotions that she boarded the plane bound for Dubai. From there, she would fly onwards to

Heathrow. In a little over twelve hours, she would step back to a world so very different from the one she had left. Hers was a world of plenty, a place of freedoms. She knew she was privileged. She knew there were so many who longed for the chance to leave Eritrea… simply by stepping onto a plane.

CHAPTER TWENTY-TWO

E VADING THE BORDER patrols was best at night, the Afghan told them. During the daylight hours, there were more guards on the ground watching for migrants. There was an aircraft too, known to patrol the frequent crossing points and the Adriatic Sea lanes from the sky. It would not be easy, but he and his family would try. They had to keep moving while their health and their resolve remained. If they stayed too long in one place, their chances would diminish and the risk of capture increase. There was no alternative.

Besides, they had come too far, and the freedom they dreamed of might only be days away. Just days. It was a warming thought. If they were not caught. It was a prize worth the risk, for already they had given up everything; worth the long, hard journey. It was the prospect of a future free from war and persecution where they might build a new life and their children would be safe.

At least the weather was kind. The promise of summer was in the air, bathing the wooded slopes of the rugged Albanian foothills in sunshine by day. But when the sun slipped beyond the mountain peaks, the chill of the evening returned as the forest fell into shadow.

The Afghan family left Daniel and Juba that evening. Javed the father, the mother and two young children, still wearing their traditional clothing, now soiled and ragged. But they had quilted Western coats. Everything else was gathered in sheets and carried in tied bundles. The children held plastic carrier bags. Juba watched them through the trees until they disappeared from view, heading towards the Montenegro border. He hoped they would make it and said a silent prayer for their safety.

As night fell, the wooded slopes grew dark and silent. There was the heavy scent of pine and a dampness in the air as the two African nurses lay on the forest floor, drawing their blankets around them. Occasionally, they would hear a rustle in the brush close by. Perhaps some animal out in the darkness. They had heard there were wolves, foxes, even bears, out among the trees, and they would draw their blankets a little tighter around themselves up to the chin. It would be the wet season in Eritrea, Juba thought. Heavy rain falling through hot and humid skies. He missed the warmth. He missed his family. They seemed a world away.

"We're going to make it," he whispered to his companion, who lay beside him.

"Yes, we will," Daniel replied, though neither man spoke with certainty.

"Then we will eat meat and drink until we can eat and drink no more," he added.

"And sleep in warm, comfortable beds."

"Yes!" said Juba. "A good life is waiting for us."

In reality, the two men were close to exhaustion. But they had to believe. They had to believe to hold the dream that drove them onwards, though they were tired and hungry. Their resources were limited, each with only a few dollars from their original bundles of cash. Already it had been many days since they had left Eritrea.

Earlier, they had shared food with the Afghans, and Juba had watched the children. He saw how the young girl helped the mother cook the food over an open fire and later how she tended her little brother. Such love, such devotion. There were smiles too in their hardship. But the girl had looked frail and hungry, he had thought, with her sallow complexion and hollow cheeks. The children were so very young to be facing such a hard and perilous journey.

The family were happy to share what they had, the father had said. It was central to his religion, and he would not allow their difficult circumstances to take that from him. In a sense, his faith was key to their survival, for their belief that God would help them prevail was essential in allowing them to continue. It gave them a sense of hope. When the family left, they offered the Eritreans an extra blanket. They needed to travel light, the father said. The two men had watched them walk into the woods and out of view towards an uncertain future.

Now they were alone again in the forest. Daniel took the penknife from his pocket and carved another notch into the plastic casing of the small torch he carried, as he did at the end of every day, though its batteries had long since dimmed and had given out.

"Nineteen," he said, rubbing a finger over the notches. "Nineteen days now."

"Then we are through the worst. We will make it, insh'allah." If God willed it so. "Amen," Daniel added.

Already they had passed through three countries, travelling more than two thousand miles by road, rail, by boat and on foot over land and sea. They could not be sure their strength would hold out. Like their cash, it was almost depleted. But they had received help along the way. Sometimes assistance came from unexpected quarters; other migrants they encountered in the woods or within a derelict house along the route. Or in small camps near the border crossings. Local groups also offered them help. For they were not the first to pass through. It would come in the form of basic food parcels or additional blankets. Sometimes there were sweets for the children and smiles. It would choke the two men with emotion almost to tears to receive such kindness in the midst of adversity. Perhaps God was smiling on them too.

In some regions they passed through, they were met with suspicion and prejudice, when they would be asked to move on. Worse still were the stories of beatings by those hostile to the migrants, or the arrests when camps were raided by the police or security forces to whom they had been betrayed. Then they had to keep moving to evade the authorities. Occasionally, there seemed no way forward. A border might be too well guarded or an area too exposed to pass through, the risk of passing close to a settlement too high. But always there was another way. They had to believe that.

One evening, they came across a cattle shed on the edge of a field that offered shelter from the chill of the night. The door was not locked and, cautiously, they had entered to discover cows inside that shuffled nervously as they moved among them. But Daniel knew about animals from his time tending cattle in Eritrea and was soon able to settle them. That night, they had slept deeply, sharing the warmth from the livestock and sinking into the hay they arranged into makeshift bedding.

In the morning, they were woken abruptly as the door creaked open and a grizzled farm worker looked down upon them as they squinted into the light of the new day. He spoke aggressively in a language they did not understand. But his voice calmed when he realised his cattle were unharmed and that the additional occupants of the shed had only sought shelter. He saw too they were hungry, and he took pity on them. Then he sat with them, and he offered them milk and bread before they gathered their scant possessions to resume their journey, heading across the fields towards the nearby woods. As they left, Juba had cried, emotionally raw from exhaustion and touched by the kindness of a stranger.

They were now making for the border. From Montenegro, they hoped to cross into Croatia and up towards Austria, if they could find a way. It would mean living rough and foraging along the way, eating and sleeping when they could. It was a desperate existence. There would be ongoing risks, stowing away on trains, hitching rides on carts, and sometimes trucks, if they would take them. But if they could make it into Austria, they knew they would be within the European Union once more and able to claim asylum.

The trick was to avoid the authorities in consecutive countries. For their goal was Calais on the French coast and to cross the Channel to Britain, where family and friends had already settled. They had heard migrants were welcome there and that the United Nations refugee agency had set up an office to assist growing numbers of refugees heading for the French port. Their aim was then a passage to the UK by any means. It was a determination which had grown ever stronger with each day of suffering during their long and tortuous journey and the hardships they had endured.

From the edge of the woods, they could see the border across the open ground and an unguarded wire fence that stretched as far as the eye could see in the fading light. They would wait until nightfall before trying to cross.

———⟨∾⟩———

Hannah Johnson emerged wearily onto the steps leading from the aircraft and, a few moments later, she was walking across the tarmac at Heathrow airport. A refreshing breeze blew across the runway under cloudy skies. She was glad to be back on English soil and looking forward to a break from the relentless heat and the gruelling workload of Eritrea. How she longed for that first cup of English tea when she would be able to sit back and watch the diversity of UK life pass by, knowing two weeks' leave stretched before her. It had seemed a long time since she had been back. In reality, it was a little over three months.

Here the air seemed cooler, fresher, cleaner. But it was surely an illusion, for Asmara was essentially industry-free and, at two thousand metres, one of the highest capitals in the world. Britain's climate was simply what she was used to, less stifling for her in every sense, perhaps; a modern, industrialised nation with better infrastructure that was still one of the wealthiest nations on the planet.

After clearing passport control and customs, she would board the train that would take her into the heart of London on the Piccadilly Line and across the city on the Underground to St Pancras station. That's where she had promised herself that cup of tea and to take some time to adjust. It was a journey of more than an hour. Then the short trip by tube to Paddington where she would meet her father.

As the train clattered and swayed, she reflected on what it was to be within her native culture once more, which she knew so well. To be among her own people. It was a comforting feeling to be 'back home'. But what was it to be British? It seemed to her there was a mixture of pride and shame in its history. She certainly felt it. It had struggled too with its sense of self since the fall of Empire. It was no longer a superpower on the world stage. But there were still things British that she was immensely proud of: Wimbledon, the Beatles, Glastonbury, the BBC. They were part of her culture, the best of British. Its humour was also quite distinctive among nations, often self-depreciating, its people able to lampoon and laugh at themselves. She liked that too. She thought of Sir Charles and smiled. She wondered idly what he might be up to. Even Cousins had it, that sense of Britishness.

Yet what was the United Kingdom, as it was still rather gloriously known? It was as Sir Charles had said. In reality, Britain was a small group of islands in a cold climate which, as a seafaring nation, had reaped the rewards of sending forth its ships in the sixteenth century to claim new lands. Its people had a tendency towards restlessness and an inclination to go it alone. They still held a reputation for resistance to their closest neighbours in Europe and a resilient 'Bulldog' spirit. It was a nation of contradictions.

Hammersmith was the first station to signal she was set to enter West London, when the train would leave daylight and enter the tunnel which would take it onwards underground, beneath the heart of the city. Then familiar tube stations came thick and fast: South Kensington; Hyde Park Corner; Green Park; Piccadilly Circus; Leicester Square; Holborn. Soon she would approach Russell Square, just a few minutes from St Pancras station. It lay close to Warren Street, where she had completed her training as a nurse at the University College Hospital. They were crazy days when she had lived, studied and worked in the capital. They seemed distant memories now.

That was before she had met Julian. Before Bosnia. Happy, carefree days, full of optimism for the future. She had liked living in North London, once she had become accustomed to the hustle and bustle of big city life, so different from the rural setting in which she grown up as a child. Londoners had seemed different. A little more sophisticated, streetwise and fashion conscious, perhaps. The train began to slow, and she prepared to move from her seat as the first signs for St Pancras flashed passed the window, and it glided to a gentle halt. She rose, lifted her case and made for the exit.

CHAPTER TWENTY-THREE

H E SAT AT a table outside and waited, staring absently across the neatly trimmed lawn. The roses were out, he noted, and their scent brought a hint of sweetness to the air in the hazy afternoon sunshine. The grey smoke curled from the cigarette burning between his fingers and drifted on the light breeze into the summer sky. A glass of beer stood on the table before him. He was anxious.

He hadn't seen Hannah since the year before she left for Bosnia. Not since the split. He wanted to get his story straight. It was all a little inconvenient. Embarrassing even. He was agitated; his eyebrows knitted over his bright blue eyes. He wasn't looking forward to seeing her. But what could he do? She had asked to meet him, and he owed her that. Besides, he felt duty-bound to return the personal items she had requested. He'd be relieved to relinquish the small box of things he had reluctantly kept in the attic all this time. He'd be glad to be rid of it. He raised the cigarette to his lips and drew the smoke into his lungs. She was late.

Most casual observers might have described Julian Andersson as handsome. His short, blond hair was neatly cut, his fringe swept back over a high forehead and a little to one side to cover the first signs of baldness. He was clean shaven with Aryan features and a fair complexion which suggested his father's Northern European blood. But his cheeks were flushed from the onset of high blood pressure from an early age and a fondness for too much alcohol. He led a stressful life in the City in pursuit of wealth from other people's investments, reflected in the clothes he wore and the car he drove. All a little garish, perhaps.

His fine cotton shirt was open at the neck, tucked neatly into his trouser waistband, with a pristine leather belt that looked as if it might never have been worn before, sporting a modest silver buckle. He wore a light summer sports jacket. All designer labels, of course. The look fitted quite neatly, he felt, with the two-seater convertible out in the pub car park.

Some might have said he was living the dream, but he was in fact a little rakish. In truth, he was feeling fatigued, somewhat life-weary, old before his time, despite his relatively young age. He was in his early thirties, but the last few years had taken their toll, and his face was less youthful than it had been. Yet he felt he was successful and that he was able to show his material wealth. That was what mattered to him.

He checked his watch. It wasn't a Rolex. But it was gold. He'd opted for the TAG Heuer at the last minute. Where the hell was she? He'd driven down from London and needed to be back for dinner with Theresa, and already it was after three. He took a sip of his beer. Perhaps she wasn't coming. If she didn't show in the next few minutes, he might head back to the City. He was weighing his options when he saw her enter the garden. He was almost disappointed. He waved and smiled, rising to his feet as she approached.

"Hello, Julian," she said.

"I'd almost given you up."

"Traffic was bad. Good to see you," she added. It was a lie. She had dreaded this moment. But she had wanted her things back. Besides, she had needed to see his face one last time, to look into his eyes. It had all ended so badly.

"What can I get you to drink?" he asked. She looked good, he thought. Better than he remembered, and there was almost a pang of regret.

"Just a fruit juice please, Julian. Orange." It felt strange to her, speaking his name.

He signalled to the waitress hovering at the edge of the garden, and she came over.

"Thanks for agreeing to meet," Johnson said.

"It was the least I could do," he replied.

"It was," she said, studying his face that had once been so familiar to her.

"I have your things in the car," he told her. "Good to see you too," he added as an afterthought.

He looked older, she thought. More jaded than he had been, and his face was slightly bloated now, with more ruddiness and more lines across his forehead. She almost felt sorry for him. But it was all still too raw. They'd had plans. She had thought they would marry. But he had been seeing another woman. Watching him now, she wondered what she had ever seen in him. Yes, he was outwardly attractive. She still thought so. But he was a vain man, too well groomed and manicured. Perhaps even too well dressed. Image seemed to be everything. That's what really struck her as her gaze rested upon him. Perhaps the difference was her recent experience overseas. First the horror of Bosnia. The contrast from life in Eritrea to sitting in a pleasant country pub garden with Julian was extreme. It all seemed so very superficial.

At least Cousins seemed 'real'. A bit dishevelled, perhaps. His hair always a little ruffled, and he was often unshaven. He wore practical outdoor clothing he might have slept in. Heavy boots of course. Not like the canvas deck shoes Julian was wearing. Cousins was ruggedly handsome and somehow more honest, even in his failings. It wasn't about image. But then there was no room for it out in the 'field'. He was a 'no frills' guy, a man of conviction, which she liked.

Julian had always been privileged. He came from what they called a 'good family'. They had wealth. Enough for a public-school education and then a place at Cambridge, even though he only scraped his economics degree. Then a master's in finance had followed. It had been so very easy for him. Even his first job in the City, thanks to his father's connections.

His first car; a flat on the outskirts of London. Always, there had been money from his parents.

"It's so very pleasant to see you again," he ventured.

"I just wanted my things back," she replied curtly.

"I have them in the car. I've kept them all this time..."

"You broke my heart," she said.

It caught him by surprise. "I never meant to," he stammered.

"You never meant to," she repeated. "But you did."

"I didn't mean to hurt you. It just happened, Hannah."

"You mean Theresa just happened." Now he was staring awkwardly at his beer. "Why didn't you talk to me at least? Was there so little trust? If you only knew the days and nights I spent wondering..."

He could see she was becoming upset. "I'm sorry." He paused, trying to find the right words. "It was a confusing time..."

He was 'sorry'! She felt an anger welling up inside her. She felt like slapping his face. "You never really told me why," she said finally as he stared vacantly, unable to meet her gaze.

"Sorry," he repeated. "You were always busy, always tired."

"I was working as a young nurse at the hospital, Julian…"
Then she stopped herself, struggling to regain her composure.

"I guess I didn't treat you very well," he conceded as their
eyes met.

She sighed. Suddenly, he seemed weak and pathetic.
Shallow. Unfulfilled. Then she realised there was a part of her
that felt sorry for him as he sat opposite her so awkwardly, so
childlike. There was no love. Not anymore. It seemed a great
weight had been lifted from her.

"I should have been kinder," he said.

"It's all right," she told him. And it was. "I just wish you
had been more honest."

He nodded. Suddenly, he seemed overcome with sadness
himself.

"It doesn't really matter now, does it? Water under the
bridge." She realised that meeting her must have been hard
for him too. But she was grateful he had come. "Thanks for
meeting me," she said as they both sat in contemplation of
things passed.

Again, he nodded but remained silent. The anger in her
was now gone. The sadness too. "Still seeing Theresa?"

"On and off. My parents would like us to marry, but I don't
know. Perhaps I will. They say she's good for me."

"Perhaps she is," Johnson said.

"How about you?" he asked. "How are things working out
for you in Africa with the aid work?"

"It is sometimes tough. But I love it," she told him.

"Is there anyone special for you over there?" He had to ask.

"As a matter of fact, there is." And as she thought of
Cousins, she realised how much she had come to care for him.

"Then I hope you find happiness with him," he said.

As she looked into his eyes once more, there was a

sincerity she had not seen before. It was a moment of genuine compassion and understanding that passed between them. "Thank you, Julian." It was all she had really wanted after they had parted so bitterly.

For a while, they talked about his family and her father. She told him about the challenges in her work. Not that she expected him to understand. Nobody really did. She didn't mind. How could they? It was something you had to see and feel. Besides, most people were consumed by their own day-to-day lives. Like Julian. He told her he didn't like the financial markets. But he still dreamed of becoming a millionaire and retiring early.

Later, as they walked towards the car park, they might even have been friends. For the tension between them had gone, and there was an easiness within them both now. Perhaps Julian had needed that too.

"That's subtle," she said as they stood beside his car. It was a bright yellow Porsche Boxster. "You could probably fund at least two schools in Eritrea with that," she added. But now she was smiling.

"You know how I like to be understated," he replied. He was, in her view, a hopeless case. "Perhaps I'll do that one day," he said. "Fund a couple of schools in Africa. And I'll name them after you in your honour."

It had been a solemn moment as he had handed her the box of personal items he had kept for her. There was a sense of finality.

"Take care of yourself and be happy," he said as he climbed into the Porsche.

"You too," she replied. Then she watched him drive off.

She felt a pang of sadness. It would probably be the last time she would ever see him. But she didn't cry. She'd done her crying a long time ago. No, it was finally done. She turned and headed over to her father's battered Saab. On the short drive back to Plymouth, where she was staying with her father, she soon overcame the sadness. It had passed quickly, for she realised she had perhaps needed to see Julian that one last time, just to put things in their proper place. It was more than reclaiming the personal photographs and trinkets he had kept for her. It was closure on a painful episode in her past.

She wondered idly how her father would receive her on her return. No doubt he would be pacing up and down. He had advised her not to meet with Julian. He worried about her, as fathers do over their daughters. He had always liked the man and had been disappointed when things had not worked out between them. Perhaps he would come to like Cousins too. She felt it was time to announce their plans for an engagement. Perhaps even a wedding in Asmara? Lord knows, she was now in her late twenties. Maybe it *was* time to settle down.

CHAPTER TWENTY-FOUR

I N ASMARA, THERE was mounting concern. Solemn-faced officials at the Ministry of Health conceded it was facing an unprecedented crisis. The wet season usually brought an increase in malaria cases, but the country was experiencing a rise in numbers not seen in recent years. Consecutive droughts and shorter monsoon patterns had resulted in reduced immunity against the parasite, particularly in young children. And this year the main monsoon had come hard and early and was forecast to stretch relentlessly into September. The field clinics were seeing scores of sick youngsters being presented on a daily basis, and the hospitals were full. The number of deaths was rising too.

Doctor David Walters wiped the sweat from his forehead and leaned back on his wooden chair. He looked away from the laptop on the desk in front of him and gazed through his office window at the rain hammering down outside. He removed his glasses and sighed. The situation was grim. Earlier, he had spoken to the minister. He knew it was a fact that a child died of malaria every few seconds across Africa. But in Eritrea, progress had been made, through the use of insecticide-treated nets, better community education and effective early diagnosis. There had been sustained investment too in the healthcare system. The current epidemic was a setback. The malaria surge was untypical and not reflective of the country's achievements in combatting the disease. Yet its healthcare system was at risk of being overrun.

Walters and his teams were at full stretch offering what support they could. In an unprecedented step, the call had gone out for other humanitarian agencies to step up and assist, including BritAid, the Italians and Catholic Relief Service. UNICEF too was on the ground. It wasn't a lack of medicines. The government invested in the drugs and was effective in distributing to its own facilities and through humanitarian agencies. Nor was it the lack of adequate and rapid screening for malaria. It was the sheer numbers of those contracting the disease in the remotest regions of the country, where the nearest basic health unit might be a day's walk.

Therefore, McKenzie and Cullen had agreed to provide additional logistical support. Essentially, that meant vehicles and drivers to ferry medical supplies where they were needed and an 'ambulance' service to take mothers and their children to the nearest hospital should they require urgent treatment. Usually, it was children under twelve. Therefore, day-to-day development work had effectively been suspended. It was a case of 'all hands to the wheel' to support the immediate medical emergency.

Cousins found himself without a vehicle and therefore volunteered to help too, accompanying Jamal on a series of 'mercy missions'. He would also cover the story, writing about the multi-agency approach to help ease the country's malaria crisis. It would do the international humanitarian community no harm in the eyes of the Eritrean Government.

Walters had two teams operating to the west in Gash-Barka from Barentu. The region was particularly hard hit. Another was drafted to work in Red Sea town of Massawa and a fourth in the large southern port of Assab, close to the border with Djibouti. The medical NGO was at full stretch. The weather conditions across the western lowlands were an added challenge, with some routes almost impassable due to the sheer volume of water on the ground which had turned the dirt tracks to mud. It made all trips out perilous, sometimes adding hours to journey times. Yet still the rain continued to fall. Over the mountains and the western plains. It was a different story along the Red Sea coastline to the east, where the relentless heat was stifling, and a heavy rainstorm was a rare and welcome phenomenon.

Walters thought of Johnson and wondered what she might be doing. Right now, England seemed a long way away, a different world. He could use some leave himself. He felt weary. The truth was, he missed her both professionally and personally. She was set to return within the next week and would be an experienced and welcome pair of additional hands during the current crisis. They could use all the help they could get. Cousins missed her too, though he was busy out in the field with Jamal most days which made for a useful distraction and the days pass quickly as her return to Eritrea drew closer.

—❧—

Progress was painfully slow as they took the tortuous route across the waterlogged track towards the tented field camp where desperate people sheltered beneath extended canvas canopies bowed by the weight of the water. The rains had turned the barren landscape into a quagmire. The dry red earth of the plains was now a sea of mud all the way from the border to the low, distant hills which marked the edge of the highlands as the water continued to fall from grey skies. But they knew they had to press on. They knew lives were at stake, and they needed to find a way through.

The Land Cruiser slipped and lurched steadily towards its destination, its occupants staring intently ahead through the driving rain to the monotonous rhythm of the wipers clearing the relentless spatter of water from the screen. Occasionally, the engine would whine in protest under the strain and the wheels lose their grip as the vehicle struggled to maintain momentum, and the driver would quickly shift to lower gears.

They were answering the call from Walters to offer additional support to his team operating in the north-west of the district, and they had set off early that morning from Barentu. On the back seats lay two boxes of doxycycline to deliver to the field clinic, which was seeing dozens of cases of malaria. Its location was an isolated hamlet, a small dot on the map, where the medical team had set up to serve the nomadic communities on the remote fringes of the district.

Cousins and his driver had no idea what they might find upon their eventual arrival or how they might assist further when they finally made it through. Yet they knew the medical team was under extreme pressure, and their immediate goal still lay several miles ahead. Already they had been driving for three hours, and Jamal estimated they should make it before lunchtime at their current rate of progress.

Suddenly, the vehicle lurched forward into a deep rut hidden by the volume of brown water and came to an abrupt halt at an awkward angle, forcing the men to brace themselves as they were thrown forward. They could feel the tyres slip and spin as the Land Cruiser was unable to drive itself forward. Jamal flicked through the gears, forwards, backwards, rocking the vehicle to and fro in a bid to regain the necessary momentum to drive the vehicle over the obstacle. But they were stuck. The Eritrean driver disengaged the gears and stared haplessly at Cousins.

"Try again," Cousins suggested. Again, Jamal tried to rock the Land Cruiser free. But the wheels couldn't grip the mud to carry it out of the deep rut into which it had sunk.

"Let me get out and try to push," Cousins told Jamal, and the Eritrean nodded. What else could they do? The Englishman climbed out and dropped into mud up to his ankles.

"OK, let's do it," he called to Jamal, leaning his back into the vehicle as once more the driver engaged the four-wheel drive and the Land Cruiser lurched forward, as Cousins pushed with all his strength, groaning under the physical strain. For a moment, it seemed the vehicle might overcome the obstacle, before it sank back again into the muddy cradle in which it was held. Again and again, they tried as the engine roared and the wheels span, spattering Cousins with mud as he pushed before sinking, exhausted, to his knees. He staggered to his feet in the rain and came to the driver's side window, signalling to Jamal to cut the engine. *What now?* they wondered as the rain continued to fall. They were miles from anywhere on a remote track, with no prospect of help.

"Shit! Shit! Shit!" Cousins cursed. He was now caked in mud and drenched to the skin. They had to get the boxes of medicine to the clinic. But now they faced the additional problem of being stuck in the middle of nowhere in the pouring rain. As Cousins leant against the side of the vehicle, gasping for breath, his gaze fell upon the boxes of medicine on the rear seat. Then he had an idea. It seemed a 'lightbulb' moment.

"We'll use the cardboard. The medicine boxes. Under the wheels," he said. He'd seen it once in a film in which wood and leaves had been used. It was worth a try. Perhaps their shirts too. Anything, in a bid to wedge material under the wheels to help the tyres grip and gain traction. It might be their only hope. Jamal stared at the Englishman while he considered, then nodded in agreement. They emptied the boxes of medicines and tore the carboard into strips, packing the material beneath the tyres. Then they took off their shirts and wedged the fabric under the wheels.

Jamal started the engine, and Cousins took up his position at the back of the vehicle. It was a crucial moment.

"Lowest gear, Jamal. Real gentle. Sustained pressure on the accelerator. After a count of three," said Cousins. "Ready! One... two... three!" he cried. The engine pitch rose, and Cousins cried out under the physical exertion, as he pushed with all his strength from the rear, his boots sliding in the mud. "Keep going, Jamal," he shouted as the Land Cruiser inched forward and then rose, its tyres slipping. But it was moving. Suddenly, it surged over the lip and lurched out of the deep rut which had contained it as Cousins roared in triumph. Once more, he sank to his knees in the mud as the rain fell about him, thankful to fate, the universe, or to God.

"Water please," he said to Jamal when, finally, he stood beside the vehicle mud-streaked, grinning and bare-chested. The driver was smiling too as he handed a bottle of water to the Englishman, and he began washing the dirt from his face.

"We did it, Mr John," beamed the Eritrean.

"Yes, we did, Mr Jamal."

This was living on the edge. It was extreme. It was one step closer to survival, and Cousins felt exhilarated. He gazed up and watched the rain falling from the sky, breathing deeply. Then he climbed into the vehicle, and it slowly moved off.

———— ❧ ————

Hannah Johnson arrived at the flat in Plymouth to find her father preparing dinner in the kitchen.

"How'd it go?" he called out to her as she entered from the hallway. "With Julian?"

"It was all right, Dad," she replied, carrying the box she had received from him and placing it on the kitchen table.

"Thought I'd cook tonight," Mr Johnson announced as he turned towards her, mixing bowl in hand and sporting a striped apron.

"Not much to show from our time together," she said, nodding towards the small box.

"I'm sorry," her father said.

"It's all right, Dad. Really it is." And it was. For she realised she no longer held any feelings for Julian. That in itself was as if a burden had been lifted from her shoulders. "What are you cooking?" she asked.

"Chicken stir-fry and green salad. Plenty for two, if you'd like some."

"Please. That'd be nice," she replied.

"About eight?"

She nodded. "Perfect. Can I help?"

"You can make the salad dressing," her father replied, nodding towards the mustard, vinegar and olive oil already out on the work surface. "Then we can eat and chat," he added.

She liked the sound of that. It had a warm, cosy feel to it. She'd tell him how it went with Julian. Also about her medical work in the field. She knew he would be interested, and as yet, they hadn't really had a chance to talk. She missed that. But more importantly, she wanted to tell him about Cousins... and that she felt she had finally found love in Eritrea.

CHAPTER TWENTY-FIVE

O N A SMALL patch of waterlogged earth, a young woman sat in her tent, staring out at the early morning rain falling from the grey sky. The infant she cradled to her breast was fussing, hot and restless. The woman's husband had not returned. He had taken their goats to higher ground. Perhaps he had been delayed by the floods which brought large flows of brown water cutting into the slopes. Or maybe there was an issue with the livestock.

Her child was ill, of that she was sure. In the night, the baby girl had cried continuously. The infant had a fever that would not subside. Nor would she take the milk from her mother's breast. Still the child whittled. The mother, known as Niyat, felt she could delay no longer.

She didn't mind the rain. The relentless patter on the tent was in some ways reassuring, for it signalled an annual cycle, which meant that life could continue. Water was plentiful and would sink into the earth, which was good, following the long dry season, and the weather was cooler. There was hope of renewal too. For after the rains came an explosion of greenery across the plains, and that heralded better grazing for the goats they kept.

That too was good, for the small family unit depended on their livestock, for milk, for meat and for trade. It was what allowed them to survive. If the herd grew, they could exchange the animals with their neighbours or sell them at the nearest market. It was a tough life, but it was the only life she knew, and she was thankful.

God had surely been good to her, for she had a strong husband who cared for her and who provided. Perhaps his delay meant he had gone to the market to trade some provisions to see them through the rainy season. Then the desert would come to life. It was her favourite season, a time of relative plenty.

She rose with the infant, which she cradled beneath her shawl and stepped out into the rain. The family camped on the far side of the rocky outcrop had told her there was a field clinic to the south near the waterhole at the foot of the hills. There they would have medicine. She also knew it was a long walk and that it would take her the best part of the day there and back. She wished her husband was with her. There was no one else.

So, she headed south towards the low mountains in the distance as the rain continued to fall, and as she walked, she whispered a silent prayer. In this way, she committed her daughter to a higher power. Therefore, she walked with a sense of hope in her heart. Allah would watch over them, and their fate rested with Him, as it was surely written. It gave her the strength to go on, as it had so often in the past in good times and bad as she set out on her journey. It was still early. She hoped she would find her way to the clinic by midday. She hoped too for a break in the weather as she began walking towards the low hills in the persistent rain.

—∞—

At the field clinic on the edge of the district, there were long lines of people who stood or sat waiting to be seen. The crowd had swelled beyond the extended canopies so that some were forced to wait in the rain. Most were women with sick children, and though the staff worked quickly, the numbers never seemed to diminish. Hannah Johnson had returned in the middle of a crisis. The nurses were at full stretch, and medical supplies were running low.

Diagnosis was almost immediate, instinctive, for it was always the same story. Malaria. Young children with fever, sickness and diarrhoea. Some with acute anaemia, listless and, in some cases, malnourished. Time was critical. The disease could be fatal for untreated infants within twenty-four hours. It depended on the child's age, health and levels of resistance.

Johnson had flown back to Asmara and headed out to Barentu the next day. From there, she was driven out to the isolated clinic on the north-western edge of Gash-Barka region, where the low mountains swept down towards the ancient waterhole. The locals knew the spot and came from miles around – through the mud, the water and the teeming rain – for treatment. They were grateful for the fortified food too, for the region often lay on the edge of famine.

Johnson worked tirelessly alongside her nursing colleagues to help with the sheer numbers of people presenting themselves with their children for treatment. Yet she felt energised. Her trip back to England had been therapeutic and restful. It had been needed. Now it was a case of all hands to the wheel. There was no respite in the evenings either, for though she could step back from the hands-on nursing, there were reports to write.

But she was refreshed and ready to meet the unprecedented challenge. She had a passion for the people which fuelled her resilience. She knew too that the emergency would begin to diminish with the onset of the dry season. Already it was almost September.

Johnson drew back from the line of people to take a water break. For although the rain continued to fall, the heat and humidity were stifling. Another child had been diagnosed with malaria. The mother was handed the pills and briefed. Her little boy should be fine. Johnson had lost count of how many cases they had seen that day.

She stepped out of the tent with her water bottle and took a mental note of those still waiting to be seen. Finally, the numbers were beginning to ease. She walked along the line of those waiting to check if there was anyone who needed to be prioritised and stopped when she came to the woman sitting on the ground cradling her baby beneath her shawl. It was the young woman who had set out earlier that day from her tent to make the long trek to the clinic with her infant.

The woman known as Niyat drew her shawl back to show the English nurse. The baby was quiet now. At rest. Johnson leaned down towards the mother to take a closer look at the infant. Then she smiled and beckoned for the woman to come with her into the tent, where she would be seen immediately. There, one of the Eritrean nurses could explain better, for there could be little doubt the baby had already died in her mother's arms.

It was heartbreaking. Though Johnson had seen it many times before, it became no easier. The infant looked at peace, almost in sleep, as if she might wake at any moment. Angelic. Perfect. Yet she was gone. It was hard to comprehend. The fragility of life hit home. The young woman listened in stunned silence as it was explained to her. Yet she had already guessed, and as the Eritrean nurse offered her condolences, a solitary tear rolled down the woman's cheek. There was nothing that could be done, the nurse told her. She was very sorry. The child was with Allah now.

The baby was washed with water and gently wrapped in a clean white sheet. But the mother did not want her little girl's face covered. She wanted to rest her eyes on her child's face so that she could remember. There was a Land Cruiser which could take her back to her home and save her the long walk, and the child could be buried quickly, according to custom. The woman was thankful. Then Johnson led her from the tent out to the vehicle, which had been acting as an 'ambulance'. She watched the mother climb in, carefully holding her dead child, then turned back towards the tent as the rain began to subside. She hoped the woman would have another child soon. She was still young. Perhaps she would be luckier next time.

She stepped into the tent to see another stunted child lifted from the scales, crying. It too was ill, the anxious mother had said. But this one was more fortunate. It was a case of dysentery, easily treated with a simple course of tablets. Yet the treatment was life-saving, costing just a few pennies. That might mean the difference between life and death. A small cost and the access to simple medicine. So often it was all that was needed. The woman's child should make a full recovery. The mother was grateful to receive several packets of fortified food too to help her infant, and she smiled at the nurses. Then she blessed them for their help and left the clinic cradling her infant to set out on the long journey back to her settlement under the dark, unforgiving sky which promised to unleash further rain.

Such was the nature of the work that the nurses continued until late into the afternoon, or until the last patient had been seen. Sometimes that would stretch into the evening. Johnson would then compile her report, totting up the numbers, listing the outcomes of the many people who had come to the clinic. They had seen more than two hundred that day. Eleven confirmed cases of malaria. One fatality. She had yet to complete her medication audit. She sighed deeply, brushing a strand of brown hair from her perspiring forehead as darkness began to fall.

She washed herself by the fading light of the torch, the kind you charged by winding a dynamo. As she stood alone in the empty clinic, she used a single small bottle of water.

It was a skill aid workers often acquired in the field. Just the essentials, but enough to freshen up. Then she sat in silence, munching on the packet of rich tea biscuits she had saved as a treat, listening to the patter of rain on the canvas above her. She was enjoying the solitude, away from the lines of mothers with their sick, screaming children, away from the unrelenting bustle of activity.

Her two nurses were already sleeping in the adjacent tent, and soon she would bed down too. For tomorrow was sure to be just as busy. Their driver had not returned. So there was no radio. Perhaps he had gone for the additional medical supplies they needed or been held up by the weather. So, the biscuits were the only 'luxury' she had, which she enjoyed in the relative peace of the night and the fading light of the torch. She reached for it and wound it vigorously until its beam grew brighter, then leaned back in her chair and sighed before taking another biscuit.

Johnson missed him. Cousins had met her at the airport, and they had spent the night together in Asmara. Their hot and frenzied embrace had been like satisfying a ravenous hunger or quenching a burning thirst for each other. Now, as she sat contemplating in the middle of Gash-Barka, she missed his touch, his smell, the sound of his breathing as they had lain together. It had been wonderful. But their time together had been all too brief.

She wanted to be with him. Their future was undoubtedly together. Of that she was now certain, and it was a comforting thought. He felt the same. He told her he had time to think while she had been away. Being with her felt natural and fulfilling. Yes, and healing too. She understood he had been damaged and was hurting still.

Perhaps he still loved the woman he had lost in Pakistan. But she seemed to understand and accept that too. What both had come to realise was that, despite their respective traumas and disappointments, they were able to feel love again. It might not be the same, but it was no less intense. And it felt good. Despite the pain they had endured in the past, there was a chance of a new life together and an opportunity for happiness which had surprised them both.

She finished the last of the biscuits and rose from her chair. For a moment, she glanced around the clinic. All seemed ready for the morning. Then she headed out into the night and hurried through the rain to the neighbouring tent. Her nurses were fast asleep. She pushed the mosquito net aside and sank onto her own mattress. She thought of Cousins as she lay in the darkness and closed her eyes. Just three more days, and she would see him again.

CHAPTER TWENTY-SIX

L ULA WAS THRILLED. Her two favourite people in the world were getting engaged. She wasn't quite sure what being 'engaged' meant, but it had the sound of something serious and permanent.

"So, you gonna be married," she said, just to be certain of the joyous news.

"That's the idea," Cousins replied, and Johnson nodded with a smile.

The girl beamed by way of approval, though secretly she wondered what had taken them so long.

"I just gotta tell Mama," she added before scampering off excitedly to find her mother and break the news.

In reality, the woman known as Mariam already knew. The story had travelled fast. Besides, she and Farjad gossiped like women at the local market, and there were few secrets, real or imagined, within their world that hadn't been discussed. Lula's mother had prepared a special stew and baked the flatbread to mark the occasion. Later, they all sat together on the floor to eat, including the girl, who watched the couple to see if the announcement had somehow changed their behaviour towards each other. But it seemed the same.

To her, Johnson was exotic. She was so white, with the fairest skin Lula had ever seen. She wore different clothes to other women she knew. Most striking to the girl, though, was the way she spoke. It sounded very foreign and refined. Not at all like the local accents she knew. She was kind to Lula too and smiled often.

Cousins was also watching. As they broke the bread and ate the stew, he observed the woman he had come to love. He watched the delicacy and refinement of her movements as they sat at a discreet distance. She was wearing cargo pants, a linen shirt rolled to the elbows and NGO boots. Yet she carried her practical clothing with grace and style. A light cotton scarf hung loosely about her neck, for protection against mosquitoes and to wipe the sweat from her face. Most aid workers were in the habit of wearing cotton scarves for the same reasons.

It was true her face was very fair, framed by dark-brown shoulder-length hair. It was a round face with pleasing features. She wore no make-up in the field, and in the heat, her cheeks would often flush red. Her lips were full and, when she smiled, revealed a small dimple above each corner of her mouth and white, slightly uneven teeth, which he found appealing. But it was her eyes that struck Cousins. Smiling eyes of a light brown with thick, long lashes that added an alluring femininity to her as she sat crossed-legged talking to the Eritreans.

She seemed utterly at ease with them, and he liked that too. She had a way of making people feel comfortable and relaxed, regardless of status, background or ethnicity. There was no doubt about it. He felt they were friends and lovers, and he considered himself a lucky guy.

Occasionally, their eyes would meet and they would be slightly embarrassed, conscious too that they were in the company of their Eritrean companions.

"Will you be living together now?" Lula asked unashamedly, and Cousins nearly choked on the mouthful of bread and stew he had just popped into his mouth.

It was Johnson who answered, looking slightly more flushed than normal.

"We would like to get married first," she told the girl as Mariam and Farjad continued to eat. "It's the custom."

"It is here too," the girl said. "But not everyone does it that way." Then she frowned thoughtfully, like a chess player contemplating their next move. "Can I come?" she then ventured uncertainly. Her mother looked up from her food and protested sharply at her daughter's unabashed persistence, but Cousins interjected.

"It's all right. We've been thinking about it, and we'd like you all to come to Asmara. We would be very happy if Lula would be bridesmaid," he said. "If that's all right with you, Mariam."

Farjad translated the happy news, and the mother smiled in agreement. Her daughter could barely contain her excitement. Lula had never been to Asmara, and it would be the first wedding she had ever attended.

"Of course, you shall have a lovely dress and new shoes too. You will look like a princess," the Englishman added.

"Like in the magic wardrobe story?"

"Just like a princess of Narnia," he added, and Johnson looked across at him adoringly. It was what they had already agreed. She thought of Sir Charles too. He'd love that. It would be the wedding in Asmara to remember. She knew he'd want to play his part with all the pomp and ceremony he could muster. Already he had offered to 'give her away' if her father was unable to travel. Yet it was a role Walters had already offered to take up, and she felt she wanted him at her side on her special day. They had been through so much together in Eritrea.

The pair's visit to Tessenei coincided with the end of the rainy season. It marked a degree of respite from the heavy workload for the medics and a slow decline in malaria cases. The drier weather also made field access easier, as the water sank into the earth and the ground began to harden once more in the burning sun. With it came new life, as vegetation that had lain dormant during the dry season burst upon the plains like a carpet of green. It was a window of abundance and relative plenty, which brought with it a sense of new hope.

While she had been away, Cousins had spent long days in the field in Gash-Barka. In some ways it had helped. When he returned to the compound, he was exhausted. Physically and emotionally, the work was draining. But so too was the heat and humidity, the long hours and irregular eating patterns. Sometimes he would flop onto his mattress at the end of the day and be overtaken by sleep. Other nights he would lay awake, unable to find rest.

He missed Johnson. He missed his family and friends in the UK too. But he also worried about his young son in Islamabad. Still, he was haunted by the memory of the boy's mother, the woman he had loved and lost in Pakistan. It was hard to let go of the memories. Afsa Ali had been his life. There were issues he had to resolve and which threw up many questions in his mind. Those nights were the longest. Yet meeting and falling in love with Johnson had changed things. It brought a new dimension to his life, a fresh hope of happiness.

But it also raised questions about his own future. Suddenly, he saw his life from a new, more positive perspective, despite the misgivings he had of himself.

He thought often about his children in England. Of course, he kept in touch and paid towards their upkeep, but it was not the same. The gulf between them was more than the geographical distance. He no longer felt he was a meaningful part of their lives. The separation from their mother had not been amicable. Was it ever? He didn't know. He hadn't wanted to hurt her, or his children, but he knew he had. He felt he had failed them. It was never what he had intended. But perhaps that was part of it. Life was what happened while you were busy making other plans.

When he had married Sarah, he could never have imagined that they would ever part, especially when the children came along. He loved them and enjoyed family life. Perhaps that is what had bound he and Sarah together in the early days. They had initially been happy years. Yet slowly, but surely, the distance in the marriage had grown like a hidden cancer, and he became restless and unfulfilled. Perhaps he was bored. Certainly, he had become lonely in the marriage as their love began to slip away, almost unnoticed.

That was the time he met her. Sarabjeet had breezed into his life like an exotic Indian goddess. He was intoxicated by her and seduced by her culture, so very different to his.

She was attractive and intelligent, and he had easily succumbed. But the excitement in the torrid affair which followed soon turned to despair. She was emotionally unstable, demanding and manipulative. Somehow, he had not seen it. In short, he had lost everything when it ended unhappily, leaving him to wonder what it had all been about. He wasn't quite sure how it had happened. But he had left the family home and now found himself on his own.

It was a prelude to Pakistan. When the opportunity arose to travel overseas, he seized it. Perhaps he was seeking redemption in aid work. A new purpose. It was an escape too, from his failures, and a bid to numb his own emotional pain. Yet it was also true that he felt a genuine compassion for those less fortunate in the world and a desire to do good. At the time of his departure to Pakistan's earthquake zone to report its devastation, he had not foreseen the impact that seeing widescale suffering on an epic scale would have upon him. He hoped his children would one day understand.

But perhaps he did want to lose himself in a different, more rewarding life. Certainly, he felt he wanted to get as far away from women as was possible; that he would be content to live out his life on his own. He thought travelling to the remote mountain areas and working among conservative Muslim communities in a disaster area was a safe bet. Initially it was. Then he had met Afsa Ali. Against all odds, they had fallen in love.

He smiled as he recalled their first meeting. Even then, though he found her stunningly beautiful, he never dreamed they might become lovers. She had been very different then. He hadn't seen her vulnerability. Quite the contrary, she seemed strong, independent and confident in her faith, and in her calling to help others, which he respected. Strange how these things happen when you least expect them. He viewed their romantic liaison as nothing less than a miracle, and so did Ali. In some ways, they were both a little lost and, in finding each other, felt a sense of purpose and fulfilment. It was the first time he began to believe in God since he had been a small child, and she had shared the enthusiasm in her own faith with him.

Cousins was suddenly seized by a terrible sadness that haunted him still. Perhaps he had failed her too. Maybe he should have seen the signs. But at least she had left him with a beautiful little boy, and for that he was thankful. He thought often about his young son in Pakistan. Though still a small child, he was healthy and strong, and his face reflected the features of Ali, though his skin was fair. He was safe and secure in the care of his mother's family. But perhaps it was time Cousins stepped up and became a full-time father to the boy; he was ready to return to England and be a better parent to all his children.

Yes, perhaps he had failed his children. But there was still time. In Hannah Johnson he had found someone who understood and loved him, despite the mistakes he had made. Despite his faults. Eritrea had helped him too. The people's suffering, their will to survive and still to smile in their pain had taught him something. Mancini had said it one night at the bar: in the midst of suffering, there is a sweetness in life. There was wisdom in the Italian's words. Perhaps, Cousins mused, it was the suffering which brought an appreciation of what is good. And the Eritreans certainly knew how to make the most of simple pleasures when they came.

His leave was due, and he would travel to Pakistan and speak to the family about his son's future. He would talk to Johnson too. She knew his past, knew his circumstances. There was an honesty between them. They had talked too about their future together. She loved children, and he knew too that she would be happy to help care for his little boy. He felt the time for a return to a more settled family life in England was approaching.

CHAPTER TWENTY-SEVEN

T HE CRATE OF gin was delivered to the office by Land Rover one morning with a note embossed with the emblem of the British Government. The team was 'magnificent', a credit to Her Majesty, it said and was signed by Sir Charles. There was a consignment of forty-eight boxes of After Eight chocolate mint wafers for the staff too, surplus from the previous Christmas. They came by way of thanks for the outstanding humanitarian effort during the prolonged malaria spike and with an invitation for a reception at the British Embassy.

Representatives from the entire international aid community were to attend, which included the UN agencies, the International Committee of the Red Cross, Catholic Relief Services, Medics International, BritAid and Cesvi. Even Locatelli, the Italian ambassador, was invited, although there was an unspoken rivalry that existed between the missions of the two former colonial powers. The gathering was to provide a platform for the country's minister of health to express his thanks in a rare public expression of appreciation. Sir Charles saw it as something of a coup. In short, everyone who was anyone in the international humanitarian community operating across Eritrea would be there in what promised to be a memorable event.

There was to be a beef 'hog roast' and barbecue, with home-made burgers from meat brought in from Kenya. Naturally, locally produced food would be provided for the national staff in attendance, if they preferred. A drinks reception would launch the event, and after the food, there would be live entertainment provided by a local band. It was hoped Sir Charles might dust down his trumpet and perform with the musicians, which was not beyond the realms of possibility.

The ambassador himself had been elusive over the last week, keeping an unusually low profile. There was whisper of a scandal in the air, or that perhaps he had contracted a serious illness. Maybe he had been struck down with typhoid, or malaria, or perhaps a serious sexually transmitted disease, given his suspected extra-marital activities. Not that the latter was ever openly voiced. It was therefore with a degree of surprise and relief that Johnson took a call from Sir Charles at the office in the days following the arrival of the invitations to the big event. Yes, he was fine. Was she free for a chat over coffee?

She arrived at the Blue Sapphire before him and sat at a table in the bar facing the entrance. An attentive waiter came to her, and she ordered a small beer. But she didn't have to wait long. She spotted the unmistakeable figure of Sir Charles as he entered, sporting a lightweight linen suit. She watched him approach and sit across the table from her.

"Sorry," he said, leaning over to kiss her cheek.

"No problem. I've only just got here myself," she replied.

He looked a little drawn and harassed, she thought.

"It's good to see a friendly face," he told her.

"Nice to see you too," she ventured, wondering what was going on in his life.

The hotel bar in which they sat was not their usual haunt. Nor were there any familiar faces. It was one of the reasons he had suggested they meet there. The place had a reputation for illicit liaisons. Usually between foreigners and local women. In essence, it was an upmarket brothel. He seemed uncharacteristically uneasy.

The waiter approached with her beer, and he ordered a double Scotch. He had told her he was 'on the wagon'. But she said nothing.

"Thanks for meeting me," he said. "I just had to talk to someone..." he hesitated for a moment, "...a friendly face."

"What's going on, Charles?" she asked, knitting her brow.

"What have you heard?"

"Nobody's seen you for days. There are rumours. And it's not the first time."

He nodded thoughtfully, as the waiter delivered his drink and placed it on the table in front of him, then discreetly withdrew. He wanted to tell her about the meetings on the border; that he was in fact working with the UK Government Stabilisation Unit. He wanted to tell her that he held secret talks with officials from the Sudanese and Ethiopian governments. Or that when trouble flared in Djibouti, he had been part of the delegation negotiating a peaceful solution on behalf of the regional powers. But he could never tell her that he had a direct line to MI6.

"What is it, Charles?"

There was a look of hesitancy in his eyes before he spoke again. "She thinks I'm having an affair," he said finally. That much was true.

"Maria?"

He nodded. He raised his glass and downed the whiskey in one.

Johnson was confused. "Well, are you?" she asked. "I mean—"

"I know," he interjected. "I know what you're thinking."

"What am I thinking, Charlie?" She took a sip of her beer and watched him over the rim of her glass.

"Truth is, she never let me love her," he said in an unexpected expression of emotion. "I never really felt it," he added.

"I'm not sure I understand..." Johnson was still puzzled. This wasn't the Charlie she knew.

"I think she was more in love with the idea of being the wife of a British diplomat. That's all. She was young, attractive and from a respectable family. I let it happen," he added. "Vanity, I suppose."

"I see," said Johnson thoughtfully, still uncertain what to say. "So, what's changed?" she asked.

"She's having me followed," he told her. "Higgins intercepted a guy."

Johnson sighed. "Forgive me, Charlie," she said. "Is it really such a surprise?"

He looked into his empty glass but said nothing. He wished he could have told her the truth. That his apparent indiscretions were part of an act to conceal other covert activities. It is not to say there had not been other women. Or that he wasn't sometimes tempted. But they were, in reality, distractions. But there had once been a girl he cared for. She was a government agent. Yet she, like the others, had been as much a symptom of a lonely, unfulfilled marriage as anything else. In truth, he still loved his wife.

"I mean," she said, "you've hardly been discreet. The times you disappear!"

"I guess not," he conceded, "but if this gets out of hand…"

"I see… who's the girl?"

"Actually," he said and paused for effect, "there isn't one."

"There isn't?"

He shook his head. "In fact, I'm really a spymaster running undercover operatives for the British Government, working on highly sensitive political issues in partnership with various foreign powers," he felt like telling her. But he didn't. He smiled inwardly. Higgins would have had a fit. London too, for that matter.

"Why don't you guys separate for a while, see how you feel?" she continued. "I mean, you said yourself Maria's not in love with you. At least not anymore. Would that be so bad?"

"Wouldn't do my career with the diplomatic service any favours," Sir Charles said soberly.

"I think that's very sad. Is that all they care about? Surely it happens," Johnson said.

"Oh, it happens all the time, my dear. But not publicly. Not to ambassadors." He paused. "Besides, I still love her."

"You do?" she said uncertainly. "Have you tried talking to her…? I mean really talking. Perhaps you can come to an arrangement. After all, it's worked for you all this time, despite your differences. And you have a daughter."

"I guess you're right," he said.

"Tell her you're not the philanderer we all think you are," she said.

"I have. She obviously doesn't believe me."

"Right!" she said sarcastically as she looked at him. Suddenly, the whole thing seemed absurd to her, and she laughed. "Come on, Charlie, who are you trying to kid here?"

"No, really. There's nobody else. Not that I care for."

"Then talk to her. Openly. Honestly. Ask her what she wants."

"What she wants?" He suspected he already knew. "It's not me she wants," he said bitterly. "A better posting. Perhaps Kenya. Maybe back in South America. Anywhere but here. But if this thing blows up, I'll be heading back to a desk job with the Foreign Office in London."

"Maybe Maria just wants to know what's going on." She paused. "Talk to her. You're supposed to be a diplomat, for goodness' sake!"

She had a point. He nodded. "You're right, of course." Then he too laughed. Maybe he should tell Maria the whole truth.

"I'm sure you can sort it out," she said.

"Another drink?" he asked. She nodded, and he signalled to the waiter. "But enough of my stupidly complicated life," he said. "How's yours?"

"All good." She smiled.

"And the wedding plans?"

"Not really started," she told him. "Not sure where to begin. Bit disappointed my dad can't make it. He's not really well enough to travel."

"Sorry to hear that. Like I said, though, if you need a stand-in."

"Walters has already agreed," she said.

"Date?"

"Last week November. Sunday, twenty-fourth. Not sure where, though. John's been married before."

"I know a vicar at a small chapel across the other side of the city. Nice cosy venue. I'm sure he'll do it. I'll have a word."

"Thank you, Charlie. That would be helpful."

"Consider it done, my dear," he said.

The drinks arrived, and Sir Charles raised his glass. "To you and John."

"Thanks, Charlie."

"Speaking of whom, how is he?"

"He's good. You know. Busy."

"Aren't we all?!"

"No, John's good. He's heading for Pakistan next week to sort things out. His boy is there, you know. So very terrible what happened to his wife."

"Yes, you told me. Very sad."

"I'm not sure how that's going to affect him. I just hope he realises how much I love him. And that…"

"And what?"

"Well, that I'll make him happy."

"Of that I have no doubt. I wish someone loved me the way you love him. Nobody ever did. He's a lucky guy. I think he knows it."

"Aww… thank you, Charlie."

"I mean it," he said, then downed the last of his Scotch. "But you guys will be at the party, right?"

"Yes, John's due back a couple of days before."

"That's a shame," he said with a twinkle in his eye. "I was rather looking forward to having you all to myself that night. Now that would give Maria something to be jealous about!"

"You are awful, Charlie!"

"I do try, my dear."

The solemn-faced official was from the Ministry of Interior, and his arrival was no real surprise to Walters, who was effectively the man in charge at Medics International.

For the bespectacled doctor, the answer to the suited bureaucrat who had arrived by official car was simple.

"We were as shocked and surprised as anyone," he said.

"But the nurses were in your employ," the official stated blankly.

"That's true. But there was nothing to indicate what would happen. They told no one," Walters insisted. "Not even their families. They simply disappeared into the desert," he added. And no, he didn't know their whereabouts. The two men had simply disappeared from the field clinic in Gash-Barka one day. It was essentially the truth. Most inconvenient, he added for effect.

"It does not look good for your organisation," the Eritrean Government official said pointedly, with a hint of menace.

"I'm sorry," Walters had replied. "I'd help you if I could." That was a lie.

The doctor was irritated by the man's arrogance and sense of self-importance. Besides, he didn't really blame the two nurses. The country's regime was harsh and controlling. Its military conscription was extreme and the cause for thousands to flee. Young men and women were often pressed into service for years. Some never came back at all.

"If I hear anything, I'll be sure to let you know."

The man from the ministry looked at him doubtfully. He said he would speak to the minister about the issue, and he rose to leave. Walters shook his hand reluctantly and watched him leave the building and get into his chauffeur-driven Lexus. What he hadn't told the official was that news had come that Daniel and Juba had made it across to central Europe.

The doctor made a call to Sir Charles's office, just to let him know. Perhaps he could put in a word at the ministry. Then he dialled McKenzie's number. The Scot sounded weary, and the doctor was concerned for his friend. Was he all right? He should take it easy. He should make sure he would be fit for the party at the British Embassy later that month.

CHAPTER TWENTY-EIGHT

JUBA STOOD AND squinted into the silver light that framed the distant hills. As he gazed towards the rising sun, he figured he must be facing eastwards towards Mecca. He closed his eyes, recited the *salah* and sank to his knees in prayer. He hadn't been able to wash as fully as he would have liked – he didn't have enough water – and he had spread his jacket onto the earth as a prayer mat. Yet he felt God would understand, especially in his desperate circumstances.

Though the words came to him automatically, he found himself suddenly overcome by emotion. Perhaps it was a reminder of his home, his family. He missed them so much. They and his faith had been a central part of his life in Eritrea. The prayers he recited in his mind resonated with unexpected force, and he realised he was crying. It was a release. He was physically and mentally exhausted; he was cold and hungry. And there he sat, sobbing uncontrollably on his knees on the edge of the forest, overlooking a meadow still wet with dew under the grey sky.

The first chill of the approaching German winter was in the air, and the gentle breeze was cold against his face and hands. The woodland which blanketed the surrounding hills was the Taunus, which circled the city of Frankfurt, the financial heart of the country, though Juba did not know it lay so close to them. He knew they were somewhere in central Germany, not far from the city. From there, they hoped to ride the train to France.

Foremost in his mind, though, was his companion. Daniel was sick. For days, he had been unwell, weakened by fever and a chesty cough that seemed to be worsening. He had lain shivering in the night, calling out in a restless sleep. It was the most serious illness either had endured on their long journey. Juba was concerned. He drew deeply from the morning air to compose himself, then prayed for his friend.

The *duas* he offered were passionate and sincere in asking for Allah's help. He asked for protection and for deliverance of his companion, as was His will. He was praying for divine intervention, for he felt without a small miracle they would falter. He hoped for guidance too to see them through the last part of their epic journey. They had come so far.

Afterwards, he sat on the ground in reflection. He thought about the many weeks they had travelled by road, by sea and by rail. Always with fear and uncertainty, paying when they had to, dodging the authorities and sleeping where they could. He thought about the birds in the sky and the fish in the sea. They were free to go where they pleased.

It didn't seem right, somehow, that human movement was restricted by race and country and that borders were often physical barriers to stop the movement of people fleeing war and persecution. Or simply wanting a safe and secure future. Was it so wrong to want a better life?

He thought too of all the beds they had slept in: on the

forest floor, in abandoned buildings, barns, hostels, baggage cars, on the streets. Wherever they found shelter. Often, they had just a single sheet and a backpack for a pillow to lay their heads on. Their dollars were almost depleted now, and they ate when they could, sometimes scavenging in the smaller towns, eating discarded fruit and vegetables from the markets. Sometimes, they took from the countryside they passed through. Once, they had come upon a field of ripening maize and gathered what they could carry for the days ahead. They had taken apples from the orchards too. But there had been days when they barely ate at all.

As they travelled across Europe, the seasons began to change. It was getting colder. Juba knew their time now was limited. He did not think they could continue during the winter. He felt too that if Daniel's condition did not improve, he would have to make the decision to surrender to the authorities. At least they had made it to Europe and would be able to claim asylum. But their dream was to make it to the French port of Calais, where they had been told they had every chance of making it across the English Channel. Others had gone before, hidden in lorries or in small rubber boats across the narrow stretch of sea. In England, they would find sanctuary. He had heard it was a civilised country which respected human rights, with a history of compassion for those seeking refuge; that the people were free.

Juba rose to his feet to check his companion, who still lay under his sheet on the forest floor. A sense of panic gripped him as he approached, for it seemed to him there was no movement, no rise and fall of the grubby white sheet in which he was wrapped. Then relief, as Daniel opened his eyes and smiled feebly at his friend. But as he tried to prop himself up, he began to cough.

"How are you, brother?" Juba asked.

"A little better," Daniel replied weakly. It was a lie.

His friend laid a hand on his forehead which still felt hot. He still had a fever. "I think we will have to look for help," he said.

Daniel had now propped himself up on his elbows and looked at his friend. "Then our journey may be over," he said. "You should leave me," he added. "You can make it without me."

Juba felt he might cry again. But this time he managed to contain his emotions. "We set off together; we will make it together," he replied. "Or our journey ends here, for both of us," he said.

Then he began to gather small sticks together to make a fire. He'd have to keep his friend warm, then break out the last of the biscuits to share before deciding what to do.

The woman was driving at speed along the country road on her way into the city in the early hours, listening to the radio. As she reached the brow of the hill, she suddenly saw two figures hunched in the road, almost as she was on top of them. She hit the brakes instantly. The vehicle screeched and slid to a halt at an angle just inches from the two men. They were just as shocked as she was, bracing themselves for a collision. Destiny had taken a hand. It might have been anyone. They might even have been killed.

Christina Schulz sat gripping the wheel, staring at the Africans, who now sat huddled in the road in front of her VW Beetle. For a few moments, they eyed each other through the windscreen. Her first instinct was relief, then concern. She realised how lucky it was that she had been able to stop in time. She flipped on the hazard lights and turned the engine

ANDREW GOSS

off. They were fortunate, for she was an educated woman with compassion. Schulz was a schoolteacher, and her partner was a Turkish immigrant. So, she knew something of the migrant story and the prejudices that existed.

Following her relief at having avoided an accident, her overriding feeling was one of guilt for having almost knocked the two men down. Schulz had been speeding. Yet her overwhelming emotion was one of compassion for the dishevelled men crouching in the headlights. She wasn't afraid. She climbed out of her car and approached the two figures in the road.

"*Mein Gott!*" she exclaimed, looking down at the two men before her. "*Seid ihr verletzt?*" She crouched down beside them as they gazed at her. "Are you hurt?" she asked them.

It was Juba who answered. "We're not hurt, madam," he said.

"What are you doing in the middle of the road? Out here?" There was a degree of agitation in her voice.

"We are lost," Juba said. It was an understatement. "We are trying to get to Calais."

"Calais?" she repeated.

"We've come across the sea…"

"You're from Africa?" she said almost in disbelief, and Juba nodded.

"But my friend is sick. He needs medicine."

What to do? Schulz felt she had to act. She couldn't just leave the men in the middle of the road. Not in that condition. There was only one thing for it, she reasoned.

"Come," she said. "I will take you into the city. We'll find an *apotheke*… a pharmacy."

Juba hesitated. "Would that be Frankfurt?"

"Yes. It is Frankfurt."

"But we must go on. To Calais," Juba insisted.

215

She nodded. "First some medicine for your friend. Perhaps some food too."

The two men rose wearily from the road, clutching their backpacks, and climbed into the vehicle.

"Thank you," Daniel croaked.

"Yes, bless you, ma'am," added Juba.

Schulz glanced at them in her rear-view mirror and turned the ignition key. How emaciated and pitiful they looked huddled on the back seat, wrapped in their grubby sheets, she thought as she pulled away and continued on the road towards the city. It was no more than a fifteen-minute drive, and she knew there was a small supermarket along the way. Sometimes she had stopped and called in there herself on her way to work, so she knew it would be open. She felt sure they would have paracetamol, ibuprofen, some hot lemon, perhaps. She could pick up some provisions for them too.

Little was said as they sped along under grey skies, and traffic was light. But her mind was racing as she drove. What should she do? Should she drop them to the authorities? She knew they would receive assistance and could claim asylum. But their dream of reaching Calais would surely be over.

"Where have you come from?" she asked.

"Eritrea," Juba replied.

"That's Africa, right?"

"Yes," he replied. "Across from the Red Sea."

She wasn't sure where that was but figured it was somewhere in the north-east.

"That's a long way," she said.

"Yes, ma'am. A long way."

"How long have you been travelling?"

"Many weeks," Juba replied.

The young woman felt a wave of compassion for the two men. She felt sure she was doing the right thing. The bright lights of the supermarket came into view, and she pulled in to park.

"Wait here," she said. "I will buy you some medicine for your friend." She stepped out of the car, and Juba watched her enter the shop.

He was grateful. But he was worried too. Would she turn them in? He didn't know. But Daniel needed the medicine, and in his weary condition, Juba was willing to let providence take its course.

"Are you all right?" he asked his friend, whose eyes were closed. His companion nodded, opened his eyes and turned to look questioningly at Juba. The woman returned with two plastic carrier bags and climbed into the front seat.

"I've brought you some medicine," she said, rummaging through one of the bags on the front passenger seat. She handed packets of paracetamol to Juba. "And some water," which she also passed to the African nurse. "Some sandwiches too," she added, handing the food into the back to Juba's grateful hands. Then she backed out and resumed their journey to the city.

The two men ate and drank greedily. They had not had a full meal for several days. As they approached the outer city from the east, she pulled into a lay-by.

"What do you want me to do?" she asked them directly. "I really don't know."

It was Daniel who replied. "You have been like an angel," he told her. "But we have come far." He paused as he struggled to contain his cough.

"We have come so far," Juba said. "We must continue. Our friends wait for us in England. So, we must try to reach Calais and cross the small English sea."

The woman understood but was still uncertain. "Then I can drop you in the city," she said finally. "Near the Hauptbahnhof, the main station. But the police watch for refugees," she told them.

"We will take our chances," Juba said. "Thank you. You have been kind," he added.

A wave of emotion swept through her. Her grandparents had known what it was to be refugees from the East, after the Second World War. They had known hunger and despair. And the kindness of strangers. Her partner too in his bid to travel from Turkey for a new life in the West. Perhaps that's why she wanted to help. It was for them. She wondered if there was anything else she could do for the Africans. Her actions seemed somehow inadequate. A small kindness.

As they entered the heart of the city, Daniel and Juba marvelled at the tall buildings, towering over the old. Traffic was now heavy, and they had not seen so many cars for many weeks. Not since Khartoum. Yet everything seemed so well ordered, so clean.

"I will pull over where I can," said the woman as she focused intensely on the traffic.

A few moments later, she swept into a lay-by next to the broad tramline in the Kaiser Strasse, a few blocks from the main train station.

"Is this OK for you?" she asked.

"Yes. Thank you," Juba replied. "God be with you," he added.

They climbed from the vehicle, dragging their bags behind them.

"The Hauptbahnhof is a few minutes over there," she said, waving her arm in the direction of the railway station, and they nodded towards her in understanding. They smiled warmly at her and slowly turned away. "Wait!" she cried. She rummaged in her handbag, then took some banknotes from her purse and thrust them towards Juba. "Take it," she said. "I hope you make it to Calais."

Then she watched the two men walk away as the rain began to fall on the city. She put the car into gear and pulled out to rejoin the flow of traffic. She could still make it to work on time, though she would be a few minutes later than usual. But her thoughts were with the Eritreans for the rest of the day and those that followed.

CHAPTER TWENTY-NINE

"PAKISTAN IS CURSED," the old woman said, turning her face from the window towards him and smiling wistfully. Despite the lines of sacrifice etched into her features, there was still a hint of the beauty that had once been hers; a youthfulness that seemed to defy her age, reflected in the way she held herself. Beneath her headscarf, a coil of plaited grey hair fell across her shoulder onto her brilliant white shalwar kameez as she sat cross-legged upon the sofa, as if she was holding court.

Her light brown eyes were bright and alert as they fixed themselves upon him, and there was still a fullness to her lips that held the trace of a superior smile. They were striking features she had passed onto her daughter, the woman he had loved.

No, it wasn't just the recent earthquake to strike Balochistan, the country's neglected province to the south-west, long since a victim of deprivation and poverty. It was the politics too. The nation's leaders were weak and clueless, driven by self-interest. She had seen the decline from when the Islamic republic still basked in the glory of hope, was still in awe of the West and anything seemed possible. At least for those with means. She had been young and glamourous then, very much in love with her husband, a rising star in the Pakistani civil service. The couple had enjoyed the privileges of the wealthy, moving within the circles of the country's elite. Life had been good.

As for the boy, he should receive an education in England. Of that she was in no doubt. Her grandson was her pride and joy, and she saw the shadow of her daughter in his face. He was his mother's son. But she was willing to give up the boy so that he might enjoy the prospect of a better future away from Pakistan. The country was going backwards, she said. Besides, she was old now and resigned to her own company. She had lived a good life. She felt she had done what was expected of her for her grandson and passed on the faith. Better he should now be with his father.

John Cousins nodded soberly, acknowledging the older woman's sentiments.

"And the woman who shall be your wife will care for and help raise the boy as we have agreed?" she asked, fixing her steady gaze upon him again. It was less of a question, more a statement.

He nodded once more in agreement. It was what his mother would have wanted, and he felt he owed her that much. It was the one thing the grandmother insisted upon: that her grandson be raised as a Muslim. She had laid the foundation for his faith, for even at the age of five, he spoke fluent Urdu, knew the pillars of Islam and had, under her relentless supervision, started to read the Holy Qur'an in Arabic, as it had been written.

"You have my word," Cousins told her.

"*Acha!* Then it is so." The woman seemed satisfied. "It is the single request of an old woman: that her only grandson should know his mother's faith and culture," she added.

It was not an issue for the Englishman. He had himself converted to Islam to marry Afsa Ali. With joy. The decision came at a time in his life when he had felt truly blessed and life was good; that some unseen force had somehow been steering his actions. He felt grateful to God and the positive forces in the universe. Indeed, it had seemed providence was smiling upon him, and he had regained a faith in the divine he had lost all those years before as a child.

"They will be here soon," the grandmother said absently, staring back towards the expansive arched window as the sun shone brightly upon the walled garden beyond. His son was being collected from school by Hassan, whom Cousins remembered fondly from his time at the four-storey villa that was the family home. Old Hassan Bhai, the smiling Punjabi, grey and grizzled by age, had been part of the family as long as anyone remembered. He had come to them as a young man and had remained, as was often the case with trusted domestic help. In effect, he had helped raise Afsa Ali and her younger sister. He knew the family dynamics and its secrets too. Yet there was an acceptance of such things with unswerving devotion and discretion, in return for an understanding that he and his family in the Punjab would always be provided for.

In truth, he felt honoured to take a new role in supporting the care of the elder daughter's child, particularly under such tragic circumstances that had recently overtaken the family he had come to love. Afsa Ali's sudden death had been so unexpected. He had grieved with the family and observed the silence over its exact details. It was in effect a cultural taboo. The funeral had been a hasty and private affair. Sometimes he visited the grave himself, where it lay in a small, forgotten cemetery, and looked upon its simple white marble headstone and the inscription in Arabic from the Qur'an which read:

To Allah we belong
And to Him we shall return.

The young woman's death perhaps hit her father the hardest. The eldest daughter had been the apple of his eye. He was genuinely fond of the Englishman too, despite his initial reservations. He was part of a generation which still respected the British for their accomplishments and their role in partition, when Pakistan was created. The arrival of his first grandchild brought a happiness to the family he could never have imagined. He was a doting grandfather, overjoyed and indulgent.

He was shocked by the suddenness with which unexpected events shattered their lives. No one could really have foreseen it. He couldn't quite take it in. Shortly after he had buried his daughter, he slipped into a state of deep depression, from which he never recovered. Perhaps he lost the will to carry on. For weeks he suffered paralysing melancholy and struggled under the stress of inconsolable grief, until finally his heart gave out and he too was dead. He had suffered a massive coronary. They said he had died of a broken heart. Perhaps it was true.

The Englishman too was consumed by grief and took a job overseas. It was his way of coping. It was pitiful how the family unit had been destroyed and their recent happiness swept away. No one spoke of the trauma Afsa Ali must have carried since childhood following her repeated abuse. But the grandmother knew. Yet she carried her guilt in silence, which flowed into her own torrent of grief. Hassan Bhai was ready to step forward to support the older woman in caring for the little boy when the time came and took him under his wing.

Now the Englishman was back to discuss the youngster's future. That almost certainly meant the father would take the child to England. Hassan Bhai would miss the boy, but he too felt it was as it should be. It was time; he felt it was written. As they walked in the sunshine from the nearby school, then under the dappled shadow of the trees in the park, the old Punjabi smiled as he trailed the buoyant youngster, excited by the prospect that his papa was home.

───── ⁓ ─────

Earlier that day, Cousins had visited the small graveyard on the edge of the city which lay in the shadow of an ancient banyan tree and was set beneath the Margalla Hills, the first fold of the Himalayas. Among the mighty branches of the sacred tree, a rainbow of tiny ribbons fluttered in the gentle breeze which blew from the mountains, each carrying the hopes and dreams of those who had gone before into the cloudless sky.

He lingered long in remembrance of happier times and what might have been and, in his mind, whispered a silent prayer. Occasionally, a couple might pass on the footway which ran along the cemetery towards the hiking trail into the hills for recreation and respite from the city. He too remembered when they had taken the same trail upwards through the forested slopes towards the ragged peaks, their little boy upon his shoulders, with Ali at his side. Sometimes they would rest by the stream which, even in the summer, ran from the hills and bubbled over the great boulders rolled down from higher ground by the fierce torrents unleashed by the heavy monsoon rains.

There they might sit, listening to the sounds of the forest, a rustle in the bushes signalling the unseen wildlife that was abundant. Sometimes their descent would be tracked by a troupe of monkeys, jabbering in the twilight treetops as the sounds of the jungle rose in intensity and shadows grew long. There were said to be mountain leopards that stalked the rocky mountain peaks. Wild boar and porcupine too on the lower slopes, which sometimes found their way across the Margalla Road at dusk and were not uncommon within the outer suburbs of the capital. It was, perhaps, a reminder of the wilderness which had once existed before the modern city was built and still lay on its periphery all the way north to the lofty heights of the Himalayas.

He sighed. His memories were like ghosts that were reluctant to find peace. He too might have tied a ribbon to the branches of the sacred banyan tree under which the graveyard lay in remembrance, so that his grief might also be carried away into the heavens. Instead, he turned from the graveside and walked towards the small mosque which lay nearby, past the rows of saplings from the tree plantation, where the path took a sharp right towards the hiking trail.

It was a small, white structure with a green dome, an echo perhaps of a time before Islamabad was even conceived. Perhaps even before Partition, when the area was scattered with small village communities across the forested plateau which ran from the edge of the hills to the old city of Rawalpindi. He approached the tiny mosque and found its rickety wooden door was unlocked. He stepped into its quiet, intimate space and found a moment of peaceful contemplation as he faced mecca and sank to his knees.

He prayed for his dead wife. He hoped she had found peace. He said a prayer for his little boy too. He asked for strength and a sense of acceptance for what had been and what was gone. Perhaps he hoped for forgiveness too, for he felt a sense of guilt for his own failings. When, finally, he stepped from the mosque and emerged back into the light, his grief had eased. In its place, he felt a new sense of purpose. His wife was gone. Yet she still lived in his son. He was grateful for the love he had shared with Afsa Ali and the son who was a product of that love, their union and of happier times.

He might never fully overcome the loss of Ali. But he still had the boy. He had found new love too, and with it came a new sense of resolve. God, in his mercy, had provided a new hope for future happiness. It was time to step up and fulfil the role he had been given and care for his son. He thought of Hannah Johnson, and he felt a pang of joy as he pictured her face.

CHAPTER THIRTY

John Cousins swept the little boy into his arms as he ran towards him. The youngster hugged his father's neck, rubbing his face against him and kissing his cheek again and again.

"Papa, Papa," the child said repeatedly.

"I've not had a shave," Cousins said, chuckling and rubbing his stubble against his son's cheek, who was giggling and struggling to break free as they laughed. The boy then tweaked his father's ear, and he set his son down. It was a game they played. Cousins then knelt before his boy as they stared, grinning at each other.

"Salman Gabriel James Cousins," the man addressed him, smiling, and the two hugged each other once more. The child had missed his father. Cousins was still studying the boy, taking in his son's features. He had grown in the time he had been away. The youngster was tall for his age. His skin was fair, like his father, but he had his mother's dark, wavy hair, which contrasted sharply with the whiteness of his complexion. His hairline was low across his forehead and temples, characteristic of the peoples across South Asia. His button nose was slightly upturned, and his eyes were wide and dark, which he also had from his mother. He was a good-looking boy.

As the youngster stood before him, he suddenly reached out and pinched his father's nose, then ran off. It was the signal for his papa to chase him. Cousins duly obliged, catching up with his son in the boy's bedroom, wrestling him to the carpeted floor as they laughed. They then launched themselves onto the bed and began to grapple, each trying to throw the other over the imaginary forty-thousand-foot cliff that was marked by the edge of the mattress. Inevitably, it was the father who found himself on the floor. After a while, they sat side by side, breathing heavily, on the bed.

"*Betu*, I need to talk to you," Cousins said, turning towards his son. "Would you like to come and live with me in England?"

The boy stared back at his father, then shrugged his shoulders, unsure how to respond. He missed his papa, but he wasn't sure what England was like. Besides, life in Pakistan was something he knew and associated with his mother. He missed her too. He couldn't quite accept that she was now in heaven. That's what they had told him. For many days he had cried for her. Sometimes he crept into the room that had been hers and went to the wardrobe where her clothes still hung. He would open the door and gather the clothes to his face, still fragrant with the perfume that was hers and lingered within the fabric. Then he felt comforted. Even now, he half expected her to come home.

"There's an English lady too," Cousins continued, "a friend of your papa's who will help to look after you. She's very kind."

"Will she be my new mummy?" the boy asked uncertainly.

"More of a good friend," he replied.

"What's she like?"

"She's pretty, and she's kind. She's a nurse in Africa."

"Is she from Africa?"

"No, *betu*." Cousins chuckled. "She's just working there, like your papa."

Cousins fished his wallet from his back trouser pocket and took out a small photograph in which Johnson was smiling straight to camera. He'd taken it one time as they'd sat and talked at the Italian café in Asmara.

"What do you think?" he asked as the boy studied the image.

The youngster smiled uncertainly. He thought the face was nice. But she wasn't like his mother. The woman in the picture was white.

"The lady's in Eritrea, where I've been working too. That's how we got to know each other," Cousins said by way of explanation. "So, I'll have to go back to Africa to get her. Then we'll start looking for a nice house in England where we can all live."

The boy said nothing.

"We'll be able to see your English grandmother. And your brothers and sisters in England. How does that sound?"

"Will I still be able to visit Nano here?"

"Sure," Cousins replied. "As often as we can."

"Will Hassan Bhai be coming with us?"

"Hassan Bhai will stay here to look after Nano."

The boy nodded in understanding.

"What's England like?"

Cousins drew a deep breath. What is England like? It was, as Sir Charles cynically said, a small group of islands in a cold climate with a dubious history of greatness.

"Don't you remember?" his father asked. The boy had barely been more than a toddler last time they had lived there.

"Well," Cousins said, "England is not as hot as it is here. There are no mosquitoes or *chipkali*." They were the geckos that clung to the white walls and ceilings inside the house that Hassan Bhai and the boy would chase with a broom and tea towel because the grandmother was so afraid of them. "And there's the Queen, who lives at Buckingham Palace in London."

His son looked thoughtful as he tried to imagine how grand the Queen's palace might look.

"Come on," his father said. "Let's get you out of that school uniform and we can go for ice cream." It was a winning move. The boy rose instantly and began to remove himself from his school jumper, aided by his father.

Afterwards, he would call Johnson on the phone before it became too late. He missed her and the comfort to him she had become. He knew the days ahead in Pakistan would be difficult. Each landmark in the city carried its memories, and they were still painful to him.

―――❧―――

That night, he dreamed Afsa Ali was with him again in Pakistan. It was inevitable, perhaps. He had visited many of the places where they had made memories together, including the family house where they had lived and where she had died. It was the same villa in which Ali had been raised. The same property where she had known unhappiness as a child. It may even have been where she was abused as a girl, which was not lost on him. He didn't know for sure. But it made him burn with anger. He felt bitterness too towards her mother and a culture of double standards that allowed such things to happen, remain hidden and steal the future of its daughters. He disguised his feelings in the presence of the grandmother. He was unsure of her part in it. But he was certain she knew. In truth, he would one day like to raise the place to the ground and, in bulldozing the villa to rubble, wipe away the evil that had once taken place there.

Yet he was dreaming of happier times. In his sleep, he was in the Punjab among the fertile farmland that lies in the shadow of the mountains near the city of Jhelum. The sun was hot, and there was a gentle breeze that caressed the fields of golden wheat. It was harvest time, and villagers headed to the fields with their hand scythes as the sun rose to crop the wheat which lay heavy on its stalks.

Rows of men, women and children took their place in the line, bent forward to cut the stalks at their base, moving across the fields, hour by hour like some synchronised human machine. Others followed in their wake, to rake together and tie the bundles of wheat and place them in baskets to be taken from the fields for threshing.

A little boy sat astride a donkey in the sunshine, smiling, taking in the frenzy of activity. For the harvest had to be done within the next few days, field by field, while the weather held and the grain was at its prime. Young and old approached him, placing their bundles into wicker paniers thrown over the animal to be taken to the ancient iron threshing machine which stood red with rust within the nearby farmyard. When the animal was fully laden, a figure in shalwar kameez with skin darkened by the sun led the donkey and its load away with the boy still astride. For he had earlier joined the croppers and was tired now. After all, he was still just a child. It was little Salman. He and his parents had been invited by Hassan Bhai to the family farm to join the harvest.

At the farm, the boy was shown how to draw water from the well, winding the rope which raised the bucket from the cool depths below. Cousins too was invited to milk the buffalo for fresh milk for the chai, as the workers were set to return from their morning's labour in the fields. There was much amusement over the Englishman's awkwardness as he took the cow's teat between his fingers and pulled tenderly downwards. And Ali had laughed too.

The people were poor, but their sense of community was strong. So too was their sense of hospitality. For they saw the attendance of the white man, his wife and their boy as an honour. Yet the feeling was mutual. To Cousins, it seemed idyllic. Hassan Bhai's family was poor. But they were ready to share everything they had with a welcoming smile. There was complete acceptance too of the Englishman. This was the Pakistan he loved. They were a gentle people whose lives were often hard. They knew what suffering was. Yet there was a readiness to smile too, often in the face of poverty and need.

Later, as the sun hung low across the fields and the work was done, they sat on the ground and ate. Simple fare of dal, rice and roti. Then they were taken across the fields that the family worked as the sun began to sink and shadows grew long. He and Ali had held hands as the children ran ahead. Then, when the youngsters became tired from walking, an 'uncle' arrived by motorcycle, and the children sat four deep behind the rider to be taken across the dirt tracks back to the farm.

Finally, as they had climbed into their car to return to Islamabad, the entire community had waved them off with smiles. It had been a wonderful day he would never forget. The sights, the sounds, the fragrances were still with Cousins as he awoke in the small hours of the morning.

Earlier, he had spoken to Hannah Johnson, and she told him about her day at the field clinic. There was excitement too among the staff, she said, when word came that Daniel and Juba had made it to Europe.

"Thank God," he said. "Let's hope they make it all the way."

He didn't tell her about his sadness in Pakistan. Instead, he said how happy he was to see his little boy and that he was looking forward to sharing their lives together. "You are sure?" he asked her.

"More than ever. I love you," she told him. "And I'm looking forward to meeting your boy."

"You know what they say," he told her, the emotion thickening his voice, "somewhere out there is someone for each of us. Call it coincidence, call it luck. But when you recognise them, it is destiny. Undeniable, unstoppable events conspire with the universe as if it was always meant to be. As if it were written in the stars. That person is you."

"You big softy," she said. But she liked the sentiment and felt it too. "You're a hopeless romantic," she added. "But I love it!" Then she blew him a kiss over the phone. She told him about her meeting with Sir Charles and that sometimes she felt she didn't know him at all.

"Hmmm... I think there's more to Charles than meets the eye," he told her. For he had heard things too. From Farjad and from Mancini. Even McKenzie, who pretty much knew everything about everybody.

"Maybe you're right," she said. "His life does seem a bit chaotic though." Then she told him Sir Charles had offered to help arrange the wedding venue and ceremony.

"That's good," he said. "I'm so looking forward to spending my life with you, Miss Johnson."

"Me too," she said. "I can't wait for you to get back. I miss you so."

"And I miss you," he said.

After the call, he felt a pang of loneliness. A long night alone lay in prospect. He'd be glad to be leaving Pakistan. Though he had once immersed himself in its customs and culture, it had become a place of lost dreams and bitter regret for him. He was sad to be leaving his son, but at least next time he would come to take the boy back with him to England. It would mark the end to that chapter in his life.

CHAPTER THIRTY-ONE

T HERE WAS NEWS upon his return to Asmara. Walters had confided in Johnson one evening as they had sat on the veranda watching the sun go down. McKenzie was resigning from his position at BritAid. He had cancer. In fact, he was dying. It was a bombshell. Suddenly, it all began to make sense to her. It explained his increasing absences from the office. Even his outlook on life.

"I'll die out here in Africa," the Scot always said, "but I'll die happy!"

Now those very words ran through her head. It was stage four cancer. Terminal. Then she had cried, for she knew his time was limited.

"How long does he have?"

Walters hesitated, frowning deeply. "Not long. A few weeks, a couple of months, perhaps," the doctor answered solemnly.

"Did you know?" she asked, and he nodded.

"A while now. I'm sorry. He didn't want anyone else to know."

Like Johnson, he was devastated. He was close to McKenzie, almost from the first day of his arrival in Eritrea. Their friend would be stepping down as BritAid country director. But he would remain in Asmara. He had the means and access to treatment, such as it was. He wanted to die in Africa, where he had been happy. There wasn't really anyone back home. He had made a life in Eritrea, with the people who had accepted him, whom he had come to love.

Cousins was equally shocked and saddened. It was true the last time he had seen McKenzie the Scot had looked thin and gaunt. But in a harsh environment in which foreigners often succumbed to bouts of malaria, typhoid or dysentery, the Englishman had thought no more of it. He had himself come through serious illness and was underweight. McKenzie was losing weight for his younger wife, he had joked.

Now the news was out, and it cast a dark shadow on the forthcoming embassy party.

It had been decided to announce that McKenzie was stepping down and make something of a celebration of his tenure at the UK aid agency. Sir Charles was only too happy to oblige. In keeping with the Scot's wishes, it would be termed a 'retirement'. The small international aid community in Asmara was stunned by the announcement. McKenzie had been a colourful, longstanding character among their ranks for more years than anyone cared to remember.

Perhaps the most memorable thing about the party was McKenzie's absence. That and the glowing tribute to the man now too sick to attend. The health minister's address featured a rare acknowledgement of the part played by Western agencies in supporting aspects of Eritrean life, particularly in the more remote parts of the country. Healthcare and education were seen as key priorities where assistance had been welcome. The official spoke of his appreciation of BritAid and the role the Scot had played within the organisation. He was universally known and respected as part of the humanitarian scene. Huge strides had been made in partnership with the international community, the minister had said, so that Eritrea was now ready to step forward and take its rightful place as a rising nation within the region.

Sir Charles too had spoken warmly about McKenzie and the role the international community was happy to play in support of the Eritrean Government's priorities. After the speech, the British diplomat announced the food was being served, and the band began to play once more. Later, Sir Charles took up his trumpet, while Higgins played the spoons in honour of their absent friend. It was a moment not lost on those who knew McKenzie well.

Next day, there was a message from McKenzie. He was sorry he had been unable to attend the event. Would Cousins visit him at home for an update on things? He should come in the afternoon. That was the best time. As the Englishman approached the house, he wasn't sure what to expect. He hadn't seen McKenzie since his return from Pakistan. He stepped up to the door and knocked, glancing back at Jamal, who would wait in the Land Cruiser parked on the driveway.

It was McKenzie's Eritrean wife who opened the door and ushered him into the hallway, and he followed her into the reception room. Her husband was not so good in the mornings or the evenings, she told him. But he was in fine spirits now. He had just received his medication. Would Cousins just wait a moment while she announced his arrival. He nodded, and the woman stepped into the adjacent room, closing the door behind her.

While he waited, Cousins stood at the French doors and gazed out into the garden, bathed in afternoon sunshine. The grass was now yellow, with the advent of the prolonged dry season, hardly a lawn at all now, with bare patches of hard-baked earth. It was difficult to imagine he had danced across the lush grass the night of McKenzie's party with Johnson in his arms as the monsoon rain began to fall. It was a happy memory, and he smiled as he recalled the evening. It was the night he finally realised how much he had come to care for her. His thoughts were interrupted as the lounge door opened and McKenzie's wife signalled for him to step inside.

He found his boss in buoyant mood, resting in his favourite armchair, sipping a gin and tonic. He looked up and observed Cousins as he approached. He was frail and drawn but raised a smile as the Englishman drew near.

"Good of you to come. Sit with me, John," he said, raising himself to lean forward and pat the chair that had been drawn up beside him. "I want to hear all the news."

"Good to see you," Cousins said. "We miss you."

"Course you do. I miss the office too. Dying to get back to work. Or perhaps I should say I'm just dying," he added cynically, grinning at his own words as he raised his glass to his lips. "Drink?" he asked.

"Thanks. Beer, if you have a cold one."

"We do," he replied, and his wife left the room to fetch the drink from the kitchen.

"So, tell me, how was it? Sorry I couldn't be there last night..."

During the update on the party, McKenzie chuckled repeatedly. "He said that? He was never that gracious in person," he said, referring to the minister, smiling at his wife who had returned with the beer. "And another one of these, please, my dear," he said, downing the last of his drink and reaching the empty glass towards her. "And what did they say about me?" he asked.

"That you've worked wonders here as part of the long-term aid and development effort; that you'll be missed."

"That's Charles. Good old Charlie," he added. He had laughed to picture Higgins accompanying the ambassador to play the spoons. He would have liked to have seen that. But he seemed satisfied with the Englishman's account of the evening's activities.

"Everyone was sad to hear you're stepping down," Cousins said.

"Aye. None sadder than me," McKenzie replied.

They spoke too of business priorities. But the Scot had already been briefed by the Kenyan. His replacement was due in post before the end of the year. He hoped he'd still be around to meet his successor. He'd heard it was to be a woman, which should be interesting, he told Cousins. A single career woman from the International Federation of the Red Cross. "And you know what they're like," he said. He wondered what the staff would make of her. Again, he grinned. Perhaps she was what was needed now.

Communications were in hand, Cousins told him, including the new drive to distribute nets in the weeks ahead. Plans to provide livestock to bolster livelihoods were also advanced. That would make for a good piece. There was a story too of the health and hygiene trainings being run in tandem with Medics International, and McKenzie signalled his approval. Head office was keen to run a feature article on his retirement, with his thoughts on the Eritrean operation and its achievements. It could wait a few days, McKenzie told him. More importantly, he said, was the business of the Englishman's wedding. "That's the story I'm more interested in."

"The wedding? All in hand. Charles is assisting," Cousins said.

"He's a good man. He'll sort things out for you."

"He's a diamond. But we're planning an engagement event first. A full coffee ceremony for all the staff next month. We'll make the official announcement of the wedding details then. You're invited, of course."

McKenzie nodded. "You know of my... my demise?"

"Yes. I'm so very sorry," the Englishman said.

"Don't be sorry. It is what it is. I'll die a happy man. I found fulfilment here and a good woman." Then he paused and looked directly at Cousins. "You and I are not so different after all," McKenzie added with a wry smile before he continued. "Find your 'happy', John. That sense of contentment."

"I will," Cousins replied.

"Live life to the full. I have. Not just for the moment, but for tomorrow too, and celebrate every day." The Scot drew a deep breath. "Sure, I've made mistakes," he continued. "I guess I did it my way. Regrets... I have a few, as the song goes..." He smiled. "But here in this corner of Africa, I found my peace, my redemption, if you like."

"I'm glad," said Cousins. "I can see why."

"I didn't know what I was looking for... but I found some answers here..." McKenzie leaned back into his armchair as the pain relief began to take effect. "You know," he said, "I've loved three women in my lifetime. That's lucky." He smiled again, closing his eyes, as if remembering the past. "The first was my childhood sweetheart in Scotland. But we were kept apart. She wasn't seen as a suitable match, and my father forbade it. She died in a road accident a few years later, I heard. I never did forgive the old bastard for that. Heather was her name."

Cousins said nothing. It seemed important just to listen.

"The second was my first wife. Good woman was Barbara. But she didn't understand the restlessness in me. I wasn't a good husband. Nor was I the best father, though I loved the children..."

"I didn't know you had children," Cousins said.

"Not many people do." McKenzie drew a deep breath. He seemed to need to talk. Perhaps it helped in the presence of a relative stranger in the way some might confide to a priest at confession. "But I failed them, I think. Yes. I failed them. That's a big regret."

The Englishman remained silent. The medication seemed to be blurring the lines between past and present as McKenzie began to slip into unconsciousness. A faint smile came to his lips as his mind wandered.

"The third woman is Capri, my dear wife, with whom I've found happiness..." He opened his eyes and gazed at Cousins through heavy lids. "Look after the woman you love, now that you've found her. Because Hannah's special. She'll help you with your children... rebuild your bridges with your boy and your older children... it's never too late," he added in almost a whisper. He closed his eyes. "It's not too late," he repeated softly.

"I'll do my best," Cousins told him, and the gentle smile returned to McKenzie's lips as the pain eased, and he slipped into drug-induced sleep as the morphine overcame him. His Eritrean wife had silently entered the room as he had been speaking and now motioned for Cousins to leave. He needed his rest, she said.

As the Englishman left the house and walked towards the waiting Land Cruiser, there were tears in his eyes. He would often recall that meeting with the charismatic Scotsman. It was the last time he saw McKenzie alive.

CHAPTER THIRTY-TWO

T HE FUNERAL SHOULD be a joyous affair, he had said. McKenzie wanted to be laid to rest with the happy memories he had made within the community he had loved, in a village just outside the city which he knew well. It was the settlement where his wife had been raised and where her extended family still lived. He wanted to be among the people he was comfortable with, he insisted. But he didn't want to be remembered with sadness. In life, McKenzie wasn't someone who stood on ceremony, but that had been his dying wish.

Like the man himself, the service was an unusual affair. A mixed group of expatriates gathered at the graveside in the low afternoon sun, standing with scores of locals, who had come to pay their respects. Among them were the national staff from across the international NGO community. They were joined by villagers and family members. Cousins and Johnson stood sombrely among them, and she reached for his hand as the six pall-bearers carrying the casket slowly drew near, led by the African minister, holding his prayer book.

Among those bearing the coffin were two ambassadors, an Eritrean Government official, a doctor, Muslim field coordinator and the Kenyan finance manager. Johnson's tearful gaze met first with Sir Charles, then Walters, the two lead pall-bearers, who stared solemnly before them. The coffin was laid carefully onto wooden slats over the open grave. She glanced at the handsome Eritrean woman that was McKenzie's wife, who stood, head slightly raised in defiance of the grief she felt, her magnificent white flowing garments fluttering in the gentle breeze as she stared before her. She was there to honour the husband she had loved; the man who had treated her with dignity, compassion and kindness.

Johnson watched as Sir Charles nodded respectfully as he approached the young widow, laid a compassionate hand briefly on her shoulder, then stood beside her. He was joined by Walters, Locatelli the Italian ambassador and the official from the Ministry of Health who flanked her in an act of solidarity.

It was essentially a Christian service. But it was perhaps typical of the country in which they gathered and the nature of the man's work that the congregation reflected all faiths to be found across Eritrea and beyond. The minister began the internment ceremony with recitals from the Book of Common Prayer.

Sir Charles spoke briefly. McKenzie had, he said, represented the best of British. "He was a champion of the people he had come to love over the many years he lived among them. He leaves his beautiful wife Capri, whose loss we share. He will be greatly missed by all of us who knew him."

Walters, too, addressed those who watched with misty eyes. "He was a great friend and humanitarian," he said, pausing to maintain his composure. "Of all the souls I have encountered in my travels, he was perhaps the most human, the most compassionate, the most joyous." He too paid tribute to McKenzie's wife, whom he said his friend had adored. "Here, among the good people of Eritrea, he found peace and happiness. God rest his happy soul…"

It was the signal for the graveside hymn that had been requested by McKenzie –'Amazing Grace' – and a sole Eritrean voice took up the first verse, joined by the other members of the small gospel choir in acapella. It was a favourite at the small chapel the Scot had sometimes frequented with his wife and her family. As the choir sang in soulful harmony, it was joined by voices from the mourners. Many were unfamiliar with the words, but everyone knew the tune and hummed, or sang, as they were able. They included Farjad, who had travelled from Tessenei to attend and had helped bear the coffin. It was a mournful and heart-wrenching tribute. It was the only time Cousins had ever seen the tough Eritrean field coordinator close to tears.

Earlier at the chapel they had sung 'The Lord's My Shepherd'. The Englishman had been deeply moved. Not just because it was a sad occasion to mark the passing of a popular colleague and friend. The service evoked memories of every funeral he had ever attended, including that of his own father several years before. He remembered too how he had watched his own wife lowered into the ground in Pakistan. There had been no voices raised in song that day.

As the last verse of the tribute came to an uplifting close, the minister stepped forward and, for a moment, there was silence before he spoke.

"'Amazing Grace'. How sweet the sound. Amen," he said, and those gathered echoed the Amen in unison. Then he drew a deep breath before uttering the final words to complete the burial service. "We therefore commit the body of your servant James Miller McKenzie to the ground: earth to earth, ashes to ashes, dust to dust in the sure and certain hope of the resurrection to eternal life."

Four men stepped forward. They passed bands of rope under the head and foot of the coffin, taking the strain as the wooden boards were removed, and, slowly, they lowered it into the ground. Cousins felt a tear roll down his cheek and, as he glanced at Johnson, he saw that she was crying too.

McKenzie's wife stepped forward. She smiled softly through her own tears as she stooped to pick up a handful of dry earth, then scattered it onto the casket in the ground, turning her face towards the gentle breeze before stepping back. One by one, other mourners followed suit, as was the custom, and the group began to disperse, offering their condolences to her as they left. Cousins and Johnson waited respectfully before taking their turn.

"So very sorry," Johnson said to the woman.

"It is a part of life. Sadly," she replied simply.

As they moved away from the grave, Walters came across to them, and Johnson threw her arms around him.

"I'm not sure we'll see his like in Eritrea again," the doctor said.

"We all knew he didn't have much time. But it was still a shock when we heard," Johnson said. "We just didn't think it would be so sudden."

"He didn't complain much," Walters replied. "Even though I knew he was in a lot of pain towards the end. In that sense, it was a mercy," he said.

"So sad..." she continued.

"Don't be sad," Walters told her. "He was ready for the end. He was content. But I'll miss him."

"What will happen to his wife?" she asked, gazing at McKenzie's widow, who now stood among her family, with Sir Charles at her side.

"She'll be all right," the doctor replied. "Charles will keep an eye on things. Besides, James left her well provided for, and she has family locally."

"They didn't have children then…" Cousins said. It was as much a statement as it was a question.

"Capri wasn't able to have children," Walters said simply. "It was one of their few regrets. But they had a good life together these last ten years or so. He adored her. He really did. And she him. As did her family."

"And his own family in Scotland?" Johnson asked.

The doctor shook his head. "He rarely spoke of them, although I believe he had children from a previous marriage."

"Sad," Johnson repeated.

"I guess so." The doctor paused. "He made a new life here. He really loved the country and the people. He felt accepted; he found his peace. Perhaps that's as much as anyone can ever hope for."

"Perhaps," said Cousins absently as he reflected on the final conversation he'd had with his boss. That was less than a fortnight ago. Clearly McKenzie had few regrets. But they had included the loss of contact with his own children. Was that what he had been trying to tell him?

"Rebuild your bridges… it's not too late," he had said. He wondered if McKenzie's children even knew their father had passed and now lay beneath the dry earth within a distant country in north-east Africa.

"Look after the woman you love, now that you've found her," the Scot had also told him.

As they turned and walked through the small grey headstones and simple wooden crosses towards the waiting vehicles lined up beyond the cemetery, he squeezed Johnson's hand a little more tightly. There was the gathering at the McKenzie house still to come, where there would be food and drink and talk. Neither he nor Johnson felt they wanted to be there. But their attendance would be expected. It would mark the final act of celebration, respect and farewell.

———∾———

The days that followed seemed unreal. At BritAid, life continued almost as before. Yet there was a sense that nothing was quite the same after the funeral. The staff seemed subdued. McKenzie was missed. Most tried to keep busy, under the direction of the Kenyan, though he was not popular or fully trusted. Perhaps there was a fear of change. After all, the Scot had been part of the aid organisation and the community in Asmara for as long as anyone could remember. Then there was the prospect of the new country director. But no one was quite sure when she would arrive or what she would be like.

Cousins was busy gathering stories from the field, travelling between Asmara and the office at Tessenei, where he would spend time with Farjad. The organisation had started its distribution of livestock across Gash-Barka's north-west. It was something McKenzie had been passionate about. This was practical help which could make a real difference to those whose lives were often a daily battle for survival, leading a nomadic, largely pastoral existence. Providing a healthy goat, a buffalo or even a few chickens could make a meaningful impact. The Englishman missed McKenzie's direction. But most of all, he missed the friendship of the older man. He was sorry he would not be at the wedding, still set for a November date.

Sometimes he and Farjad played chess in the evening at the field office, watched by Lula. She lifted the Englishman's spirits, for she was making good progress at school, and she would often seek him out and tell him of the wonderful things she had learned that day. When she had finished her chores, she was there, like his shadow. But he enjoyed her company and, above all, her enthusiasm for all things, including the books he continued to read to her.

Johnson too continued to oversee the health programme, which often took her to the field clinics operated across the plains. But in a sense, they were simply going through the motions, for they were set to leave Eritrea before the end of the year. Occasionally, they would meet at Tessenei, where Johnson was a welcome visitor, or at Barentu where Medics International had its field office. But the days they enjoyed most were back in Asmara, where they would spend time with Walters or Sir Charles, and there were dinners, or parties, and the UN barbecues that continued as before. Or they would browse the bazaars and boutiques, then meet at one of the popular Italian coffee shops.

Slowly, the sadness following the death of McKenzie began to recede. Not least of all as their marriage plans began to take shape. It would be a small, intimate affair, attended by members of the aid community in Eritrea they had become a part of. It was not as Sir Charles might have wished. He had bigger plans for them, yet they were able to curb his enthusiasm. It would be a memorable event, nonetheless, held at the small church which was used by those international staff that were not Catholic.

There was further good news with the arrival of a cryptic message which found its way to Walters' email inbox one slow day early in November. It was remarkable in two ways. Firstly, it was written in French. But there was no mistaking its meaning.

Magnifique vue sur la Manche de Calais. On va bien. J'espère
voir bientôt des falaises blanches. Tes amis.

It roughly translated as: wonderful view of the Channel in Calais. We are well. Hoping to see famous white cliffs soon. Your friends.

It was in essence a coded message. Daniel and Juba had arrived in the French port of Calais, despite all the odds. It would make for a double celebration during the forthcoming coffee ceremony at which Cousins and Johnson would formally announce their wedding plans.

CHAPTER THIRTY-THREE

T HE TWO RAGGED figures approached a small white caravan parked alongside the muddy track on the edge of the tented encampment under unwelcoming skies. They were bent forward into the wind which blew across the dunes from the sea, clutching their blankets around them against the cold. A sign painted in blue lettering proclaimed that refugees were welcome. Behind a small window, inside the caravan, a young woman watched the men draw closer with a heavy heart. They were a pitiful sight as they hobbled towards her. Such arrivals of men, women and children in similar condition were becoming more frequent.

She was one of several young volunteers working for a handful of small charities from England, France and their neighbouring countries, moved by the desperate plight of migrants converging on the ports of Calais and Dunkirk. In Calais, a growing community of refugees from troubled corners of the world converged on the expanding tented community dotted with ramshackle huts constructed of recycled wood and tarpaulins at the former landfill site on the eastern edge of the town. They all shared the same hope: that they might make the short passage across the English Channel for a new life in the UK.

The illegal encampment was to become known as the Calais 'Jungle' and would eventually swell to almost ten thousand refugees who arrived with little more than the clothes on their backs, carrying with them the hope of a life free from war, persecution and economic hardship. The volunteers were also beginning to see children as young as eight or nine years old whose parents had made the agonising decision to set them in a small boat to cross the Mediterranean, perhaps with a relative, or friend, in the hope they might have the chance of a better life inside the European Union. They, like Daniel and Juba, travelled thousands of miles from their homelands in search of safety in the UK, where most had friends and relatives. It made sense to them, not only in joining family and friends already settled in Britain, but because English was often the most familiar language to them.

It was a hot political potato which neither the French or British authorities seemed willing to grasp or commit themselves to resolve. Therefore, arrivals grew steadily under the watchful eyes of the local authorities. As did the numbers of illegal crossings from Calais, by small boat, by stowaway, in the back of trucks boarding the busy ferry routes, Channel Tunnel or by any means possible. There was a network of traffickers too to facilitate the increasingly desperate and spiralling numbers of migrants who still had any cash. For there were no safe, or legal, routes for them to cross the Channel.

Though reluctantly tolerated, it was a headache for the local administration, which seemed paralysed by indecision and therefore content to 'kick the can down the road'. There was simply no political will to find a solution either side of the Channel. Therefore, the Calais Jungle continued to expand. With it came growing fears and frustrations within the local French community and sometimes violence towards the migrants borne from prejudice and fear.

The woman inside the caravan slid the small window open as Daniel and Juba approached. She was tasked to offer assistance to new arrivals. She would take details of the men's names, age and country of origin. In return, she would hand them a tent, sleeping bags and whatever other donations she had to hand which might be useful. She would signpost them to further support, including the large tent where they would find something hot to eat and drink. At that time, there were several hundred migrants within the settlement – mainly from Eritrea, Somalia and Syria – camped at the site. With support from volunteers, they were beginning to organise themselves and put basic amenities in place to serve the escalating need.

The two weary men gratefully took the tent, the sleeping bags and blankets offered by the young woman. They made their way towards the larger tent further along the muddy track as directed. Raising the entry flap, they stepped inside. There were perhaps a dozen men who raised their faces towards the two new arrivals as they entered, mainly African. But there were Arabs too, from Libya, Iraq or Syria.

"Come," said a cheerful voice with a heavy Tigrayan accent as a young African man wrapped in a blanket raised himself from the wooden crate on which he sat and beckoned them in.

"Welcome to Calais bistro." He grinned. "We have tea, we have coffee and hot soup. And we have bread," he added cheerfully.

Looking at the faces of those who sat, or lay, inside the tent, the two men felt reassured. It was the first time since travelling across the Sudanese border that they felt among friends as they stepped inside to join them. Mohammed, the Iraqi, took his place behind a table, upon which a steaming pot of soup simmered on a gas stove, and beckoned for them to come over, as he began ladling the hot brew into small bowls.

"Please," he said. "The hot soup will warm you, brothers. You look as if you have travelled far."

They lay their baggage against the side of the tent and approached.

"Where are you from, pilgrims?" one of the Africans asked them.

"Eritrea," Daniel replied.

"That is a long way," he said. "Which district?"

"Asmara," said Daniel, taking a steaming bowl of soup from the Iraqi. There were bread rolls too.

"The mountain capital," said the African. "I know of it. We call it the Italian city."

The man was from Gash-Barka, and he welcomed them in the language of his people. It was Tigrayan dialect, but both men could understand. And they felt welcome.

There was an Ethiopian among them, a lay preacher with a dream to build a church on-site. There was a need for faith, he said. He was one of dozens of his countrymen, with more arriving every day. There were scores of Eritreans too who had made the long trek. They should have somewhere to pray.

"But here we have just one nationality. We are all refugees, migrants," said the Iraqi with a grin, and the others murmured in agreement.

"Here we survive as brothers. And we look for a way to cross the Channel," he added. "There are ways."

To Daniel and Juba, it seemed almost unreal. They had reached Calais. Here, there were others who had endured similar hardships on their journeys. For the first time in many months, they felt a sense of renewed hope. After they had eaten, there was sweet tea. Then they were directed to the dunes where they could pitch their tent. Two Africans helped them raise the small frame and pull its nylon covering into place, pegging it to the ground as the wind began to howl across the sand and the long grasses. It was barely large enough for the two Eritreans and their scant possessions. But it was shelter, and it was safe. Then, as they lay within it, gathering their blankets around them, they were finally able to rest. And as they lay among the bedding within their small tent, they were sure they could hear the sound of the sea crashing against a nearby beach as they drifted into a deep and restful sleep. It was the first time they had slept soundly in many weeks. Their biggest comfort lay in the knowledge they were among others who had made the long journey with the same aim and that their final destination lay just a few miles across the English Channel.

———❦———

It is hard to imagine what hardships were endured along the way. There were stories of beatings and of loss, hunger and exhaustion. There were arrests, kidnappings and exploitation. Even deaths. In this sense, Daniel and Juba were among the lucky ones. They had made it this far. The Ethiopian preacher was right though. Faith and hope were essential companions. The two men were grateful for their deliverance to the French port. They knew there were still challenges. Yet they now heard stories on a daily basis of those who succeeded in their bid to reach the shores of southern England. There were those too who continued to try and fail. But at least there were ways, and therefore there was hope. So, they gave thanks to God.

The volunteers also helped them. They were moved by the kindness of strangers. They were 'angels', the refugees said.

There were distributions of shoes, clothing, blankets and food on a regular basis. The days that followed were still difficult, but at least they could survive with a degree of support within the camp. The migrants were becoming better organised too. Each day seemed to bring more people and additional expertise within the camp. New temporary structures were being planned and built as the migrant numbers increased and the crisis rose in prominence across Europe, fuelled by conflicts across the Middle East, South Asia and North Africa.

Soon there would be makeshift shops, soup kitchens, a barber, ashram, a legal centre, even a school under canvas or housed within temporary wooden shacks. There was a mosque too and the Ethiopian church that rose out of the mud. It was the start of the community which, in time, would also see the arrival of two international medical NGOs, Médecins Sans Frontières and Médecins du Monde, to help protect the welfare of hundreds of vulnerable refugees.

It was as he was praying that Daniel reflected not on the harshness of their journey and the many challenges they had faced. Instead, he gave thanks for the unexpected kindnesses he and Juba had encountered along the way. He remembered the Sudanese trafficker. He remembered the Syrian family they had met in the woods. He thought too of the Albanian farmer who had discovered them in the barn and brought them food. Then there was the young German woman who had skidded to a halt before them on the road outside Frankfurt in the early hours, then bought them food and drink before taking them to the city.

On the streets of Frankfurt, they had been embraced by black Africans selling cheap jewellery who had shared food with them. They had given them advice on where to bed down safely and how to dodge the authorities. Even how to board the train for Paris and ride ticketless, avoiding rail and border officials. It had seemed a fateful day as they said farewell to their new companions and walked through the main entrance of the city's Hauptbahnhof under the shadow of Atlas, holding the world aloft upon the building's magnificent arched frontage. For after many weeks of travel, Calais seemed within their reach, perhaps only a day or two away.

At the French border, they had hidden under seats in case of document checks. In Paris, they had found people on the fringes of society, buskers and beggars at the Gare du Nord who helped direct them. There, they were able to board the train north to the French port, but narrowly escaped detection just before Abbeville. It was here that they stepped onto the station platform to avoid a railway official. But the train moved off before they could climb back aboard, and they found themselves stranded, some eighty miles short of their destination.

Should they wait for the next train and risk it again? After all, they felt they were now adept at travelling without a ticket. It was just another hour or so by train. The alternative would be two days on foot, perhaps less if they could hitch a ride. In the event, they decided to wait and risk the next train to Calais. There was no one checking tickets, though they were anxious minutes as they gazed at the rural landscape rushing past the window as it clattered through the open countryside, drawing ever closer to the French port. As a precaution, they left the train one stop before Calais-Ville station at Fréthun, south of the town. They then made their way by foot under grey skies into the centre of Calais, where they found other migrants. Some were newly arrived. But others were able to direct them to the eastern side of the town, where there was a bustling migrant encampment and those who might help them. Their money was gone; their clothes were ragged and their possessions few. But it was here, more than ten weeks since leaving Eritrea that fateful day, that they finally found respite.

———❀———

Word came one evening that a group of Sudanese men were planning a bid to board lorries bound for England parked up near the ferry terminal. Hundreds of trucks were at a standstill, following a dispute with border officials. It was an opportunity. Those who were ready to make a bid to cross the Channel should camp in the nearby woods and then make their way before dawn to the lorry park. There, they would attempt to open trailers and conceal themselves inside. Daniel and Juba had been at the encampment for several weeks and had been able to rest and regain their strength. But how long should they stay and languish there? It wasn't much of a life. Now they felt perhaps their time had come to attempt their first bid to make the crossing. They packed up only what was needed for the night and left the camp with three Sudanese men for the woods. And there, on a cold November night, they waited for their chance…

CHAPTER THIRTY-FOUR

IN GENEVA, CONCERNS were mounting. Up to three thousand people were fleeing Eritrea every month along precarious escape routes of 'a life-threatening nature', the United Nations said in an expression of increasing frustration issued by its special rapporteur. The lawyer from Mauritius had been continually denied access to the country by the Government of Eritrea since her appointment in 2012. Patience with the regime was wearing thin.

She had been tasked by the UN to examine widescale human rights abuses that were said to be continuing, fuelling the exodus of young people running from forced conscription into the country's army for indefinite periods. International pressure on the Eritrean national administration was growing. It could go either way.

Sir Charles smiled wryly as he viewed the report on his desk at the British Embassy in Maryam Gmbi Street. He rose to his feet and walked to the window, where he gazed down at the sun-drenched avenue below. It might pose a problem for his own diplomatic mission, he mused. Of course, London was aware of the ongoing situation in Eritrea. He himself had relayed information from a network of operatives across the country and described the situation in-country in candid terms. Sometimes he had personally attended meetings at the border to gather intelligence from his people on the ground.

Certainly, he regularly heard stories of those who crossed into the Sudan. He also knew directly from Walters about the Medics International nurses who had disappeared. He was also aware that those who were caught were subjected to beatings and torture, or even worse. It could mean lengthy jail sentences and reprisals against family members. There was a real fear of the government and its machinery that persisted on the streets, even along the temperate and pleasant boulevards of Asmara.

His was therefore a difficult line to tread. He had to maintain cordial relationships with senior government officials, smooth the way for trade and represent British interests with a regime known for its human rights abuses. The latest UN statement of dissatisfaction from its special rapporteur would need careful handling, not least some guidance from his Foreign Office superiors. The Eritrean Government could easily make life difficult with visas or withhold business permits. He picked up the telephone and asked Higgins to join him in his office.

—❧—

Across the city, Cousins and Johnson were on a mission of their own, as they strolled hand in hand along the palm-lined avenues of the shopping district. Life for the small number of expatriates was comfortable in Asmara. There were few signs of poverty on its streets, and the oppression of its people by an austere, conservative government went largely unperceived. They were browsing the boutiques along Harnet Avenue which lay in the shadow of the magnificent cathedral. Their purpose was to buy an outfit for a young lady in Tessenei who was wildly excited by the prospect of attending their special event in the capital. That was the wedding ceremony of her two favourite people in the world, and the person in question happened to be Lula.

Already, there had been an endless stream of questions. Where would it take place? Who would be there? What would happen at a wedding? Especially a Christian wedding. Was it the same as a Muslim ceremony, she wondered, which she knew from her community was a religious service and required a promise before Allah to live together forever? She liked that idea. Perhaps there would then be a baby. That was usually what happened. She'd look after the child anytime. She giggled happily at the thought.

She was excited too by the prospect of a beautiful dress to wear. And shoes! Her mother had suggested a mixture of traditional and European styles. Mariam was also thrilled by the forthcoming event. She had never travelled to the mountain capital, though she had heard stories of how beautiful the streets and buildings were. Not least the Our Lady of the Rosary Cathedral, which served as a national focal point for the country's Christians. She would like to see it, pay homage and offer prayers. She would pray for her family and give thanks for the good fortune that God in His mercy had bestowed upon them.

She was also grateful to the Englishman and his kindness to her daughter. For though she would never openly say it, she had become fond of the white aid worker, despite her initial misgivings. For she saw the change in her daughter. Lula was thriving. The mother was therefore happy that her daughter was able to receive the additional schooling. She herself had not been so fortunate as a little girl. Instead, she had helped support her own mother at home. But she saw the value in education, which made the prospect of a better future that much brighter.

She liked the woman too and she could see that she was good for the Englishman. You could tell just by seeing them together. Besides, she *felt* it and had good intuition in such matters. She hoped they would be happy and have many children together. But she knew they would not remain in Eritrea, even before Farjad had told her they were set to leave. For she had seen it when she kneeled in prayer and had a strong sense that their destiny lay in a distant land. It was surely written.

In Asmara, Cousins and Johnson stared into the shop window at a selection of traditional dresses on display. There was a range of ready-made garments, but there was a rainbow of coloured fabrics too and the option to have something tailor-made, as was commonplace. They were looking for something of length, perhaps in white cotton, that could be drawn in at the waist. Maybe a coloured shawl as an accessory. And that's what they bought. An outfit for a young Eritrean lady with a dash of vibrant colour. With smart leather sandals to match.

Cousins prided himself as a man with good taste in women's clothing. Yet in this instance, he was happy for Johnson to take the lead. She was clearly enjoying the shopping expedition and seeking out the child's outfit. For she had also grown fond of the girl. Besides, Cousins had an agenda of his own that day. He was yet to present Johnson with an engagement ring. In fact, he realised he hadn't yet proposed to her formally and was a traditionalist at heart. He fully intended to go down on bended knee when presenting the ring to her. He knew too it would have to be displayed at the forthcoming coffee ceremony.

Already, he had seen a ring that he liked. But he was practical too and wanted Johnson to help decide. Above all, he wanted her to wear it with pride. She had to be happy with the choice. Besides, he had been unsuccessful in trying to obtain her exact ring size and had found himself gazing at her slender fingers, trying to gauge what it might be. No, it had to be done properly at the expense of surprise.

It was after they had bought the outfit for Lula that they found themselves standing in the small jewellery shop just off the main thoroughfare with their bags from the boutique. It was a family business that had been recommended by Sir Charles. The man behind the counter smiled as they entered and now stood before him.

"Good morning, sir," he said, recognising the Westerner and glancing approvingly at the woman beside him.

"Hello," Cousins replied. "I'd like to see the ring again. The one I looked at the other day."

The jeweller nodded, for he remembered the recent visit and the ring in question. He turned and opened a small drawer in a cabinet behind him, upon which a set of scales rested. The ring he had retrieved and then held out towards the couple comprised a delicate band of gold with a beautifully set blue sapphire. There was intricate feathering on the band which rose to the setting in a series of delicate Islamic crescents which held the stone. The gold was yellow, suggesting it was a high level of purity and came from the East.

"I love it," Johnson exclaimed excitedly, turning to Cousins.

"The lady will try it on?" the man behind the counter suggested.

"Of course," Cousins replied as the jeweller handed the ring to him, and he slipped it onto the finger Johnson held expectantly towards him.

"It's beautiful, John," she said, raising the ring closer to her face, then gazing at him adoringly. It was a little loose, and the man behind the counter produced a ring sizer. He took the ring from her hand, then slid a steel hoop upon her finger in its place. Then he tried another, before nodding. He could have the ring resized and ready for collection by the evening, he said.

"Thank you," Johnson said as they stood outside the shop, and she kissed Cousins tenderly on the mouth. "I can't wait to show it off," she added, and he smiled at her. He would collect the ring later.

From there, they wound their way across town to the Medebar Market, a few blocks from Afabet Street, a bustling hive of commercial activity with traders of every description. They included the recycling workshops where craftsmen made coffee pots from old olive tins or fashioned corrugated iron into metal kitchenware. Johnson had long held a wish to have a pair of 'Shida' sandals made from an old tyre, which was one of the country's 'must haves'. The black rubber sandals had been a trademark of the Eritrean freedom fighters during the long war with Ethiopia and had become a national symbol of pride.

The young Eritrean sat on a wooden crate beside his battered workbench, upon which a dubious selection of tools lay scattered. He wore a grubby, white, sleeveless T-shirt and shorts, which displayed a lean and muscular physique, and was barefooted. Old tyres were stacked high to one side of him. On the other lay a heap of rubber sandals. His name was Kebede, and he could make a pair of Shida especially for the lady, he said. The price was a hundred nafka, roughly equivalent to ten dollars, he ventured with an infectious grin. But neither Cousins or Johnson had the heart to haggle.

Having agreed the price, they watched him as he took an old tyre, wedged it between his knees and began to cut away its outer rim with a Stanley knife, working quickly and confidently. Within a few moments, he had the rubber for the soles. He asked Johnson if she would remove her boot and place her foot upon the material he had cut from the tyre which he had laid before her. She duly obliged and watched him as he swiftly drew around its contour with a chalk pencil. If they would like to browse the market and return in a short while, the Shida would be ready, he told them. So, they left the young man to his work.

They were keen to look for some traditional fabrics and perhaps pick up some of the intricate woven reed basket ware that was such a feature of Eritrean life. They felt like tourists, but perhaps in a sense they were. They knew their time in Asmara was now limited and the intensity of their work had seldom allowed them the luxury of shopping for such items.

When they returned to the sandal workshop, the Shida were ready. The man had worked deftly and skilfully, fixing the interwoven ribbons of rubber across the top of the sandals and ankle straps, complete with steel buckles at the side. The Eritrean insisted that the lady try them on. They were a perfect fit, and Johnson marvelled at the accomplishment, adding another fifty nafka as she pressed the notes into the young man's hand. For although American dollars were the preferred black market currency, they were not legal tender and were never exchanged in public. The young man thanked them and watched them walk away before he returned to his work. He would make another ten pairs of sandals in various sizes before the day was done. Perhaps he could finish early.

Laden with shopping bags, the couple decided to take one of the battered yellow cabs back across the city to the compound as the sun rose to its highest point. They returned tired but satisfied and retired to Johnson's room for an afternoon nap.

Lula would be thrilled with the outfit. They flopped onto the bed fully clothed and lay gazing up at the mosquito net.

"I'd say that was a successful shop," he said, and she nodded, before sighing deeply. He reached an arm around her, and she snuggled closer to him, resting her head against his shoulder before they fell into a satisfying sleep.

❧

When she awoke, he was already gone. He had scribbled a note which she found on the small coffee table which stood in the centre of the room. She looked beautiful as she slept, it said. He had just dashed into Asmara on an errand.

I love you, my angel, he had written and signed off with a string of kisses. She smiled and felt a rush of emotion for him. It must surely be love. She kissed the note, folded it carefully and put it on the bedside table. She liked to keep such things and was sentimental that way.

For a moment, he had watched her as she slept, noting the gentle rise and fall of her chest and the look of contentment on her face. He blew her a silent kiss from where he stood, then turned and slipped quietly from her room, pulling the door slowly closed behind him.

When he returned from the city, he found her sitting outside on the terrace, sipping a cup of green tea. She tilted her face up towards him as he approached, and he kissed her.

"Rested?" he asked, sitting down beside her, and she nodded.

"Didn't hear you leave. Thanks for the lovely note," she added.

"You were flat out," he said.

"Had to pick up something important from the city," he explained. And suddenly, he was down on one knee looking up at her. He retrieved a small jewellery box from his shirt pocket, flipped it open and held it out towards her. "Will you marry me, Miss Johnson?"

"If you'll have me, Mr Cousins." She laughed, taking the ring from its box and sliding it onto her finger. He watched her as she spread the fingers of her hand before her and gazed at the ring approvingly. "Thank you," she said and slipped from her chair to kneel before him. Then, as they faced each other on their knees, he wrapped his arms around her, and they kissed long and deep.

CHAPTER THIRTY-FIVE

T HE GIRL SAT in the dirt at the entrance to the compound on the outskirts of Tessenei and waited. She was wearing her Batman T-shirt because Cousins had told her the 'Caped Crusader' was a superhero, and that was how she felt today, in anticipation of their arrival. She was drawing images in the dust with her forefinger under the warm November sun when the two white Land Cruisers approached the open gateway.

She jumped to her feet and waved as the vehicles passed, then ran behind them as fast as she could as they swept up to the main house and came to a halt. And there she stood with the broadest grin to greet Cousins and Johnson as they climbed from their respective vehicles. A moment later, Farjad stepped into the yard from the office to welcome them, following the long drive from Asmara. There were cold colas in the icebox, he said, and Mariam would make some tea. Lula then ran to tell her mother the Westerners had arrived.

They took the sweet tea in the shade of the terrace. It had indeed been a long drive in the hot sun from the capital. They had a few busy days in prospect, Farjad said, with distributions to take place across Gash-Barka. The long dry season was taking its toll on the nomadic peoples of the plains. There were plenty of stories to tell, he added. He was delighted to see Johnson. How were the wedding plans progressing? They had a date, Cousins said, and the small chapel was booked.

"All will be well; such a happy event," the Eritrean said. "Insh'allah."

Lula had talked about little else, he told them, shaking his head. "That girl... she has been very much excited. Indeed," he added, "we are all looking so much forward to the marriage and will wish you many blessings."

"Thank you, Farjad," Johnson said. "It will be lovely to have you there. We have Lula's outfit," she added and the girl, who now stood beside them, beamed with joy.

"You must try your dress." Johnson smiled. "That's why I have come today, to see how beautiful you will look."

Then, looking at Cousins, she asked: "Are the bags in yet?"

"I have them here," he replied. "Can you please ask your mama to join us?" he asked the girl, and she scuttled off to fetch her mother. As they approached, Cousins reached under the table and lifted two carrier bags up towards the Eritrean woman, who nodded in thanks as she took them from the Englishman.

"I think it will fit perfectly," Johnson said, eyeing the girl. "We hope you like it. We think the dress is beautiful."

"Fit for a princess," Cousins added, and the mother and daughter withdrew.

Indeed, they were right. When they returned, Lula was a vision of loveliness in her white flowing dress. The sandals just lifted the hemline from the ground, and the patterned red and orange shawl set the whole thing off. Lula was bursting with happiness. She looked less a camp urchin, more like the daughter of well-heeled parents in Asmara.

"You are a picture of loveliness," Cousins told her, and she felt herself flush. "Speaking of which..." and he reached for his camera bag to take a shot of the girl. "With your permission, Mariam," he added. He raised the camera and clicked several images. They were pictures he would come to treasure: Lula smiling with happiness straight into the lens. Johnson too was thrilled by the transformation.

"I will be honoured for you to be my chief bridesmaid," she said.

Sadly, she added, it was time for her to leave. But she looked forward to seeing everyone in Asmara for the wedding. Then she rose from her seat and said her goodbyes. Cousins followed her to the Land Cruiser in the yard, where Samuel the driver was already waiting. It was almost two hours back to Barentu. But Johnson felt the detour had been worth it.

"I'll miss you," Cousins said, and they embraced, a little self-consciously. For they were both aware they were being watched from the terrace.

"It's only a few days," Johnson said, and he nodded. She would head back to Asmara on the Friday, and he would join her at the compound in the capital for the coffee ceremony the following Sunday afternoon. There was a story he had to cover the day before. It couldn't be helped. He opened the door for her, and she climbed into the vehicle.

Cousins waved and smiled, then watched the Land Cruiser pull away. For a few moments he stood there, as if lost, gazing at the open gateway to the compound as the dust settled. She was now a part of his life, and even a few days away from her felt like an eternity. He sighed deeply, then headed back towards the main building. He still had to discuss his schedule for the week ahead with Farjad. Later, he would read to Lula. Tomorrow was likely to be a busy day.

⌘

The small town of Barentu was a hub for Medical International and the International Federation of the Red Cross. For it was here that the Government of Eritrea distributed the supplies needed to operate the field clinics both organisations provided across Gash-Barka region. Johnson watched as two vehicles were being loaded with medicines. She was tasked with auditing the drugs and equipment on a regular basis, working with Walters, who was mainly based in the mountain capital some 150 miles to the east. It was his job to liaise with senior officials from the Ministry of Health.

This particular week, Johnson would oversee the set-up of three clinics across the plains. It was a gruelling schedule over the next few days, but at least she would be busy, and time would fly. She would set out from Barentu to Asmara on the Friday. The coffee ceremony was set for Sunday afternoon, when most staff would be able to attend the event at the Medics International compound. Already, there was a buzz of excitement among the staff. Walters was coordinating the event. Cullen from CRS would be there, as would Mancini from Cesvi and, naturally, Sir Charles. National staff too.

The doctor had already enlisted several members of his team to help and had suggested a meeting with Johnson on the Saturday to discuss the arrangements. Besides, he felt he needed some time with her. He was desperately sad that she would be leaving Eritrea, not least because she was an integral part of his team. She was more than just a colleague, whom he had grown fond of. He had half a mind to ask her to remain in-country, at least until the spring. It would give him more time to find a replacement.

He knew her leaving had been inevitable. Yet he had always pushed the thought away. It would be painful for him. He would miss her. He missed McKenzie too. As yet, there was no date for the arrival of his replacement. He had heard there was still no visa. He wondered how Joe the Kenyan was coping at BritAid. He decided to give him a call. Perhaps Cousins might be offered an extension to his contract until the arrival of the new country director. He'd sound him out, for he knew Cousins and Johnson were now a package: neither would stay without the other. It might be worth a try.

⚭

The Kenyan sat at a desk upon which the documents and folders were scattered before him. For a moment, he paused from his work and leaned back towards the gently whirring fan. The figures didn't quite add up. Not that it was unusual. But there were gaps between expenditure and outputs. Some discrepancies which needed to be accounted for. Fuel costs were high, as was food expenditure. Did they really use that much cooking oil? McKenzie had been onto it. But he had taken a relaxed and pragmatic view. Things did 'go missing'. A crate of cooking oil, a sack of onions, a jerry can of diesel... or two. It was surely to be expected in Africa, particularly in a country experiencing acute poverty. It was part of the cost of 'doing business' in such countries. It was an acceptable, perhaps inevitable, loss which was borne for the greater good. At least that was how McKenzie viewed it. Besides, who was he to judge? As long as the margins fell within acceptable levels.

He felt it was somewhat hypercritical for Westerners – outsiders – to take an inflexible, zero-tolerance approach to such things, especially when they were paid Western wages which allowed them an unprecedented level of wealth on 'mission'. Yes, there were hardships and deprivations in the field. But was their work really any more difficult than that of the national staff, who were essentially paid local rates? The locals were perhaps the real unsung heroes of humanitarian work. Often, they had to support small armies of extended family. It was expected.

No, McKenzie understood. He had hinted as much to Cousins when he had first arrived in Eritrea. It was about context. There was generally an unspoken understanding across the international humanitarian community. It was accepted that poor people would be tempted to take from a Western NGO, given the opportunity. That was obvious. Therefore, it was about having robust systems of accountability in place to limit that opportunity and ensuring those mechanisms were enforced.

The Kenyan understood too. He counted himself fortunate, for by virtue of his nationality, he was paid as an expatriate. Yet his own country of birth was not a million miles away from the Eritreans with whom he worked or their culture, which was similar to his own. Some therefore viewed him with suspicion. He might have commanded more respect had he been Eritrean. He knew it. He was perhaps kinder than the national staff imagined.

The ring on the phone was a welcome interruption to his work. It was Doctor Walters from the neighbouring compound. Was he free to discuss the forthcoming coffee ceremony? It would be a pleasant diversion. Besides, he had earlier received the news that the incoming country director's arrival had been delayed. Her visa had not yet been approved. There was time to work the figures and cover obvious irregularities.

A sweet tea next door with the New Zealander would lift his spirits. The two men knew each other well. He was, however, caught unaware by the doctor's suggestion to offer the Englishman a short extension on his contract. At least until the arrival of McKenzie's replacement at BritAid. Cousins had been a useful member of the senior management team and his communications work had been well received at head office. The Kenyan agreed it was perhaps worth pursuing.

———

Walters watched her face as she considered his proposition, squinting into the bright sunlight, then brushing a strand of her hair from her face before shielding her eyes with her hand.

"It's a bit of a surprise," she said, gazing at him from beneath her fingers as he grinned sheepishly at her. He liked to look at her. It wasn't just her face but how she acted and the way she moved. He liked her honesty and compassion too, reflected in her light brown eyes. Perhaps he was a little in love with her.

"Just another eight weeks or so." He paused. "Hannah, I'm not asking you to run away with me." He smiled disarmingly. He knew he had put her on the spot.

"At least talk to John about it, please," he continued. "You could always spend Christmas together in the UK, then come back."

"I will consider it, David, but I can't promise anything," she told him. She knew Cousins was anxious to collect his son from Pakistan. But, as yet, there was no new job to go to. She would talk to him.

"Thanks," the doctor said, and they sat grinning at each other.

"You know I've always been fond of you," he said. "We've been through some stuff together…"

She nodded and took a sip of her tea, watching him over the rim of her cup. She knew he had always carried a torch for her. He might even have feelings for her, and she wondered what he was going say next. But he was far too discreet to reveal his true feelings. Instead, he simply told her she would be missed. He would miss her. Things wouldn't be the same.

"I'll miss you too," she said and reached across to squeeze his hand.

"I'm very happy for you," he told her. And it was true. He could have said more, but she was thankful he left it at that. "The coffee ceremony," he said, clearing his throat and changing the subject, "everything's in place," he assured her. "It's all set to kick off at around three," he added. "Everyone's very excited, especially Charles!"

"Bless him!" She laughed, shaking her head. "Such a child… it'll be good to catch up." Cousins was to travel from Tessenei in the morning, she said, but was set to arrive in plenty of time. She couldn't wait to see him.

CHAPTER THIRTY-SIX

G OADING THE LIVESTOCK along the wooden ramp
onto the truck began before sunrise. The goats were
stubborn, and additional hands were needed to lure, push
and pull the troublesome animals into place as they bleated
in protest. Eight was deemed the maximum load for the
small, flat-bedded truck, with each goat tethered by rope to
the side panels. One Eritrean herder would sit on the back of
the battered open-topped Fiat to keep an eye on the livestock
as they rumbled along the rugged lowland terrain. Two
isolated settlements had been identified to receive animals
during the day's round trip across the challenging landscape
encompassing some two hundred miles.

Cousins had risen early, waking to the commotion outside
even as he lay beneath his mosquito net. He hurried a light
breakfast of toasted flatbread and jam as the first orange
glow fell upon the flat-roofed buildings on the edge of the
ragged frontier town. He'd barely had time to make himself a
green tea before he was out in the dusty yard with his camera

bag and knapsack. Farjad was already outside, directing the activity, stepping forward to help pull one of the goats towards the truck.

He and Cousins would take the Fiat and the Land Cruiser across the parched desert terrain, where the single dirt track would peter out to nothing, and they would continue across the sun-scorched earth to reach the isolated family groups. But they needed to be on the road before the sun rose.

He downed the remaining green tea and, handing his empty cup to Lula, who had come to stand and watch, then moved towards Farjad to help load the last of the animals.

"The beasts are moody," the Eritrean said as Cousins joined him.

"They would rather stay home today," the Englishman replied, taking hold of the guide rope around the animal's head to help Farjad steer it towards the vehicle as it began to pull against them.

"It is a good game to start the day." The Eritrean grinned and, finally, the animal began to move.

"And good morning," the Englishman said, gazing up at his African colleague who had suddenly run the goat up along the ramp onto the truck and now stood bent forward, hands on his thighs, breathing heavily as he squinted down at the Westerner.

"Yes... yes, my friend." The Eritrean smiled, gasping for breath. "It is a good morning." Then he straightened himself to draw deeply on the cool morning air as he gazed towards the sunrise. "Allah be praised," he added, standing among the animals. The last of the goats was loaded and tied.

The herder raised the wooden ramp, slid it onto the flatbed of the truck and slammed the tailgate into place. Cousins watched him climb onto the back of the Fiat, then turned and strode across the yard towards his own vehicle. He opened the passenger door and glanced back to see Farjad standing beside the truck and raising a 'thumbs up' before stepping into the cab. The Englishman raised his hand in acknowledgement, then nodded towards Lula, who beamed back at him before sliding onto the passenger seat of his own Land Cruiser as the engine roared into life. Jamal put the vehicle into gear, and they began to roll, falling behind the battered truck which swept slowly across the yard towards the compound gateway.

They would take the road north to Sebderat, then leave the single dirt track to head deeper into the Forto district, the northernmost part of Gash-Barka, picking up the trails across the lowlands which Farjad knew like no other. But there would be stretches when they too would simply disappear, and they would literally drive across the hard, dry terrain.

To witness the first rays of brilliant light fall upon the plains as the sun rose above the distant hills to the east, breaking across the empty expanse of land which lay before them, was truly breathtaking. It was a majestic beauty that inspired faith and belief in something greater as the new day chased the shadows across the vast and silent panorama. At least that's what struck the Englishman as he gazed out across the emptiness and breathed the morning air. Farjad had ordered a halt so that he could take his bearings. Cousins felt choked with emotion and moved almost to tears. There was incredible beauty in the world, he mused. He wished Johnson was there to see the sunrise too. Suddenly, he smiled to himself. He could use a smoke.

"There is time," Farjad said, nodding as Cousins held up his pack of cigarettes. The Westerner then took one from the crumpled carton, placing it between his lips before lighting up.

"It's beautiful," he cried out to the Eritrean as he squinted across the desert.

"This country I love," the African said simply.

"Know where we are?"

"Of course. This the land of my people," he told Cousins and walked towards him still clutching the compass in his hand, taking a cigarette from the pack offered to him. "We find the way. Insh'allah," he added. And the Englishman laughed.

———

The women were squatting on the ground, cooking over an open fire outside the tents pitched among the low, stunted trees as the vehicles approached. The men were tending their livestock nearby. The older of the women rose to her feet and drew her headscarf across her face when she saw the trail of dust climbing from the flat expanse of the desert landscape, signalling the truck and Land Cruiser slowly drawing nearer, now travelling abreast.

She was a handsome woman, more Arabic in her features than African, though her skin was dark. Her face was finely chiselled, framed by long, finely beaded braids, and above her forehead there was a band of circular golden jewellery just below her hairline. The colourful, loose-fitting dress she wore was gathered at the waist and her sleeves rolled to the elbows, showing an assortment of shining bangles against her brown arms as she placed her hands onto her hips and squinted into the distance as she watched with an air of defiance.

Several small, barefooted children wandered from the palm-thatched tent behind her to stand, clutching the folds of her garments that blowed softly in the gentle breeze from the plains as they fixed their gaze upon the approach of the strangers. The woman cried out to alert the men that visitors were approaching. The two younger women rose and retreated to the safety of their tents as the men joined the family matriarch.

This was an extended family group of three brothers, their wives and their children whose nomadic lifestyle was largely reliant on their livestock and the turning of the seasons. They were the people of the Beja Hedareb who dismantled their tents and moved across the landscape with their animals when the weather and available resources dictated. They were excellent herders and often kept an assortment of cattle, goats, sheep, donkeys and camels, depending on the family fortunes. Usually, they lived in family groups and practised a form of Islam blended with traditional beliefs reaching back to tribal customs predating ancient Egypt.

The vehicles drew to a halt a respectable distance from the encampment. Farjad was the first to jump from the truck and offer his salaam, raising a hand in greeting to the small group of people that stood and stared. The Land Cruiser had drawn alongside the battered Fiat, and Cousins climbed out and now stood with the Eritrean field coordinator. The older of the men, with a shock of greying curly hair, stepped forward from the family group and nodded in recognition as he approached. He seemed to be the head of the family. Farjad smiled and moved towards the man, while Cousins watched them 'bump' shoulders and shake hands, as was common among the Eritrean peoples. He had brought the livestock, as promised, and the Beja man smiled to reveal the gaps in his brown teeth. The nomad looked over Farjad's shoulder to meet the Westerner's gaze. He was curious about the fair-skinned man and wanted to be introduced.

The field coordinator told Cousins the Beja was named Isyan, for his wisdom. The Englishman would take some photographs, as had been agreed, to show people from his country, Farjad explained. Cousins would observe their customs, he added. That would exclude pictures of the younger women. The white man's name was John. The nomad nodded and smiled in acknowledgement. The older woman might agree to a photograph. As the family matriarch, she held a status of her own. But what was the meaning of his name? he enquired. The Englishman had to think. John, it was a Biblical name meaning 'graced by God', he seemed to recall, and again Farjad translated. It was an answer which seemed to draw approval. He was welcome, the Beja said, and gestured for the two men to approach his family. He was very grateful they had come.

The family group moved forward and gathered around the visitors, curious about the Westerner from outside. Minutes later, the livestock were being unloaded from the truck and the distribution became a joyous affair, with the smiling faces of those who watched. The family was to receive four goats to bolster their existing herd. It was a help during hard times, Isyan and his brothers said.

Cousins was in his element as he snapped away, asking the family to pose, pointing to his camera before raising it to take each rapid succession of shots. Then he would show them the digital images he had taken on his viewer, a kind of wonder the children had never seen before. Even the older Beja woman agreed to be captured on camera, though she adjusted her headscarf and turned her face from the Englishman. But it was a striking image, showing the full magnificence of her frame and her flowing garments as she posed with one of the goats under a twisted acacia tree. The men too were obliging, pictured happily receiving their new animals.

Then there was an offer of sweet tea, when the younger women emerged cautiously from their tents and the children felt confident to approach the Westerner without any sense of suspicion. The barefooted youngsters were natural models and provided Cousins with some wonderful images of Beja family life. He felt privileged.

The offer of refreshment was politely declined. It was very kind and, ordinarily, they would be honoured, Farjad said. But they had to press on. There was another family to visit, and the remaining animals were growing restless in the rising heat of the day. They would be delighted to return when they were next in the area and would look forward to accepting the family's hospitality. The Beja understood. One of the brothers climbed onto the truck and assisted in soothing and watering the remaining goats, and the visitors said their farewells.

The next family group due to receive the remaining livestock were camped just beyond the small ridge. They should see the small oasis marked by a cluster of stunted trees. The Beja family then wished them a safe onwards journey, insh'allah, and waved them off.

───❧───

It was late in the afternoon when, finally, they reached the outskirts of Tessenei. The vastness of the arid plains had lain like a petrified expanse of ocean between the distant hills, shimmering in the heat and punctuated only by a single twisted tree or scattered patches of low scrub which rose from the dry earth. Occasionally, they might spot a splash of colour on the horizon that signalled a solitary figure in search of water or firewood.

Now the single dirt track had delivered them to the edge of the frontier town where they would be able to rest after the long trek. Lula was at the gate as they pulled into the compound, and she ran across the yard to tell her mother they had returned. In the morning, Cousins would set out on his way back to the capital where Hannah Johnson was waiting for him. But first, he needed to quench his thirst, then take to the shade of his room. He hoped there was a cold cola in the icebox.

CHAPTER THIRTY-SEVEN

I n Asmara, she awoke with a flutter in her heart. She
was enjoying a lazy Saturday morning at the compound in
the capital. It had been a busy week in the field. She was in no
rush. Instead, she took joy from waking without the sound
of an alarm clock beeping in her ears. In truth, it was still
relatively early. But by now, he was surely on the road from
Tessenei.

She threw the cotton sheet back and emerged from
beneath the mosquito net draped above her bed. Yet she did
not feel inclined to hurry. It was a rare moment of leisure she
felt she had earned. She was due to meet Walters at ten, but
there was plenty of time to shower and breakfast.

When, finally, she joined him on the terrace, the doctor
was drinking his second cup of tea, reading a book with
knitted brow. It was a little after the appointed hour, though
his look of concentration melted into a smile as he looked up
and removed his glasses to observe her approach.

"So sorry," she said, acknowledging her lateness.

"No worries," he replied. "There's still tea in the pot," he added as she joined him at the small table and drew a cup towards her.

"The ceremony's all set," he told her as he watched her pour herself a tea. The roasting of the coffee beans would begin around five, he said. That's when everyone was set to gather at the office, and it would allow Cousins to arrive in good time, if not for the first serving, then perhaps for the second, he thought.

"Thank you," she said, gazing into his eyes. "For everything."

"It will be good to get everyone together," he said.

"No. I mean thank you for *everything*," she repeated.

It was true they had been through thick and thin together. But he was a man not comfortable with showing emotion. They had become more than colleagues. Certainly, they were friends. Extremes of common experience brings a closeness. Especially working in the 'field'. A year was indeed a long time in Africa, he mused. He would miss her.

"I'll miss you too," she told him.

"Are you sure I can't persuade you to stay?" But even as he posed the question, he knew her mind was made up, and her leaving was as inevitable as the coming of the rains.

"He's a lucky guy, that man of yours," he said. Then he paused. "I'm very happy for you," he added. He might have said more. Expressed his true feelings for her, but he left it at that. Besides, deep down, she knew, and sometimes these things were better left unsaid. "They called in on the radio before setting out early this morning," he said. The Kenyan had let him know.

"Must be passed Barentu by now," he added.

With any luck, they should arrive in the capital not long after lunch. She could hardly wait to see him. The sun was shining as she sipped her tea, and all seemed well with the world.

—⚬⚬—

Cousins watched the children from the roadside as they made their way across the hard earth with their bright plastic buckets. They stopped and stared back. Then they waved, and he raised a hand in return. He couldn't quite tell how old they were across the distance that separated them, but he could see from their clothing it was a girl and a smaller boy. The girl might even have been Lula. She was of a similar age and build. Perhaps they were brother and sister going for the water.

The Land Cruiser was on its approach to Barentu when they had halted. The town was the main city in Gash-Barka region but still bore the scars of heavy fighting from the war, when it had been besieged by Ethiopian forces. The area had been heavily mined by both sides, and they were still fetching them out of the ground.

Something didn't feel right with the front wheel, Jamal said, and they had stopped on the track which rarely saw much traffic, particularly as the heat rose in intensity. Now the Eritrean driver was frowning; then he kicked the nearside tyre.

"This one needs some air," he said, rubbing a hand thoughtfully across his face.

Cousins was smoking a cigarette, still watching the children as he leant against the vehicle.

"Do we have a hand pump?" the Englishman asked.

"In the back, I think," the driver replied.

Cousins was still observing the children, who were now making their way across the ground towards him.

"Wasn't this where the fighting was?" he asked.

"Yes," the Eritrean, who had moved to the back of the vehicle, replied absently.

"Many died," he added solemnly, opening the back door and searching for the pump. That's when the stark realisation suddenly hit the aid worker, and he leaned forward from the vehicle. There was a reason Jamal had not pulled off the dirt track. A sense of panic rose within him as he searched for signs of danger. Too late he saw the battered red sign up ahead, leaning against the roadside, twisted away from him.

He didn't need to see the white skull and crossbones painted roughly across its surface which signalled the hidden menace. A feeling of dread gripped him. He had to act. They were in the middle of a minefield.

"Stop!" he cried out to the children, waving his arms frantically in alarm as they continued to approach, excited by the prospect of meeting a Westerner. Cousins instinctively moved towards them, calling out to them to stay where they were, could even see their faces when the mine exploded beneath them with a devastating thud, and he was thrown to the ground by the impact.

As he hit the dry earth, blinded and numbed, with the blast ringing in his ears, he felt it was the end. A sense of helpless resignation swept through him. But he wasn't afraid. In those moments, as he lay dazed and shattered on the ground, he thought of his children; he thought of Afsa Ali, the woman he had loved and lost in Pakistan a lifetime ago. Yet the person he longed for more than any other was Hannah Johnson as he slipped into unconsciousness, bleeding into the dust.

In a suburb on the western side of the city, they were already gathering at the Medics International compound. The women had prepared the bread and the popcorn, and the smell of roasted coffee beans mingled with the sweet perfume of the frankincense that hung in the air of the late afternoon. The female nurses and the admin staff were in their finery, with their white *zuria* dresses, their distinctive jewellery and their hair tied back. The men too wore traditional *jelabiya*. Even Walters was sporting his best linen suit and seemed uncharacteristically relaxed. He was smiling as he chatted to Mancini, the Italian field coordinator from Cesvi.

Hannah Johnson came to join the two men. All was well in the kitchen, she said. The coffee had been ground and was doing the rounds, with the guests invited to take in the aroma as it passed before it was brewed over an open flame and served from traditional earthenware jugs into small handle-less cups.

"All we need now is for John to get here," she said.

"Not heard any more," Walters replied. "But I'm sure he can't be far out now." Strange that they had not checked in again.

Sir Charles was mingling, smiling and complimenting the women before he too stood with them. "It's good to see you, Hannah. You look ravishing," he said, and she felt herself blush.

"Why thank you, Charlie. You're looking quite dapper yourself," she replied.

"One does one's best," he said, grinning at her.

Then a jubilant cry rang out, and they turned to watch the first serving of the coffee. Johnson never seemed to lose her sense of wonder at the reverence displayed during the procedure and then, when the time came, the skill of the server pouring the steaming brew into the tiny vessels, though she'd witnessed the ceremony countless times. It was ever a moment of celebration. They were sixteen people. But always there was an extra cup or two that was served. No one knew why. Perhaps for the departed, for absent friends or for anyone who arrived late. In this instance, two additional cups stood awaiting the arrival of Cousins and his driver, though there had been no further news of their progress along the hot and dusty road. But their cups would be left to go cold. Later, the ritual would begin again, and fresh coffee would be brewed for a second, sometimes even a third, serving. Cousins was sure to make one of them.

Outside, the atmosphere was relaxed, as those who had gathered sat on their rugs taking their coffee, helping themselves to brown sugar and ginger to taste, with plates of food being passed from hand to hand. The Kenyan from BritAid arrived as they were finishing their first cup. For a moment, he stood soberly and scanned the yard. He was looking for Walters. The doctor was chatting to the Eritrean nurses but saw him approach. The African leaned forward and spoke into his ear, and the New Zealander's expression changed to one of concern.

The moment she saw Walters walking towards her, she knew something was wrong. "Hannah, I have to talk to you," he said with a troubled look in his eyes.

"What is it, David?"

"Not here," he said and took her gently by the arm to lead her away from the party, towards the main building, followed by the Kenyan.

"Tell me..." she insisted.

As soon as they were inside the building, he stopped and turned towards her. "It's John," he said.

"There's been an incident," the Kenyan added.

The colour drained from her face. "He's not coming," she said in a voice that sounded alien to her, her mind racing.

"He's at the hospital in Barentu..." Walters told her.

"God, no," she cried as she felt her knees go weak, and the Kenyan reached for a chair so that she might sit down.

"Is he… is he…?" She was unable to say the words, looking up at him expectantly. Desperately.

"A mine went off. And he was caught in the blast." He paused. "He's in pretty bad shape, but we're waiting for further news from the hospital," Walters told her, and she felt a tear roll down her cheek as the enormity of what had happened began to sink in.

"So sorry," he said, laying a comforting arm around her shoulder, and she leaned towards him, now sobbing pitifully, watched helplessly by the Kenyan.

Out in the yard, the ceremony continued, blissfully oblivious of the drama unfolding within the main house. Only Sir Charles guessed something terrible had happened, as he had seen Johnson being led away. He'd seen the look on Walters' face. For a moment, he was unsure whether to follow them into the building.

Instead, he stood and observed the women pouring the coffee into rows of small cups, then watched as they were offered one by one into grateful hands. He took one himself as the tray was extended towards him. Yet there were several cups of coffee that remained unclaimed, left to go cold as the orange sun began to paint long shadows out across the yard. He drew a deep breath, then turned and slowly walked towards the main house.

EPILOGUE

S HIDA SQUARE WAS quiet. Traffic was light as the couple stood in the gentle sunshine, dwarfed by the colossal sandal sculpture before them. The dark-haired man was tall and lean but stooped slightly forward, as if bearing an unseen burden upon his shoulders. The woman was young and fair, with auburn shoulder-length hair, and her arm was locked in his. Both were casually dressed, as if they had just returned from their work on the parched plains which swept westwards to the border with the Sudan. They were foreign aid workers.

John Cousins shifted his weight from his walking stick and leaned towards the woman beside him, as much for physical support as emotional comfort, oblivious to the scattering of pedestrians crossing the square as they went about their business. For a few moments, they both gazed in silent reflection at the giant structure upon which the sun reflected dully from its black metal finish.

The striking monument pays tribute to Eritrea's long and bitter struggle for independence and the simple footwear worn by freedom fighters, a symbol of resistance, of determination and ultimately of triumph. And there it stands since 2001, casting its defiant shadow across the traffic island upon which it stands in the middle of one of Asmara city's main thoroughfares. A reminder of prolonged sacrifice.

Neither could really comprehend fully the many years of struggle and the suffering it represented. For they were white Westerners; visitors passing through. At least, that was the man's perception, though his time in Eritrea had taught him something about its people's pain, their resilience and their capacity for kindness. Perhaps about life itself. He felt grateful. Not least for the woman at this side, Hannah Johnson. But he was overcome by a pang of sadness too.

Earlier, at the nearby Italian café along Beirut Street, they had sat with Sir Charles for the last time. He had arrived a little late on foot from the embassy, which lay just a few minutes away in Maryam Gmbi Street in the heart of the government quarter. As ever, it was good to see their friend as he sat with them, ruddy-faced and perspiring in his lightweight linen suit from the exertion of his brisk walk to meet them.

It had been at the embassy party during the Independence Day celebrations that he had taken up his trumpet and famously accompanied the local band. That was their first vivid and joyous memory of the ambassador. And McKenzie had played the spoons.

Later, they had taken an impromptu stroll to that same monument in Shida Square, still awash with a flag-waving crowd, singing and dancing to the banging of drums into the early hours. Higgins, Sir Charles's long suffering personal secretary, and the security team trailing them, had not been overly impressed.

The trio now laughed over their coffee as they recalled the evening.

"Happy days," exclaimed the woman, sweeping a strand of hair from her face as she smiled. It was a habit she had. "You were *very* drunk that night, Charlie."

"I'm drunk every night, my dear," he replied.

"Do me a favour, though, when we've gone. Be kind to yourself," she told him, and he nodded.

"Yes, Nurse Johnson. I'll try."

Then, as if suddenly remembering, he reached into his breast pocket and fished out a narrow, white envelope, handing it across the table to Cousins. It was a letter from the British Government. "Just in case there is any unforeseen problem getting out."

"We've got the exit visas," the aid worker said, taking the envelope from the ambassador's fingers. "But thanks. Thanks for everything, Charles," he added, reaching across the table to shake his friend's hand.

"Is it time?"

The man opposite nodded. "Soon," he said, glancing at the woman. "We'll take a slow walk across the town, take in a few sights. Then some last-minute packing, and we'll be off."

"Do let me send a car to take you to the airport."

"It's OK, Charlie," Johnson said. "Land Cruiser's booked. Walters will insist."

"Of course." The British diplomat took a deep breath and sighed. "So, this is 'goodbye.'"

"More like au revoir... or perhaps I should say *arrivederci*," Cousins said with a grimace as he reached for his stick and struggled to his feet.

"Right," said Sir Charles. He drained his espresso, raising himself from his chair. "And, sadly, I have to get back to the office. Higgins wants to go through tomorrow's schedule. Packed programme. Bloody nuisance."

There was a sadness in her eyes as Johnson stood before him.

"Never did get to see that wedding," he told her.

"We'll send you an invite." She smiled. "You'd better be there."

"I will. Wouldn't miss it for the world."

She didn't believe him for a second. Then she stepped forward to embrace him. As they hugged, he spoke to her in a low voice which Cousins couldn't quite catch. His hearing had been impaired by the blast.

As she drew back from Sir Charles, there were tears in her eyes. "Thank you," she whispered.

"I'm going to miss you both," he said.

"We'll miss you too," she replied, regaining her composure. "Be good, Charlie. And give our best to Maria."

"I will." He paused. "When I see her."

"Thanks again, Charles," said Cousins, laying a hand fondly on the ambassador's shoulder. "Been a privilege. I won't forget your kindness. Nor indeed Eritrea. It's been an adventure."

"It has, hasn't it?"

"I certainly have the scars to prove it." The aid worker grinned.

"Shattered leg, broken ribs, dislocated shoulder and a few scratches. Not bad for a beginner out here," said Sir Charles. "Good job we were able to put you back together." Then he paused, as if suddenly overcome by the moment.

"Well…" he said finally, looking at them both. "I'd better be off. Safe travels." Then he left them for his 3pm meeting with Higgins back at Maryam Gmbi Street. He'd have to hurry. Already he was late. He upped his stride to 'power walking' mode as they stepped out into the sunshine from the café, and they watched him disappear from view.

"He's a good man," Johnson said. "Despite himself."

"He is," Cousins replied. "What was it he said to you before we left? I couldn't hear."

"Nothing much," she said, blushing as she recalled his words. "He told me I was the most beautiful woman he had ever had the pleasure to call his friend."

Cousins raised an eyebrow.

"And that he thought you were the luckiest guy alive," she added.

Her partner smiled faintly. "I'd say the man is right on both counts," he said, and he kissed her on the cheek.

They crossed Beirut Street and approached Shida Square arm in arm, where they stood at the monument one final time to reflect on their days in Eritrea. He thought of the children who had died in the explosion. He thought of McKenzie. And he thought of the long-suffering people he had come to know. He reflected too on the many kindnesses he had encountered along the way. Most of all, he felt grateful and hopeful for a future with the woman at his side. It had indeed been an adventure...

Somewhere out there is someone for each of us. Call it coincidence, call it luck. But when you recognise them, it is destiny. Undeniable, unstoppable events conspire with the universe as if it was always meant to be. As if it were written in the stars.

ABOUT THE AUTHOR

Andrew Goss is a former print journalist, aid worker and humanitarian reporter. His work has led him to travel extensively across Europe, South Asia and Africa. For several years he lived in Pakistan, where he supported the aid and development sector. He is a passionate advocate of education for the world's poorest, and specifically girls and young women.

Andrew lives in Leicester, in the heart of England, with his partner Claire, a nurse and former aid worker. His dream is that one day the poorest across the Global South are freed from poverty through greater equality of opportunity and fairer distribution of wealth – and that finally we learn to live as one. He hopes one day to return to Pakistan.